The Bass Wore Scales

A Liturgical Mystery

by Mark Schweizer

Advance Praise for *The Bass Wore Scales*

"...A rollicking rhubarb of a tale...a real bodice-ripper with pirates, harem girls, a beautiful princess, killer monks, and a dashing hero—all tied together with an intricately woven plot worthy of John Grisham in his prime. Something like that would have been really good."
Christopher Schweizer, son

"If this book is ever made into a movie, Tom Selleck should play the lead, and Schweizer should make a cameo appearance as 'third idiot on the right.'"
Annie Mahre, Bookkeeper

"A heartwarming adventure...well, maybe not exactly heart-warming—but pretty good. Hmm...that may be overstating it. I'd say that you could certainly read it if you were stuck in a doctor's waiting room for a few hours. I mean, if you didn't have an old *People* magazine or anything."
Dr. Karen Dougherty, Pediatrician

"There are two ways to dislike the *mystery* genre. One way is to dislike it. The other way is to read this."
Dr. Richard Shephard, Chamberlain, Yorkminster

"This book is 'unputdownable!' It is 'laughoutloud' funny and can be described with these and many other made-up words!"
Alice Carpenter, poet and book editor

"As a writer, Schweizer is a fine musician. As a musician, he is a fine writer. He is deeply committed. Or *should* be."
Clifford Hill, President, Cliff Hill Music Company

"I believe that everyone has a book inside them. Sadly, Schweizer's has escaped."
Sandy Cavanah, English Professor

"Never come to my home again."
Elaine Hicks, retired teacher and incidental character

"Having been unpopular in high school is not just cause for book publication."
Jay Goree, high school friend and lead singer with "The Carburetors"

The Bass Wore Scales
A Liturgical Mystery
Copyright ©2006 by Mark Schweizer

Illustrations by Jim Hunt
www.jimhuntillustration.com

Published by
St. James Music Press
www.sjmpbooks.com
P.O. Box 1009
Hopkinsville, KY 42241-1009

ISBN 0-9721211-8-8

Printed in the United States of America

1st Printing January, 2007

The Bass
Wore Scales

a Liturgical Mystery

by Mark Schweizer
Illustrations by Jim Hunt

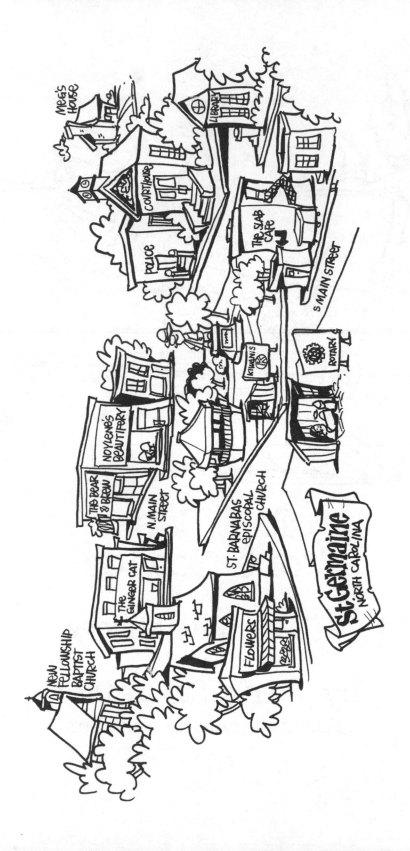

Prelude

Pie Pelicane, Jesu Domine,
Me immundum munda tuo sanguine:
Cujus una stilla salvum facere
Totum mundum quit ab omni scelere.
Sixth Quatrain—*Adoro Te Devote*

May is a fine month in the Appalachians—cool, green and slightly damp, with clouds hanging so low that you could brush them away from your face if you had a mind to, their smoky essence heavy with the bouquet of fir trees and mountain laurel. Yes, I thought, looking across the blank paper in my typewriter and out the open window, my chin resting in my hand and my elbow planted firmly on the desktop, May is a fine month. I liked March and April as well. June's okay. July stinks. August, too. It's way too hot—even up here in St. Germaine. But it was still May, and August was a world away. I took the cigar out of my mouth and looked at it in disgust. It had gone out during my chronological musings. My cigars don't usually go out when I'm writing. I generally chomp down, light up, and pound furiously at the worn keys of the old Underwood, puffing away like a fat man on a treadmill. Now, here I was contemplating the merits of various months and having to spend valuable writing time re-lighting my stogy. I growled and reached for the matchbox. Like many cigar aficionados, I preferred a wooden match to light my Cubans. I slid the matchbox open, removed one, but paused mid-strike. Meg would be here shortly, and the rule was no cigar smoking when she was in the house. I sighed and tossed the match into the ashtray. The cigar wasn't helping anyway. I had to face facts. I was up against the most dreaded of the wordsmith's phobias—writer's block.

I heard the screen door in the kitchen bang open and counted myself lucky to have had the cigar go out when it did. It's not that Meg hates cigars. Well, yes it is. It's that Meg hates cigars. I, on the other hand, love them. It was Rudyard Kipling who penned the immortal line, "A woman is only a woman, but a good cigar is a smoke." Rudyard Kipling never met Meg.

Megan Farthing and I were introduced five years ago—I, in my capacity as police chief of St. Germaine and officer on-duty—Meg in her capacity as wanton criminal motorist. She came zipping past my old Chevy pickup in her late-model Lexus like I wasn't even there. Everyone in town knows my truck, and even though Meg had only moved to St. Germaine a month earlier, I still find it hard to believe that she didn't see me. I've often accused her of speeding on purpose that evening, knowing that I was on the job and lying in wait for a foolish motorist. I further point out that in the five years since I've known her, I've never seen her exceed the speed limit. Not even once. She denies everything, of course, and looking into her beautiful blue-gray eyes, I almost believe her. Almost.

I tore up the ticket, invited Meg back to my place to see my etchings, and the rest is history. Now, we celebrate this anniversary every July 15th pretty much the way we began—listening to Bach on the stereo and eating knockwurst. Meg is fortyish, divorced, and the best looking woman in three counties. Maybe four. She lives in town with her mother. I live about twelve miles farther out on two hundred remote acres.

"Hayden," Meg called from the kitchen. "I've got dinner."

"Great," I yelled back. "I'll be there in a second."

Rudyard Kipling, although probably never plagued by writer's block, also never had the pleasure of Meg Farthing's company. Otherwise, he wouldn't have made that crack about the cigar. Kipling was good, all right (I thought *Gunga Din* a minor masterpiece, especially when read aloud with a really bad English accent), but my real literary hero was the mystery writer extraordinaire, Raymond Chandler.

I opened one of Mssr. Chandler's books and tried typing one of his famous lines, hoping the gesture would be the impetus that might inspire me to conjure up one of my own.

```
    She opened a mouth like a firebucket and laughed.
That terminated my interest in her. I couldn't hear the
laugh, but the hole in her face when she unzipped her
teeth was all I needed.
```

I looked at the sentence. It was good. Something that I wished I had written. I tried another one.

8

I'm an occasional drinker, the kind of guy who goes out for a beer and wakes up in Singapore with a full beard.

I sat for a long moment waiting for the muse to interject, but nothing happened. Nothing. The typewriter had never failed me before. I had come to believe that there was magic in the old contraption because these were the actual keys that Chandler had used to write those lines and a multitude of others including some of his greatest works—*The Long Goodbye, Farewell My Lovely, The Lady In The Lake, The Little Sister*—all of them typed on this very machine—Raymond Chandler's 1939 Underwood Number 5. I had bought it at auction after I made a few million dollars with a little invention that I sold to the phone company.

"Hurry up," called Meg. "The pizza's getting cold."

"Coming."

I headed for the kitchen, leaving the unsympathetic, antique typewriter sitting alone in the room.

"Put on some music, would you?" Meg said, as I wandered dejectedly into the kitchen. Then she noticed my slumping shoulders. "Hey, what's wrong?"

"Writer's block," I said.

"So," quipped Meg, "the eminent Hayden Konig—police chief and word-slinger—has writer's block. There *is* a God."

"I'll have you know that my detective stories have been very well received." I clicked on the Wave stereo, and the piano music of Eric Satie filled the house.

"And by 'well-received,' you mean...?"

"Umm...well...no one has burned the house down yet."

"Not yet," agreed Meg. "How's your blog doing? Getting any hits?"

I had put my first four liturgical detective stories up on a blog entitled *The Usual Suspects*.

"Not very many," I admitted with a sigh.

"That's a nice choice of music," offered Meg, delicately changing the subject and nodding toward the stereo, her hands busy with two beers and an opener.

"I was listening to it this morning. It's one of my BMG club selections." I belonged to several music-of-the-month clubs—just one of the many perks of being frightfully rich. Another perk was that I did not have to work for a living, a perk that I exercised when I gave up my part-time job as organist and choirmaster at St. Barnabas Episcopal Church. Yes, as is not uncommon in churches of any denomination, I'd had quite a rift with some of the parishioners. The priest, Father George, hadn't helped the situation. So I had quit, but the vestry had chosen to categorize my leaving as an "extended leave of absence." I kept my other full-time job as police chief because I like it. I like it a lot.

"This is from the new pizza place in town," Meg said. "The Bear and Brew. You know—the one going into the old feed store."

"I wondered when they we   re going to open up and start serving."

"Friday. Day after tomorrow. This is from their open house. I dropped by after I took Mother over to Noylene's to get her hair done."

"Why wasn't I invited to the open house?"

"You were, Hayden. I told you yesterday."

"Oh, yeah," I said, my chagrin hopefully apparent. "I forgot."

"Nancy was there. Pete. Dave. They asked where you were."

"I was trying to work up at least one good sentence."

"No luck?"

"No luck."

"I shall try to generate some sympathy," said Meg, putting a piece of artichoke and goat cheese pizza on my plate, "but it will be tough. However, I affirm your pathetic endeavors because I love you."

"You've always been jealous of my typewriter."

"Allow me to point out that your last attempt at a detective story ended with your musical gum-shoe drinking beer at a bar named *Buxtehooters*."

"Brilliant!"

"Humph," said Meg. "Hardly brilliant."

"I think I have at least one more story to tell. Sometimes literary genius isn't recognized until long after the author is dead."

Meg wiped the corner of her mouth with a napkin. "That's one theory, sure. Okay, you've finished *The Alto Wore Tweed,*

The Baritone Wore Chiffon, The Tenor Wore Tapshoes and *The Soprano Wore Falsettos*. What's the title of the new one? *The Castrato Wore Lifts? The Mezzo Wore Flannel?*"

"All good suggestions. But I think I'm going with a bass."

"That is, if you can somehow find some inspiration."

"Maybe *you* could inspire me," I said, suggestively arching my eyebrows over a second piece of pizza.

"Maybe I could," Meg agreed. "But I have to ask myself, do I really want to have one of those detective stories on my conscience? I'd have to ask for absolution on my deathbed."

"I'm sure it would be granted."

"Not necessarily. What if the priest has read your work?"

I ignored the barb. "A true writer is secure in the knowledge of his inevitable success."

"And you are secure in this knowledge?"

"Absolutely."

Meg smiled. "Then I'd better do some inspiring."

Chapter One

The Bass Wore Scales

It was a dark and stormy night--a night just like any other night, except it was a Tuesday, so it was really a night just like 1/7 of any other nights; a night when the air was just as hot, the streets just as mean, and second chances just as likely as a beret-wearing donkey named Wotan tapping out the exact number of Rossini operas with his hoof and taking my last sawbuck. Yeah. It was one of those nights. A Tuesday. I oughta know. I'm a detective. A Liturgical Detective, duly licensed by the Bishop. I needed some answers, some hymns, and a couple of theological insights. What I got were questions. I was thumbing through the Book of Occasional Services, looking for the Liturgy of Revirgination, when I heard a knock at the door.

Not bad, I thought. I'm back in the groove. Now all I needed was a dame—a looker, a babe, a twist, a chippy, a broad, a dolly, a skirt. I looked down at the typewriter, and there she was.

My heart jumped into my mouth like a frog into a pond full of fly soup as I looked up at a dish that was flaunting the kind of body that made married men wish they were single, single men wish they were better looking, and every Red Sox fan wish the starting lineup swung their bats the same way she swung her hips as she crossed the threshold of both the doorway and bad taste.

"My name is Betsy," she said in a voice so grating it could have scraped the warts off the bottom of my feet and still had enough rasp left to shred a half pound of cabbage. "I need a detective I can trust."

"You can trust me, Kitten," I said, lighting up a stogy, "for two hundred a day plus expenses." Long before Betsy ever walked through my door, I knew she'd show up-- and show up just when I was down to my last pair of clean shorts.

"Two hundred? I'll give you thirty." She sashayed flouncily across the carpet toward my desk. I bit my cigar in half.

"Okay, twenty," I compromised. "But I get to buy you dinner."

"Well...I don't know." She was hesitant, but I was ready to close the deal.

"Look, Toots," I said, pulling out my wallet. "I can't pay you more than ten."

"I accept your terms," Betsy purred. "Pick me up at eight."

Breakfast at the Slab Café has become a tradition for the St. Germaine Police Department and friends. The SGPD is comprised of myself (the chief), Nancy Parsky, and Dave Vance. Friends include Pete Moss, the owner of the Slab and mayor of St. Germaine, Meg, and whoever else happens to pass by and wants to sit for a while.

"Morning, Hayden," said Nancy as I pulled up a chair and sat down at our usual table, recently adorned with a cheery red tablecloth and three lovely plastic daffodils. I knew that Nancy had procured our seating arrangements as soon as I walked up to the Slab. I saw her Harley-Davidson parked in front of the building—a present from a grateful and rich police chief after one particularly dark episode involving an insane rector's wife. Since this bequest, Nancy's been motorcycle cop—at least when the weather was good.

"And a beautiful morning it is," I responded, maybe a bit too cheerfully for the six-o'clock hour. "Anything interesting happening in the world of law enforcement?"

"Nope," Nancy said, waving an empty mug toward Collette in hopes of flagging down the busy coffee matron. The Slab was full this morning, and Collette seemed to be the only waitress on duty. "Dave said he'd be here in a minute. He's checking his e-mail over at the office."

St. Germaine is a beautiful little town in the mountains of North Carolina. Our resident population is small, but grows significantly during the summer as the reverse snowbirds come up from Florida and south Georgia to escape the heat. Our other influx of tourists comes during October and November when the leaves start to change color. But those folks are usually only here for a couple of days—the summer residents stay until Labor Day or, in some cases, until the first snowfall. A crime wave in St. Germaine generally consists of some fraternity pledges from Appalachian State coming over and engaging in some nefarious cow tipping, so the three of us can handle the constabulary duties fairly easily.

"By the way," Nancy said, as Collette filled her cup with coffee, "I was looking through the job descriptions like you told me to."

I nodded. We had to update the personnel records for the city council every five years or so.

"And it seems that you're still a lieutenant. And a detective as well."

"That's not what my business card says," I said. "It says 'Chief.' 'Hayden Konig, Chief of Police' to be exact. And 'Detective Extraordinaire.'"

I had moved to St. Germaine at the behest of my college roommate sixteen years ago when the city was looking for a highly qualified individual to run its Police Department. It turns out that I was that individual despite the fact that my first two college degrees were in music. My third was in criminology, and that was the one that did the trick. My college roommate was none other than Peter Moss, said mayor of the town and owner of the fine eating establishment in which we sat.

"I'm hereby giving myself a promotion," I said.

"How about me?" asked Nancy. "I need a promotion, too."

"What does your job description say?"

"It says 'officer.'"

"You want to be a lieutenant?"

"Sure. Do I get to boss Dave around?"

"You do that now," I said, finally sipping some much-needed coffee.

"Yes, but this would make it official. And I want a new badge."

"Speaking of badges, have you seen mine?"

"Not for years."

"Well, I sure don't know where it is. New badges for everyone," I said magnanimously, as Collette, who had put down the coffee pot, appeared at the table with her order pad at the ready. "And some country ham biscuits."

"We don't have no badges," Collette answered, confusion clouding her face.

"Just the biscuits then," I said, "with a side of grits."

Collette nodded, wrote down the order and looked timidly at Nancy. Collette had recently become engaged to Officer Dave, and Nancy, being Dave's former infatuation and a formidable personality in any case, was still very intimidating. It's not that Nancy was ever interested in Dave. She wasn't. But it rankled her to no end that Dave's veneration, however unreciprocated, should have been so easily transferred.

Nancy's eyes narrowed, and she gave Collette a wicked grin. "Give me an Adam and Eve with the eyes open, burn the British, bossy on the hoof, a short stack in the alley and some Sweet Alice."

I snorted into my coffee and glanced up at Collette. She was writing the order on her pad, seemingly unperturbed.

"You want me to pin a rose on that bossy?" she asked Nancy. "And maybe grease the British?"

Nancy looked as though she were trying to decide. "Sure. Pin a rose on it. And the other thing, too."

Collette nodded, smiled and made her way back to the kitchen.

"What was *that* about?" I asked.

"Rats," said Nancy in disgust. "I thought I had her. I've been practicing since last night."

"Did you really want to pin a rose on bossy?"

Nancy shrugged. "I have no idea. I hope it tastes good."

Dave came in a few moments later, walked up to the counter, leaned across and gave Collette a kiss.

"Oh, puhlease," growled Nancy under her breath. "Get a room."

Dave pulled out the chair opposite Nancy and sat down. "Morning, all," he chirped.

"Well, someone's in a good mood," I said.

"Hey Dave," said Nancy, her voice switching from caw to chirp. "Guess what? We're all getting promotions and new badges."

"Wait just a second," I said. "I didn't agree to that."

"You mean I get a promotion, but Dave doesn't?" asked Nancy, a look of false innocence on her face.

"Okay," I said. "Everybody gets promotions and new badges."

"And raises," added Nancy.

"Now just wait a minute..."

"That's okay," said Dave. "I don't need a raise."

As far as I knew, Dave not only didn't need a raise; he didn't even need to work. When I hired Dave some five years ago, he told me that his trust fund provided a very comfortable income for him. He was just looking for something to do. Dave is the guy who answers the phones, fills out the reports and tends to be "on-call" more often than the rest of us. He's still listed as part-time, but I may have to upgrade his status in our new report.

"How big's my promotion?" asked Dave. "Sergeant? Lieutenant?"

"I'm the Lieutenant," said Nancy. "You can be the officer-in-charge-of-donuts. Now about my raise..."

"But he's gettin' married," chimed in Collette, reappearing with the coffee pot. "He needs to have some respect."

"She's right, Dave," I said. "You need to become respectable. You can be an officer with the respectable rank of corporal."

"Oooo," sighed Collette. "Mrs. Corporal Vance. I do like the sound of *that*."

I watched Nancy's nostrils flare slightly, but she saw me looking at her and composed herself quickly. "Yes, Mrs. Corporal Vance. You should put it on the wedding announcements," she said sweetly.

"Thanks, hon. I think I will," said Collette, pinching Dave's cheek and heading back to the kitchen. "I'm so proud of my Snookie-Pie."

"Snookie-Pie?" guffawed Nancy as I stifled a chortle of my own. "My GOD! Snookie-Pie?!"

"No pinching the customers, Collette." Pete was coming out of the kitchen, wiping his hands on a towel. "Not even Snookie-Pie, here. You want to pinch someone, pinch me."

"Hey, Officer Snookie-Pie," said Nancy as Pete sat down. "Pass me the sugar, will you?" Nancy didn't take sugar in her coffee. She was just looking for an excuse to say "Officer Snookie-Pie," and who could blame her?

"That's *Corporal* Snookie-Pie," corrected Dave.

"Breakfast will be right up," Pete said.

Pete had taken over the Slab Café, aka the family business, after his college career and a stint in the Army Band. His major had been philosophy, but he could blow a mean tenor sax and although Army life wasn't suited to him, he still enjoyed playing and gigged from time to time in some regional pick-up groups. He hadn't changed much since college, still sporting a ponytail, now gray, and the occasional earring. He favored brightly colored Hawaiian shirts, jeans, and sandals, and, according to his own admission, hadn't worn any underwear since 1975. I knew this was true in college, but thought he might have grown out of the predilection for unfettered hedonism during his years in the service. Pete explained to me, though, that once you have experienced such freedom in your youth, it's tough to go back into confinement. He was a raving Democrat on environmental issues, a screaming Republican on social reform and a crazed Libertarian when he had to pay his taxes. Pete had, over the years, become a capitalist hippie, and we loved him for it.

"Hey Pete," I said. "What's it mean when you say you want to pin a rose on bossy?"

"Hmm," said Pete thoughtfully. "I guess it means that your prom date isn't going to win any beauty contests."

Dave and I laughed.

"That's just freakin' hilarious," snarled Nancy.

"Order up," called Collette as she came out of the kitchen carrying an oversized tray of food. "Here y'all are." She put a basket of country ham biscuits in the middle of the table, furnishing me with an empty plate and a steaming bowl of grits. Dave had his usual breakfast of a western omelet and toast, an order he didn't have to verbalize as long as Collette was the waitress on duty. Pete was having waffles.

"Here you go, hon," Collette said, placing Nancy's order in front of her. "Adam and Eve with the eyes open, burned British with grease, bossy on the hoof with a rose pinned to her, and a short stack in the alley." We all looked over at two eggs sunny-side up, a buttered English muffin, a rare steak with onions on top and two pancakes on the side.

"Oh," said Collette, setting down a glass of milk. "Almost forgot. Here's your Sweet Alice. Can I get y'all anything else?"

"Nope," I said. "I think we're good."

"I'll be back with some coffee in a bit, then," said Collette with a smile. "Y'all give a yell if you need anything."

"Can you eat all that?" I asked, looking over at Nancy's place. "Or were you just trying to stump her?"

"Oh, I'm *gonna* eat it all right," muttered Nancy. "Every bit of it."

"Another sumptuous repast," I said, dabbing a napkin at the corners of my mouth in the most genteel fashion I could muster. "Excellent work, Mr. Mayor."

"Oh, I'll take all the credit," said Pete. "But Bud's doing the cooking. He's been working mornings since school let out."

"Well, send him out here so we can give him a round of applause," I said.

"Hey, Bud," Collette yelled from the register. "Come out here for a second."

Bud appeared a moment later, first poking his head through the swinging door of the kitchen and then walking out into the dining room, all the while wiping his hands on his stained apron. True to his nature as a shy, self-conscious sixteen-year-old, he turned red at the applause that greeted his entrance, but smiled nevertheless.

Bud was the eldest of the three McCollough children. Their mother Ardine, a hard-working woman, had lived a tough life. Their father, PeeDee, was an abusive good-for-nothing who thought that welfare was the best thing the government had come up with since the free cheese program. He disappeared about seven years ago and hadn't been heard from since, the rumor being that Ardine might have had something to do with his vanishing act. Up in the hollers of the Appalachians, beating your wife and kids was an offense that was frequently taken care of in-house, and when PeeDee McCollough disappeared, no one looked very hard.

Although PeeDee didn't do much in his life, one thing he did do was name all three kids after the thing dearest to his heart—beer. Bud was the oldest. Bud's sister, Pauli Girl, was now fourteen and as beautiful as her mother might have been in her youth, before life had taken the color from Ardine's cheeks and the spring from her step. The youngest was a gregarious eight-year-old boy named Moose-Head—Moosey for short.

Bud, in addition to his newly discovered culinary talents, had an encyclopedic knowledge of wines. No one was sure how he came by such proficiency. He explained that it came from extensive reading at the library, but none of us bought *that* story. He knew too much. It was Bud who put me on to a pinot noir that he described as "bland, yet dishonest; virginal, yet tarty; grudging at first, but evolving into gingerbread. It has a bit of dirty-sock overtone and sharp aftertaste." I tried it and, to my surprise, he was right. Yep. Bud had the whole package—knowledge, taste buds and most importantly, the lingo. Anyone in St. Germaine who wanted just the right wine for a dinner party came to Bud first. He never duplicated a suggestion and never disappointed.

"Did Moosey get hold of you?" Bud asked me, as he came over to the table.

"I haven't seen him for a couple of days."

"Well, he's hot to go fishing. He said you promised him back in February."

"I did indeed," I said. "If you see him, tell him I haven't forgotten."

"Are you still coming on Tuesday?" asked Billy Hixon, the Senior Warden of St. Barnabas. I recognized his voice as soon as I answered my phone.

"Tuesday?" I said, trying to remember what Billy was talking about.

"Tuesday afternoon—three o'clock. At St. Barnabas! Don't tell me you've forgotten?"

"Give me a hint."

"The Blessing of the Racecar!"

"Oh, of course!" I said.

"Junior Jameson is bringing the racecar up on Tuesday morning. Maybe you heard that he hasn't been doing so well. He had it re-painted before the season started, but, so far, having St. Barnabas as the main sponsor of his racing team isn't garnering him any holy mojo. Those're his words, not mine."

Last year, St. Barnabas came into a lot of money—sixteen million dollars, to be exact. It was an unexpected windfall and after several fairly hostile congregational meetings, it was decided that the church could not decide. That is to say, some wanted to invest the money and live off the interest, never having to take up a collection or worry about a pledge drive ever again. Then, there were those people who felt that financial security of such a degree would be a detriment to the spiritual life of the church. As Father George so eloquently put it in his speech to the congregation, "It is important for the people that are St. Barnabas to know that they are needed, that their gifts and their tithes are what sustain the church and that their talents are appreciated and invaluable."

In the end, it was decided that one person, and one person alone should make the decision, and this trustee would be the one who had given the most money to St. Barnabas over the years. We all assumed that the person named would be Malcolm Walker, the richest man in the congregation. Much to everyone's surprise, the person named as the trustee was none other than Lucille Murdock, an eighty-seven-year-old widow who'd been giving half her pension to the church since 1938.

To make a long story short, Lucille Murdock finally decided, after much prayerful consideration, that St. Barnabas Episcopal Church would use the money to fund a NASCAR racing team. This decision was helped along, in no small part, by several coversations with her nephew, Junior Jameson, a NASCAR driver who just happened to be looking for a sponsor. In the end, they concluded that putting the church emblem on the top of the racecar would be the perfect "vehicle" (if you will) to spread the Word of the Lord. "After all," Junior said, "isn't NASCAR racing the number one spectator sport in the country? And don't those people need to be exposed to the Gospel?"

"I'll be there," I said to Billy. "Who's doing the service?"

"Well, Father George doesn't want to do it and Tony said he's going to be out of town, so I'm going to try to get the Bishop."

"That sounds like a tall order. Do you have a back-up plan?"

"Yeah," Billy said. "You."

Chapter 2

"How's the writing going?" asked Meg. "I don't hear any clacking going on."

"I'm thinking," I said. "The twin poniards of my craft—percipience and perspicacity—are delicately balanced on the spire of my intellect."

"There you go!" laughed Meg. "That's the ticket! Write some more stuff like that. Sentences with three-dollar words that don't mean anything. You're like Tom Wolfe, only without the talent!"

"Harumph."

I pulled my flivver up to Betsy's place at eight on the nose. I hadn't had a steady job since the Bishop pulled me off the Tuna Hotdish Caper. It was a Lutheran scam to get the Episcopalians involved in running bootleg potluck suppers. I exposed it easy enough, but now the Lutherans and the Episcopalians were in bed together, and it wasn't the result the Bishop was after. He was my meal ticket, and it didn't do to make him mad. The sign on my door read "Liturgical Detective," but I was at the Bishop's beck and call.

Betsy came down the steps of her apartment, looking like a million bucks and change. I was there to open the car door for her, a practice I usually neglected, but, eyeballing her graceful form squirming down the landing like an anaconda on stilettos, it seemed that the evening might be worth a few manners. Yeah, I'd been to charm school—one of the best. Lady Diedre's Ettiquetorium and Beanery. I even had the certificate in my wallet. I just didn't like to flaunt it.

"Wow, what a gentleman," said Betsy in a squeaky yet sultry tone—a modulation that incorporated the twin timbres in equal measure, like Lauren Bacall chewing chalk; not the soft, colored chalk of childhood that one might eat in kindergarten where consuming chalk (and paste!) was a delightful pastime and a necessary source of

21

fiber, but the white, bitter chalk of adolescence that was gnawed nervously in front of the class while entreating the Almighty (even though prayer in public schools has been forbidden since 1962) for divine help in discovering the value of f if f has a vertical asymptote at x=5, a single x-intercept of x=2 and f(x) contains quadratic functions in both its numerator and denominator--that kind of chalk. "I ain't never had no car door opened for me before."

"You ain't been around me, Doll-Face," I said. "I got manners I ain't even used yet."

"Did you hear the news?" asked Georgia, barging into my office at the station without even a never-you-mind. "Father George is outta here!"

"What do you mean, outta here?" I asked. "He's leaving?"

"He's got another gig." Georgia Wester was a stalwart member of St. Barnabas, a lay Eucharistic minister, and to say that she had never warmed to Father George Eastman in his year with us would be an understatement.

"You mean another *appointment,*" I corrected.

"Yep," said Georgia, a smile splitting her face. "He's going to teach at a seminary in Virginia. He just got the word."

"What's he going to teach?"

"Homiletics," Georgia answered with a snicker. "He's teaching homiletics. Anyway, he starts in a couple weeks. They want him to teach the summer courses, so he's outta here."

"Bad news for us, I suppose. Now we have to start looking for a priest all over again."

"Not necessarily," said Georgia. "We still have that résumé from the woman we were going to interview."

"I thought she'd withdrawn her name."

"She did, but Beverly's kept in touch with her, and says that she might still be interested."

"Didn't she take a teaching position at Lenoir-Rhyne College in Hickory? To be close to her parents, as I recall."

"I think so," said Georgia.

"Anyone here?" called Bev Greene, banging open the front door and coming around the receptionist's desk into my office. "Oh. There you are. Did you hear the news?"

"Isn't anyone working out there?" I asked. "Where's my crowd control? I can't just have people charging in here whenever they choose."

"Maybe they're at lunch," said Bev, with a shrug. "I don't know. But guess what?"

"I couldn't even venture a suspicion."

"Father George Eastman is *leaving!*"

"I never would have guessed," I said.

"I already told him," said Georgia. Bev glared at me.

"I didn't want to ruin your fun," I explained. "You both seemed positively mirthful."

"Tell him about Gaylen," said Georgia.

"She's really good," said Bev. "We were going to interview her last year, but she withdrew her name from consideration, and Father George was the only other person we had scheduled to come in."

I nodded and heard the front door open again.

"Hayden? Are you here?" called another female voice—one that I knew very well.

"In here, Meg," I called back. Meg came into the office a moment later.

"Hi, you guys," said Meg, acknowledging my visitors before getting quickly to the point of her pop-in. "I couldn't wait to tell you. Guess what?"

"Father George is leaving. That's what!" said Bev and Georgia in unison and followed the outburst with a laugh.

"Hmm," I said. "I give up. What?"

"Harumph," sniffed Meg. "I see you have spies all over town."

"We just couldn't wait," said Georgia. "Tell Hayden about Gaylen."

"Gaylen Weatherall," said Meg.

"I remember looking over her vitae last year," I said. "It was very impressive."

"Hey, guess what?" called Elaine Hixon, coming through the front door.

"Father George is leaving!" everyone yelled back.

"Oh, brother," sniffed Elaine.

"She's got a doctorate from the University of Georgia, and she's published extensively," said Meg.

"Who?" asked Elaine.

"Gaylen Weatherall," I said. "The next ex-priest of St. Barnabas."

Bev took over the narrative. "Her mother was sick, and she took the job at Lenoir-Rhyne to be close to her, but she passed away in January. Her father is doing fine, and she's decided that she doesn't like teaching as much as she likes being a priest. So she's looking for a parish again."

"Don't get too far ahead of yourselves," I said. "You know that all this has to go through the proper channels."

"Oh, I know," said Meg. "But we've already done all the legwork. She was our first choice last year, and unless the interview reveals something that we're not expecting, the whole process may go quite smoothly."

"Have you ever known the process to go smoothly?" I asked with a grin.

All four women fell silent.

"I guess not," said Georgia dejectedly.

"Nope," said Bev, shaking her head.

"There was this one time..." started Meg, then looked over at Elaine who was shaking her head. "Oh," she said, remembering. "Never mind."

"Well, never fear," I chirped. "I'm sure that she'll get no other offers since she's been waiting for this position to open back up. She'll be happy to come straight-away for an interview. I'm confident that she'll really love St. Barnabas and our fair city, and the vestry will take to her like a ferret to a French-fry. They'll offer her the job, and she'll be here by July."

"Well, when you put it like that," said Elaine, "it doesn't sound too hopeful, does it?"

"No," said Meg, "but I like her. I liked her last year, and I like her now."

"Me, too," added Georgia. "There's no reason why we can't have a priest that's good for our parish. We deserve it. I'm getting on that committee. I have ways."

"Keep me informed," I said. "I'm always happy to be kept in the loop. May I take you gals to lunch?"

Bev shook her head. "Not me. I've got a meeting over at the church."

24

"Ah, yes," I said. "The Parish Administrator." The role of Parish Administrator was a relatively new position at St. Barnabas enacted by Father George so he could, in my opinion, avoid conflict altogether. Bev Greene was in charge of writing checks, scheduling the building, keeping up with pledges, handling all personnel issues (at the behest of the rector), and all sundry chores that fell under her job description as "other duties as required." She also had to attend worship meetings.

"You wouldn't forget if you were still employed," humphed Bev. "I hand out the checks."

"I already ate," said Georgia, with a sigh. "I could eat again, I suppose." She reconsidered. "Nah. Better not."

"That just leaves us," I said, looking at Meg hopefully.

"Oh, yes. I can just manage to get some lunch in before my next appointment," Meg said.

"When's your next appointment?"

"A week from yesterday."

The Ginger Cat was, as always, doing brisk lunch business. Located on the north side of the square in St. Germaine, they specialized in coffee, soup on Thursdays, and a variety of upscale yuppie sandwiches on unpronounceable bread. Cynthia Johnsson was darting to-and-fro in the graceful dance of the experienced waitress. A new, college-aged waitress whom I didn't know seemed to be struggling to keep her head above water. We sat down at a table next to the front window, and Cynthia glided by—moments later—with a couple of menus and a water pitcher in one hand, a tray with two bowls of soup and some bread in the other.

"Be right back," she said, putting down the menus and pouring two glasses of water, "as soon as I deliver these."

"Take your time," Meg said with a smile. "We're in no rush." The other waitress—I suspected she was a student at Appalachian State—was standing in the middle of the restaurant, flipping back and forth through her order pad as though she was looking at lunch orders written in ancient Greek, another shell-shocked victim of the noon rush.

"What looks good to you?" I asked Meg, as we peered over our menus.

"I think I'm going to have a grilled Gruyere and roasted red pepper sandwich on Kalamata Olive bread."

"What?"

"Don't be snide. You heard me perfectly well. It's the special."

"How about this black walnut bagel with seared tuna, Daikon sprouts and Wasabi cream cheese?"

"Nope. I always like to have the special. It's good for my self-esteem. 'I'll have the special,' I say to Cynthia, and then, when she brings it, I actually *feel* special."

"Well, if that isn't the dumbest thing I've ever heard."

"Yes it is, isn't it," said Meg. "But since I'm feeling special, I shall affirm you in your selection, no matter how commonplace and boring it may be."

I sighed and stared at the menu. I always had a problem trying to decide on a designer lunch, so I was still undecided when Cynthia hurried up to the table and asked if we were ready to order.

"I'll have the special," said Meg, closing her menu and handing it to Cynthia. "And a glass of ginger-peach iced tea." Cynthia nodded and looked in my direction.

"I'll have the egg sandwich," I said, finally seeing something that I recognized.

"That comes with Parmigiano-Reggiano cheese and Crimini mushrooms," Cynthia said.

"Okay."

"Would you like that on Asiago Cheese bread?"

"Great," I said.

"Perhaps with a side of cranberry compote?"

"Now, look here..."

"Never mind," she giggled. "I'll bring you a regular egg sandwich, chips and a cup of coffee."

"Put some snooty mayonnaise on that, will you?" I called after her.

We were finishing our lunch just as Ruby, Meg's mother, walked in the front door of The Ginger Cat. She spotted us right away, or, more probably, spotted us from the street since our placement in the front window was more than a little conspicuous.

"I thought you might be here," said Ruby. "I tried calling your cell phone, but you didn't answer."

"I have it turned off," said Meg. "It's my lunch hour."

"Well, I have two messages for you. Actually, one for you and one for Hayden."

Meg and I looked up at her expectantly.

"But first," Ruby said, sitting down in one of the two vacant chairs at our table, "how about a little dessert?"

"Sounds good to me," I agreed.

"I'll skip it this time," said Meg.

Cynthia, overhearing Ruby's comments, was at our table in two shakes of a lamb's tail with the new waitress in her wake. "I'm getting ready to leave for the day, so Lisa will take your dessert order." She ushered Lisa, an obviously shy girl, front and center.

"What's on the dessert tray today?" I asked.

"Umm," she started, wracking her brain to bring the desserts back from memorized obscurity to the frontal lobe where she could access the information. "There's blackberry cobbler, bread pudding, cheesecake, blackberry cobbler..."

"You said that already," said Ruby, having missed seeing the poor girl struggling earlier and therefore lacking the patience that Meg and I were so admirably demonstrating.

"Let me start over," said Lisa. "Blueberry cobbler..."

"I thought you said 'blackberry,'" interrupted Ruby.

Lisa nodded and blinked hard. Twice. "Blackberry cheesecake, bread..."

"Blackberry cobbler!" said Ruby.

"Mother! Please!" hissed Meg.

"What?" hissed Ruby back.

"It's her first day," I whispered, hoping that it was.

"Oh. Take your time, dear."

Lisa nodded and started again, this time looking at her pad. "Blackberry cobbler, bread pudding, cheesecake, key lime pie and chocolate torte."

"Very nice, dear," said Ruby. "I'll have the chocolate torte."

"I'll have the bread pudding," I said. "With rum sauce."

Lisa wrote down the orders as she made her way to the kitchen, bumping into only one table that seemed to leap in front of her when she wasn't looking.

"Poor child," said Meg, looking over toward the door. Since we had chosen to be front and center in the window, we had as fine a view of the pedestrian traffic as they had of us, and we could see the customers just as they opened the door of the restaurant. "Elaine's coming in."

"Afternoon," said Elaine. "I couldn't help noticing you three from the square. You look like a Piggly Wiggly window display of Country Chic."

"Very clever," I said. "How long have you been working on that one?"

"Since I saw you guys a couple of minutes ago. The first time I walked by. You were talking to that little waitress."

"I like it," said Ruby. "The whole Piggly Wiggly/Country Chic thing really works."

"Oh, please," I said. "Don't encourage her. Next thing you know, she'll think she's a bad writer."

"Hey," said Elaine. "I can write just as badly as you. I mean...I can write just as *bad* as you. I used to be an English teacher."

"Huh," I sniffed." I don't *think* so. *My* writing has been panned on three continents. *And,* as you know, I own Raymond Chandler's typewriter."

"Maybe," Elaine countered, "but I made a D in creative writing in high school."

"I once dated a clown at a grammar rodeo."

"I was kicked out of my writing group for excessive run-on sentences."

"I shot the editor of my college yearbook just to watch him die," I said smugly, sipping the last of my now cold coffee.

This comment brought a startled look from Lisa, our waitress, who had just shown up at the table with an order of key lime pie and blackberry cobbler à la mode.

"Umm," she said. "Who had the key lime pie?"

"Why, I did dear," said Ruby. "Thank you so much."

I rattled my coffee cup on the table, indicating its non-active status, but it did no good. I was about to say something about our dessert order when I felt Meg's foot on my shin under the table. I glared over at her, but she returned my gaze with sweet innocence.

"It's her first day, dear," she said, as I looked down at my blackberry cobbler.

"You want this?" I asked Elaine, pushing my dessert over toward the empty place. "I really wanted some bread pudding."

"Don't mind if I do," she answered, sitting down. "Could I get some coffee as well?"

"Apparently not," I growled. "World-wide acclaim in the field of bad writing doesn't count for anything anymore."

"Oh, I could write worser stuff than you ever could write," said Elaine.

"To badly write is something I can well do," said Meg, seductively splitting an infinitive twice in one sentence.

"Me, too," said Ruby. "Listen to this. 'After being whipped fiercely, the cook put the cream into this key lime pie.'" She smiled. "That's a dangling participle."

"Bad writing is much more than dangling participles and obese gerunds," I said. "It's an art form. And, by the way, splitting an infinitive, no matter how provocatively, is no longer considered a grammatical offense."

"How hard can it be to write a bad sentence?" asked Elaine. "I mean, if *you* can do it?"

"This sounds like a challenge," I said, looking around for Lisa who had seemingly decided that it was time to go on her break. "What's the bet, and what are the rules?"

"Let's make this interesting," said Elaine. "What's the deadline on the Bulwer-Lytton Fiction Contest?"

"Officially, it's April 15th, but they usually take submissions till June I think."

"What's the Bulwer-Lytton Fiction Contest?" asked Ruby.

"Ah," said Meg, "now you've done it."

"Edward Bulwer-Lytton was the famous author who penned the immortal lines 'It was a dark and stormy night,'" I explained. "That opening was part of a longer sentence that has been dubbed one of the worst first lines of any novel ever written—or at least published. The Bulwer-Lytton Fiction Contest asks for submissions of the worst opening line to a novel that you can come up with."

"What's the prize?" Ruby asked.

"A couple hundred bucks, I think. But it's the prestige we're all interested in."

"Have you entered before?" Elaine asked.

"Yep. No luck though. But I haven't entered this year, so they haven't even seen my good stuff."

"Here's the bet then. Whoever wins the B-L contest has to buy the other three supper at the Hunter's Club."

"But that means that the winner is out a couple of hundred bucks," I protested.

"As you said," explained Elaine, "it's the prestige of winning that's important. And besides, I'll have the two hundred dollars from the prize money. I won't be out anything."

"Okay," I said. "There are a couple of sticky wickets to work through. Firstly, there are thousands of entries every year, and although there are different categories, any of us would be lucky to get a dishonorable mention, much less win. Secondly, after I *do* win, the pressure to give radio and newspaper interviews will be enormous. I don't know that I'll have the time."

Meg laughed. "Oh, you've got the time. It's me I'm worried about. I'm too pretty to be on the radio. I'll have to do television appearances. That means new clothes, a new hair style...it may all be just too much."

Ruby put her fork down on her empty plate. "Sounds like you all have the contest wrapped up. How many prizes are there?"

"Well," I answered, "one grand prize. Then there's a grand runner-up as well as winners, runners-up and dishonorable mentions in each category. You know—adventure, romance, detective—that sort of thing. Then there are miscellaneous dishonorable mentions as well. Quite an assortment of honors. They're all listed on the Bulwer-Lytton web page."

"Why don't we do it this way?" said Ruby. "Whoever gets the highest award wins. Grand Prize Winner is the top, Grand Runner-Up next. Then, winner in any category. Runner-up trumps a dishonorable mention."

"That sounds fair," said Meg. "Do I get a trophy as well as the two hundred dollars?"

"Wait a minute," said Ruby. "What about the magic typewriter? Hayden shouldn't be allowed to use it."

"I should, too," I argued.

"I have an idea," said Elaine. "There are three or four old manual typewriters in the basement of the church. Let's get them out, clean them up and use those. Hayden can use his, and we'll all be on equal footing."

"I still think it's an unfair advantage," said Ruby. "Anyway, I don't need one. I've been typing on my old Remington for years."

"I'll take one," said Meg. "Do we happen to have the one that Moses used to write Leviticus?"

"The very one," laughed Elaine. "I'll go and dig them out this afternoon."

Lisa managed to struggle back to the table and present me the bill. She'd charged us for two pieces of cheesecake and four cups of coffee. I left ten bucks on the table.

"I'll come back and settle up with Cynthia later," I said. Meg nodded.

"I almost forgot," said Ruby. "Your messages. A man named Harris called. He wants some advice on his stock portfolio."

"Precisely the reason I turned off my phone," said Meg. "He's calling me twice a day since he opened his account."

"And Moosey McCollough called looking for you, Hayden. He said you were supposed to take him fishing."

"I am and I will," I said. "But first I must think of the most delectishous, horriblest sentence ever constructed in the history of the English language."

"That's a good start," said Elaine. "Good luck."

"The game is afoot," I replied.

"What about your detective story?" asked Meg, as we walked out the door of the Ginger Cat into the sunshine. "You've already started it. And, as I recall, our pertinacious detective is on a hot date with some floozy named Betsy."

"She's not a floozy," I said. "She's just misunderstood."

"That's what all the floozies say."

"I guess I'll just have to leave them on their date until I knock out a couple of obvious winners for the competition."

"How many are you going to send in?"

"At least two or three," I said. " I intend to win this bet."

Chapter 3

Moosey McCollough was waiting for me as I walked into the police station. He was sitting on the bench in the waiting room, chomping on a Zagnut candy bar, a departure from his usual Milky Way, his legs dangling and his tattered high tops barely scuffing the linoleum. Moosey was eight but small for his age.

"Hayden! You ready to go fishing?" he called out as he saw me open the door. "I been waitin' all summer."

"Moosey, it's only the end of May. Summer hasn't even started yet."

"It has for me! School got out two days ago."

"How about tomorrow morning? I still have to go pick up Pete's boat."

"Okay," Moosey said, his mouth full of chocolate and peanuts. "What time?"

"I'll pick you up at six."

"Five," said Moosey. "I'm usually up at five. I wake up whenever the sun comes up."

"Six," I said. "Now scoot on out of here and go dig up some worms. We need about a hundred."

I checked in with Dave at the station and, as usual, nothing of a felonious nature was happening in St. Germaine—nothing that we were aware of, at least. The summer crowd would start appearing in town about the second week of June as school holidays began and the heat and humidity began to exact its inexorable toll in Georgia and Florida. But, for now, all was quiet.

I wandered down the sidewalk and made my way around the town square. The square was built around Sterling Park, named for Harrison Sterling, a mayor of St. Germaine, who in the early '60's, ramrodded zoning ordinances down the city council's gullet, resulting in the preservation of the downtown area in an era when most small towns were tearing down old buildings and putting up architectural monstrosities. Now, of course, Harrison Sterling was a hero. As the statue said, "A man of vision."

Since The Slab Café was in my path, and I had little else to do, I stopped in to see if Pete was busy. He wasn't. The lunch crowd had abated, and the lone stragglers sitting at the tables didn't look as though they'd be ordering anything else.

"Need some lunch?" asked Pete as I came in, the bell on the door jangling behind me.

"Nope. I had an ostentatious lunch with Meg over at the Ginger Cat. I just came in to borrow your boat."

Pete frowned. "You come in here telling me you just had lunch at my competition's place and now you want to borrow my boat? You've got some nerve."

"If it makes you feel any better, I didn't pay for it," I offered. "The new waitress is a little ditsy."

"Well, that's okay then," said Pete. "As long as I'm not the only one comping your meals."

"I may have to go back and pay," I admitted. "Meg might shame me into it."

"Yeah, yeah, whatever," said Pete, already losing interest in riling some guilt out of me. The Ginger Cat wasn't a threat to the Slab Café, and Pete had good reason for wanting them to stay in business. Pete Moss was, as they say in investment circles, a generator of multiple cash streams. Over the past twenty years, he'd been buying the old buildings on the square, renovating them and renting them out to the merchants of St. Germaine. This strategy was starting to pay off in a big way. The Ginger Cat was in one of Pete's buildings.

"Which boat do you want?"

"How many do you have?" I asked.

"Three," said Pete. "No. Four."

"Four?"

"I've got the sailboat over at Emerald Isle. I've got that bass boat. The cabin cruiser—it's in the shop—and the rowboat."

"I need the rowboat."

"It's tied up on the lake. Been there since Easter."

"Down at the dock?" I asked. Our little mountain lake was just outside town and surrounded on three sides by the Mountainview Cemetery. The remaining adjacent property had belonged to Malcolm Walker and was now in the possession of his ex-wife, Rhiza. Malcolm was doing prison time and wouldn't be seeing this or any lake for quite a few years to come. The Mountainview

Cemetery didn't offer an access road to the shore, but anyone could park up on the hill overlooking the lake and walk down. A small dock, set on piers, jutted about eight feet into the water. There were "No Swimming" signs every fifty feet or so, but every once in a while a couple of kids would sneak down there to cool off. And cool off they did. The water came right off the mountains and was usually about sixty-eight degrees or so.

"Yep," said Pete. "It's tied up at the dock. That is, unless someone's stolen it."

"I kind of doubt that," I said. "Where would they go? The lake only covers a couple of acres. And anyway, I'm a detective. If it's stolen, I'll find it."

"I was just kidding. It's not stolen," said Pete. "I was there yesterday. I took Molly out for a nice boat ride just about dusk."

"Molly Frazier? Kenny's sister?"

"The very same."

"Are you two an item? You working on wife number four?"

"Well, you never know," said Pete, thoughtfully. "Love seems to be in the air."

"Speaking of love in the air, have you talked to Noylene lately?"

"Actually, I have," said Pete. "She's doing a brisk business at the salon, but she's going to close on Mondays and Tuesdays. She says that ever since she opened Noylene's Beautifery, she doesn't meet as many people as she used to when she was waiting tables. So she's going to come back to work here on Monday and Tuesday mornings."

"I'm sure you'll be glad to have her back. If the help at the Ginger Cat is any indication, good waitresses are mighty hard to come by. But that wasn't the news I was talking about. It seems that Noylene has a beau."

"Really? Who?"

"Meg said his name was Woodrow DuPont. He just bought Kenny Frazier's farm."

"Oh sure," said Pete. "Wormy DuPont. He's lived around here off and on since he was born. I went to school with him."

"Wormy?"

"Yeah. Wormy. He got the nickname in second grade. The school nurse got on the intercom and told him he had to come to

34

the office for his worm medicine." Pete laughed. "I remember it like it was yesterday."

"Poor kid."

"Oh, he never seemed to mind," said Pete. "Wormy is better than Woodrow anyway."

"How about 'Woody?" I offered.

"Never thought of it," Pete shrugged. "And 'Wormy' sort of fit him, you know?"

I stopped by Noylene's Beautifery and Dip 'n Tan on my way around the square. Noylene Fabergé had graduated from an on-line beauty college and opened her salon a couple of months ago. She and her son, D'Artagnan, had invented the immensely popular "Dip 'n Tan"—a contraption that allowed the customer to hang from a trapeze and be gently lowered into a vat of tanning fluid. Noylene's first few attempts at getting the recipe just right had resulted in a rash of orange-colored St. Germainians, giving some substantiality to the scuttlebutt around town that we had been invaded by giant mutant carrots, or, at the very least, Yankees.

There were three cubicles in Noylene's Beautifery, and they were all in use. Noylene was in the one furthest from the door. The other two were staffed by a couple of young ladies from Boone—the signs on their mirrors identified them as Darla and Debbie. These name-tags were decorated with various cute personal items and complimented their officially framed licenses to practice the art of beauty in the state of North Carolina. Noylene looked up as I came in and waved me back.

She was diligently teasing the hair of a woman I didn't know. I smiled and nodded, trying to avert my eyes as the woman glared up at me. I had forgotten the one rule of beautiferies—a visitor is not allowed to see a woman whose coif is in a state of disrepair. If you're there getting a haircut, that's one thing. But you mustn't wander in off the street without an appointment and gawk in horror. It's bad form. Noylene didn't seem to mind, however, and started talking to me as soon as I walked up.

"Man, what a day! I'm ready for a break. My dogs are barkin'."

"Fridays usually this busy?" I asked.

"Oh, yeah," answered Noylene, the rat-tail comb flying in her hand. "Summer's here, and everybody wants a cooler 'do."

"I heard you were going to work over at the Slab a couple of mornings a week."

"Yeah," said Noylene. "I miss it, you know. I mean, here I get to talk to folks, and this is my life's work...doing hair...but I miss seeing the regular people. And anyway, Brother Kilroy says that we are supposed to find our gifts and use them. I have two gifts. The gift of beauty and the gift of getting your breakfast out on time."

"Well, I'm sure Pete and Collette will be glad to have you back."

"That's the other thing. Collette's got to plan her wedding. She's going to be busy enough with that."

"That's true," I said. "By the way, I heard you have a new boyfriend."

"Wormy? Yeah, he and I go way back. He just bought Kenny's farm you know."

"I just heard."

"I think he's got big plans," said Noylene with a smile.

Five-thirty in the morning comes early—especially on a Saturday—but I'd told Moosey that I'd pick him up at six and, by golly, a promise was a promise. I was ten minutes showering and getting dressed, five minutes eating breakfast and pouring a thermos of coffee from the coffeemaker that, luckily, I'd remembered to set the night before, and two minutes throwing a couple of poles and my tackle box into the back of the truck. Baxter, the Burmese Mountain Dog that shared my house, heard me rummaging around and was happily waiting by the truck, his entire hindquarters a-wag at the prospect of a ride. I'd gotten Baxter for Meg as a Christmas present, but now he stayed at the cabin where he had the run of the mountain.

"Not today, boy," I said and handed him a dried pig's ear. The big dog chomped on it delightedly and made his way to the front porch, apparently appeased.

It was a fifteen-minute drive to the McCollough's trailer, so I'd probably be right on time. I didn't worry about being a couple of minutes late, though. Moosey would have been on the front porch waiting for me since the sun came up. It was foggy and a little chilly at six in the morning, but the weatherman had promised a beautiful seventy-degree day with just a few clouds. I figured he might get lucky. I started the old truck and slipped a CD into the player—just about the only thing that was up-to-date on this dinosaur. The Chevy had no power steering, power brakes, power windows, power door-locks, fuel injection, air conditioning or computer chips. I also suspected it had no springs in the seats or shocks to speak of, and a family of mice was living in the air cleaner. The sound system was top-notch though, and I was treated to the sounds of Anton Bruckner's *Te Deum* sung by the Berlin Philharmonic Chorus. I knew the text well enough that, even though my Latin was as rusty as the tailgate latches on the truck, I had no trouble being drawn in by the poetry as well as the music.

Te Deum laudamus: te Dominum confitemur.
We praise you O God: We acknowledge you to be the Lord.

The *Te Deum* was heading into the fourth movement as I pulled into Ardine McCollough's drive. Moosey, as I expected, was sitting on the edge of the porch, his chin in his hands, tapping his tennis shoes on the dusty ground. He had his old cane pole wedged upright against the porch post, and as soon as he saw me, he stopped counting the ants (or whatever was consuming his interest at the moment), grabbed the pole and ran toward the truck.

"Hey there," I said. "You ready to catch some fish?"

"You bet!" exclaimed Moosey. "Hey, can I ride in the back?"

"No, you may not. Put your pole back there though unless you want to use one of the rods I brought."

"Can I?"

"Sure. Do I need to tell your mother we're leaving?"

"Nah," said Moosey, leaning his cane pole back against the porch. "I'll tell her. She's prob'ly still in her drawers."

"Go tell her then."

Moosey disappeared into the trailer and banged out of the door a minute later carrying a large coffee can.

"Almost forgot our worms," he said. "I've been keeping them in the fridge, but Mom says she'll be glad to see 'em go. She says they've been causing a racket."

37

"Really," I said. "I didn't know worms carried on so."

"It weren't the worms so much. Pauli Girl reached in there to get some coffee."

"I see."

"She screamed for about a minute, and now she won't go near the fridge." Moosey's ears perked up. "Hey, what's that music?"

"That is the *Te Deum* of Anton Bruckner for chorus, orchestra and organ."

"What're they saying?"

"Hmm," I said, listening harder to pick up the text. *Per singulos dies benedicimus te.* "They're saying 'We bless you every day and we praise your name forever until the end of the world.'"

Moosey nodded thoughtfully. "Are they talking about God?"

"Yep."

"That's a good song."

"It is indeed."

The fog was still heavy on the lake as we walked down the hill from where I parked, but we could feel the breeze beginning to pick up. I had the two rods and the tackle box; Moosey was carrying the can of worms carefully with two hands. I'd taken Pete at his word when he said the boat was tied up to the dock, but now, not seeing it where I expected to, I'd wished I'd taken the time to walk down and make sure the rowboat was where Pete had left it. I needn't have worried though. It was there, just as Pete said, tied fore and aft to the pier. It was an old fashioned wooden rowboat, about twelve feet long with two bench seats, a pointed bow and a flat stern with a place to mount a small motor. It had been painted red, but was now in need of another coat. I looked it over as Moosey set the worms down on the dock. The oars were in the locks, everything was ship-shape and, as my good friend Pete once remarked, "the boat bobbed lightly on the water just exactly the way that a bowling ball wouldn't."

"Mom says to wear a life jacket," said Moosey. "I can swim, all right, but she says I might hit myself in the head with the bait bucket and drown."

"She knows you pretty well, Moosey. The life jackets are under the seats. Get mine out, too. Who knows? You might hit *me* in the head with the bait bucket."

"Naw. We don't even have no bait bucket. Just this ol' can of worms."

"Even so," I said, helping Moosey with the straps. "We don't want any accidents. It would put a damper on the whole weekend."

"I guess," said Moosey. "Oh yeah—I forgot to tell you. I'm helping with the birds tomorrow."

"The birds?"

"You know. For Penny...umm..." Moosey thought hard. "Penny somethin'," he finally said. "At church."

"Pentecost. You're helping with the birds for Pentecost?"

Moosey nodded and we both got into the boat. I untied one of the ropes, he untied the other and we pushed off from the dock into the still lake.

"Are you going to St. Barnabas tomorrow?" Moosey asked, as I dropped the oars into the water.

I hadn't been back to church to play since the third Sunday of Easter. It had been a month of Sundays, and now Pentecost was upon us. I was still on an extended leave-of-absence from the church, and Father George had hired another substitute organist on the advice of several vestry members. Unfortunately, the only organist available in this part of the world was a one-legged, retired music teacher named Henrietta Burbank. Meg was less than impressed by her skills. She might have been a pretty good pianist, but, in Meg's opinion, an organist should, ideally, have the use of both legs. Oh, she could walk around well enough, but space was tight up in the choir loft, and her prosthetic limb wasn't constructed to bend in all the directions needed to situate oneself on the organ bench. Her solution to the problem was to unstrap her leg and lay the appendage up on the console like some kind of medieval relic— the leg of St. Henrietta the Untalented. Marjorie, a choir member since the middle-ages, said that the plastic prosthesis was just "grossing the choir out." Meg told me, in an effort to guilt me into ending my sabbatical, that almost all her playing was done on the manuals (although she'd throw in a few pedal notes if they were above middle C) and consisted of hymn arrangements written for piano. I had heard from a number of parishioners that things in the music department were less than satisfactory, and although I hadn't been back to church to play, I *had* gone with Meg to the Ascension Day service. The choir didn't sing, but Henrietta had been in fine form, the Feast of the Ascension being an opportune time to play a Josh Groban arrangement of *You Raise Me Up*.

"Told you," whispered Meg.

"Yes, you did," I whispered back.

"Can you see her leg from here?"

"If I spin around. She's in the back you know."

"Everyone can see it when they come back from communion. And also when they leave at the end of the service and she's playing the postlude. You know how you're not supposed to look at an accident, but everyone does? That's what it's like. You can't help but stare. It's right there!"

"Why doesn't someone ask her to put it on the floor?"

"Everyone's embarrassed. I mean, it's not every day you have to tell the organist to get her leg off the console."

"Reminds me of my organ performance class in college," I said, and was rewarded with an elbow in my ribs.

"*Are* you going to church tomorrow?" Moosey asked again, and my attention snapped back to the task at hand—rowing us to the center of the lake.

"I guess I will. It's the birthday of the church."

"How did you know what we were doing?" asked Moosey suspiciously.

"Huh?"

"We're having a birthday cake."

"Really? When?"

"Miss Brenda says when she calls us up to the front for our time with Father George, we're gonna have cake and sing *Happy Birthday*."

"Ah," I said, finally understanding. "The Children's Moment."

"Yep."

"Is that when the birds come in, too?"

"Nope," said Moosey. "That's later. Did you bring any candy bars?"

"Yes," I replied. "But you can't have one until at least seven o'clock. I promised your mother."

It was a glorious morning once it got started. There were a couple of herons stalking us along the lakeshore, pausing just long enough in their inspection of us to skewer whatever frog or fish ventured into their reach. Moosey and I had our lines in the water, but enjoyed no luck. Not even a nibble. We'd even switched worms several times as our wrigglers became waterlogged. After a couple of hours of fruitless angling, we decided to call it a morning and head in for some breakfast. As I rowed to shore, the turtles that had come out to take advantage of the sun splashed back into the water, disappearing in the concentric circles that marked their departure. It made for a very pastoral tableau. We tied the boat to the dock, shelved the oars, stored the vests under the seats and made our way back up the hill.

"Sorry we didn't catch anything," I said to Moosey.

"That's okay. We'll catch them tomorrow."

"Umm...I can't tomorrow, Moosey. We have church. Remember?"

"What about after church?"

"Well, fish usually bite early in the morning. If they're hungry, that is."

"What about Monday? You said you'd help me catch a fish," reminded Moosey.

"I did?"

"Yeah. So what about Monday?"

"How about next Saturday?"

Moosey pursed his lips. "Well, okay. But if you want to go fishing before that, you'd better call me."

"That's a promise."

It was a night for bratwurst, sauerkraut, Anchor Steam beer, Cuban cigars and Prokofiev—specifically, my new recording of the *Classical Symphony* and the *Third Piano Concerto*. I sat at my typewriter, sipping my cold beer and contemplating what passed for a plot. Meg was reclining on the overstuffed leather couch, reading a magazine, and I could smell the bratwurst starting to simmer in the beer. I'd take them out in about ten minutes and put them on the grill.

"Are you working on your Bulwer-Lytton entries?" asked Meg. "I think I may have a good one."

"May I hear it?"

"Nope. Not yet. It needs a little refining."

"I'm actually working on my detective story," I said. "And if there happens to be some overlap, well, so be it. Two birds with one stone, as it were."

"Do you have a plot yet?"

"Not yet, but that's never stopped me before."

I drove up to the Chartreuse Chapeau and flipped the valet a sawbuck. The Chartreuse Chapeau was out of my league, but I was here to make an impression. I took Betsy's arm and walked her toward the doorman. She smelled like the bus station by moonlight.

"Now tell me, Toots, what's your problem?" I asked once we were seated.

"What about dinner?"

"Yeah," I said. "Sorry. Order whatever you want."

I hoped she wasn't too hungry. After the valet, the doorman and the maitre d', I had about six bits left. Luckily, I had a dead woodchuck in my pocket. I figured that dropping it in my salad and covering it up with a slice of tomato not only guaranteed splendid service, but a couple of free meals as well.

"I'll have the Lobster Picador," said Betsy to the waiter. "On the hoof."

"I'll have the Penguin Platter," I said. "And a salad." Then I turned my attention to Betsy. "You wanna tell me now?"

She nodded. I waited, then waited again.

"It's my husband," she said, the tears suddenly streaming down her face, her shoulders heaving with tiny sobs, like the sound of Snuggles the Fabric Softener Bear getting his leg caught in the lint trap. "I think he's being unfaithful."

I sighed. The old unfaithful husband routine. "Tell me about him." I tried to sound sympathetic, but I knew this night was going nowhere fast.

"He sings in the church choir," she sniffed. "He's a bass with real low notes."

"Low C?" I asked.

"Low A," she said. "He's been highly recruited."

"What's his name?"

"They call him Fishy Jim."

"Fishy Jim, eh?" said Meg, looking over my shoulder. "I suggest you come up with something better than that if you want to win the contest. Sheesh. Fishy Jim..."

"This isn't my actual contest entry," I reminded her. "I'm working on my detective story."

"Fine," she said with a toss of her black hair. "I'm going to get another beer and put the sauerkraut on. Care to join me?"

"On my way. I think the bratwurst is about ready for grilling."

"I was talking to Elaine and Mother, and we've agreed that we should meet every once in a while and read each other our entrics. It might be good to get some input from each other." Meg plopped the sauerkraut in the saucepan, scooped in a small spoonful of black current preserves—an old Konig family recipe that Meg found as delicious as I did—and put the pan on the stove.

"Nervous?" I asked. "Starting to feel the pressure?"

"Not at all," Meg said, "and if you'd rather not, we girls will be happy to meet without you."

"Nope. I'm in. I need to keep track of all of you." I reached into the refrigerator and pulled out a coffee can that had a large note duct-taped to it. The note said simply "Archimedes."

"Have you fed him today?" Meg asked.

I shook my head, put the can on the counter and glanced around for a small white saucer. "I looked for him this morning, but he wasn't around."

"Better give him three then."

"Okay."

I opened the can and carefully shook three dead mice onto a saucer.

"Are you going to put them outside," asked Meg, "or wait for him to come in?"

"I'd better put them on the sill outside. He hasn't wanted to come in for a few weeks. I think he's enjoying the weather, but he still drops by every day or two."

Meg nodded and waved her hand in front of the window by the sink. The electric eye activated and the window opened. I reached through and placed the saucer with the mousey victuals on the windowsill.

Archimedes is a barn owl. He's been a resident of these two hundred acres for a couple of years now. Archimedes showed up one evening outside my kitchen window, and since I happened to have a couple of dead mice handy (I'd just cleaned out the barn traps that afternoon), I opened the window, enticed him into the kitchen and fed him supper. He visited so frequently that I installed an automatic window so he could come and go as he pleased. Archimedes spent much of the winter indoors, ignoring Baxter who had become quite used to the sight of an owl flying through the house. Come spring, though, and he was out and about, hunting squirrels, mice, rats, the occasional snake, and whatever else suited his fancy.

I took the bratwursts out to the gas grill and laid them over the flames in a neat row. Then I went back into the kitchen.

"Have you heard anything about the service tomorrow?" I asked. "It's Pentecost, you know. I thought I'd go to church and see how things are going."

"I was going to ask you if *you'd* heard anything."

"Moosey told me that he was helping with the birds. Do you know what *that's* about?"

"No, I don't," said Meg. "I haven't been privy to the internal workings of the Worship Committee."

"Do you know anyone who has?"

"Sure," said Meg. "Carol Sterling, Bev Greene, Joyce Cooper, Father George and, of course, Princess Foo-Foo. Any of them can probably tell you. I'm not on that committee."

"It'll probably be better if it's a surprise."

"What?"

"Whatever's going to happen on Pentecost."

Chapter 4

The feast of Pentecost (named for being the fiftieth day after Easter) is the birthday of the Church and has traditionally been a lively occasion at St. Barnabas. It has always been difficult to reenact the appearance of the Holy Spirit descending and manifesting itself as tongues of flame resting on the heads of the Apostles, but that, essentially, is what liturgy is all about—representing our faith through symbol and ceremony and making the encounter meaningful to modern worshippers. Charismatic churches reenact the glossolalia experience on a weekly basis, although I've never actually seen, or heard stories of, tongues of fire coming in and resting on the heads of the congregation. Episcopal congregations, however, not fully embracing the gift of "speaking in tongues," attempt to reenact the original Pentecost in other ways.

"Remember when we were doing helium balloons?" said Meg. "That was kind of good."

"Ah yes," I said, recalling the Ghost of Pentecosts Past. "I remember the balloons. I also remember the banners and the streamers. I remember mimes and liturgical dancers. I remember sparklers, kites, red carnations, and wind machines. I even remember the fire baton."

"That was excellent," agreed Meg. "Well, until our twirler dropped the baton and lit the carpet on fire. As I recall, we had to replace the whole center runner. We don't seem to be able to get a handle on Pentecost. How did they do it in the old days?"

"Let's see," I said. "In France, it was customary to blow trumpets during the service. You know, to recall the sound of the mighty wind. In Italy, rose petals were dropped from the ceilings of the churches to bring to mind the miracle of the fiery tongues."

"Why don't we do that? I like rose petals."

"You know," I added, "there's an old English custom of having boys crawl into the vault of the cathedral and drop bits of flaming rope soaked in tar onto the worshippers."

"I don't think we'd like that."

"It's not all about what we like. Sometimes we have to do what's best for the congregation."

"This is all Princess Foo-Foo's fault, isn't it?"

Yes, it was true. Pentecost was a mess, and the Christian Education Directors were to blame. I tried to assign the priests their share of the responsibility, but it wasn't really their fault. In my experience, a priest could be talked into anything. It was the Christian Ed Director. I imagine it all started in Assisi when Isabella, the resident CED, said "Listen, St. Francis. We need to have a living nativity scene in the church, and it needs to have a real camel."

So, given all our history, I wasn't a bit surprised by what happened.

The morning started out like so many other Sunday mornings. Meg and I walked up the front steps to St. Barnabas just as the prelude was starting. Benny Dawkins, St. Barnabas' champion thurifer, was warming up on the steps outside the church. He hadn't lit the incense yet, so the smoke wasn't billowing around him, but he was going through the motions of some of his signature gyrations. Benny had been to the finals of the International Thurifer Invitational for five years running and, although, he'd never won, he was recognized as one of the top pot-swingers in the world. Benny only worked on major feast days since some of the parishioners complained about the smoke, but, as far as I was concerned, the more smoke the better. If the altar disappeared altogether while he was censing it, I was happy.

"Morning, Benny," I said as we passed him. "What are we going to see today?"

"I'm working on a couple of new ones," Benny answered, not looking at me, but concentrating on the arc of the thurible. "Watch for one I call 'Over The Falls' on my first turn. Then coming back up the aisle, I'm planning to do the 'Jericho Twister' and when I get up to the altar, a 'Triple Spin Double Back-Loop' in honor of the Trinity. It's a revised shamrock pattern."

"Sounds great," I said. "I'm looking forward to your artistry."

We shook a few hands in the narthex and found a seat in the back, just under the choir loft, as the processional started. *Hail Thee, Festival Day* was the traditional St. Barnabas opening hymn for Pentecost and today was no exception. It was a tune that the congregation knew pretty well, although Henrietta Burbank's rendition seemed to be a little thin, due, I expect, to the lack of any pedal notes.

"Why doesn't she just reverse the great-to-pedal coupler and play the pedal part on the keyboard?" I whispered to Meg in between stanzas.

"Why don't you go up and show her how?" Meg whispered back. "I'm sure she has no idea. She's a piano teacher."

"I'll show her after the service," I said, "after she puts her leg back on."

"Blessed be God: Father, Son, and Holy Spirit," coughed Father George after the hymn had concluded. Benny had done his job well. We could barely see the front of the church for the smoke.

"And blessed be his kingdom, now and forever," the congregation coughed back. "Amen."

"Alleluia. Christ is risen," continued Father George.

"The Lord is risen indeed. (Cough) Alleluia."

The service continued as we sang the *Gloria*, heard the story of Ezekiel and his valley of dry bones in the Old Testament reading and sang the psalm refrain in response to the choir's bold attempt at chanting the verses. I was settling in for the Epistle reading, the story of the mighty wind and tongues of flame, and wondering what Father George and Princess Foo-Foo had come up with to bring the gospel to life, when the Princess stood up and invited the children to come forward for the Children's Moment.

"Ah yes," I said to Meg, under my breath. "The Children's Moment."

Princess Foo-Foo was the nickname that Meg had given to Brenda Marshall, our Christian Ed Director. Brenda was not an Episcopalian by birth or by choice, a fact that she pointed to on a regular basis with a certain amount of pride. Her theology, Meg was convinced, was guided by her confidence in the power of a warm and fuzzy Spirit Force with shoe-button eyes. Elaine was less kind, calling her—and I'm not using Elaine's exact words here— "ecumenically promiscuous," and it was Georgia that suspected that she was a touchy-feely Uni-luther-presby-metho-lopian. In addition to her duties in the worship-planning department, she taught the elementary Sunday School class, telling Bible stories with the help of a furry hand puppet named Gladly the Cross-Eyed Bear.

The children popped out of the pews and headed up the aisle to the front of the church where Father George waited for them, his hands clasped together as though in prayer. Meg elbowed me as we watched the children walk slowly to the front. There were the three or four little children from the nursery school class...and then there were the Children of the Corn...Bernadette, Moosey, Ashley, Robert and Christopher. Father George didn't stand a chance, and the whole congregation knew it.

"How many of you know what today is?" began Father George. All the hands went up, and we all knew that the gesture meant that the whole group had been threatened by Princess Foo-Foo during Sunday School.

"Ashley," said Father George, confident of his control. "Why don't you tell us?"

"It's the birthday of the church," said Ashley, matter-of-factly. "Everyone knows *that!*" She twirled around and sat down. "*My* birthday is next month. I'll be eight."

"Ooo, ooo," said Robert, frantically waving his hand in the air. "Ooo, ooo, ooo!" Father George chose to ignore him.

"That's exactly right. So now we have a surprise for St. Barnabas. Look! Miss Brenda is bringing us something. Can you guess what it is?"

"Ooo, ooo," said Robert, one arm still flailing and the other hand supporting his elbow.

"Bernadette?" said Father George. "Can you guess what it is?"

"Well, duuuhh," said Bernadette, rolling her eyes. "It's a birthday cake."

"*My* birthday cake is going to have SpongeBob on it," announced Ashley, now reclining on the top step of the chancel.

"How many candles does it have?" Moosey tried to look past the priest. "Huh? It doesn't have *any!*"

"Well, we didn't want...we didn't think it would be a good idea..."

"Ooo, ooo," said Robert.

"On *my* birthday, I'm having *lots* of candles. I'm going to blow them out and make a wish," said Ashley. "I'm wishing for a pony."

"I wished for a pony last time," said Christopher, "but all I got was a baby brother. No, wait a minute. It was a puppy."

"Yes," said Father George. "That's nice. But this is the church's birthday, so..."

"You got a puppy?" asked Moosey.

"No. I got a baby brother."

The organ suddenly boomed out the opening strains to *Happy Birthday* and everyone turned around and looked.

"Not yet!" shouted Brenda from halfway down the aisle. The music stopped as suddenly as it began, and Brenda continued her journey carrying the birthday cake sans candles.

"Is it true you have to do unto others like they do unto you?" asked Bernadette. "'Cause if it is, I'm gonna get my little brother good."

"Ooo, ooo," said Robert.

"Can I have some cake?" asked Christopher, sticking his finger into the frosting just as the cake arrived.

"Yes...umm, I mean no..." said Father George in exasperation. "What *is* it, Robert?"

"Momma says that Daddy won't get in heaven if he uses his golfing words in the house. She says that Satan's gonna have a field day."

"Here," said Father George, grabbing a handful of cake and handing it to Robert. "Happy Birthday."

The organ started up again, and this time we all sang *Happy Birthday* to the Church. I'm sure its heart was strangely warmed.

The choir sang an anthem following the Children's Moment, presumably to set the stage for the Epistle reading from the Book of Acts. It was a little unaccompanied medieval carol using the text "Holy Spirit, Truth Divine."

"That was nice, wasn't it?" asked Meg, quietly.

"Yes, it was."

"But, now what?" she asked.

"Now what" was a reading of the Pentecost story in different languages by members of the congregation. I was unimpressed. This had been done many times before. We were hoping for something new.

"When the day of Pentecost came," said Father George, the only one of the readers using a microphone, "they were all together in one place. Suddenly a sound like the blowing of a violent wind came from heaven and filled the whole house where they were sitting.

Gretta Schmidt stood up about halfway back on the right side and started reading in German. *"Und als der Tag des Pfingstfestes erfüllt war,"* she said loudly, *"waren sie alle an einem Ort beisammen."*

"De repente vino del cielo un estruendo como de un viento recio que soplaba, el cual llenó toda la casa donde estaban." It was JJ Southerland. I didn't know she spoke Spanish, but there she was, standing near the baptismal font.

"Og det viste sig for dem tunger likesom av ild," came another voice, this time from a man I'd never seen before.

"What language is that?" asked Meg.

I shrugged. "Maybe Danish? Or Norsk."

"They saw what seemed to be tongues of fire that separated and came to rest on each of them," read Father George. "All of them were filled with the Holy Spirit and began to speak in other tongues as the Spirit enabled them."

It was just at this point in the service that the worst happened. The church newsletter, *The Trumpet,* said that we were going to celebrate Pentecost in a new and meaningful way. It neglected to tell us we'd need to wear hard-hats. I found out later, after talking with an expert, that most birds actually need to learn how to fly. Oh, they will certainly flap their wings by instinct, but unless they have flying experience, once they hit the open air they'll pretty much drop like rocks. So when Moosey tossed the eight birds over the edge of the choir loft, these birds, having been raised in captivity specifically for the Hunter's Club Restaurant, didn't stand much of a chance.

It was a good bet that when Princess Foo-Foo and Father George planned this extravaganza, they were thinking about Garrison Keillor's story about the Gospel Birds in which the birds flew gracefully around the sanctuary, doing tricks and lighting gently on each member of the congregation, bestowing God's blessing on every person. At the very least, they were probably counting on the birds flying around for a few minutes and then coming to roost in the rafters, making for a nice, feel-good moment. This would pose a whole different set of problems, of course, but ones that could be dealt with at leisure. Unlike the Birds of St. Barnabas, however, Garrison Keillor's Gospel Birds had the advantage of being both highly trained and fictitious.

The first one of the unfortunate symbols of Pentecost hit Thelma Wingler right in the head. It happened right in front of us. There was a flurry of feathers followed by a light thunk. Thelma didn't say anything; just jumped up, screamed and grabbed her hair with both hands. As the bird bounced off her head and into the pew beside her, we could see that it was a dove. The second bird to come down was a pigeon. A big pigeon. It was, as they say in the hills—eatin' size.

It was another direct hit, this time clobbering Calvin Denton, little Robert's father, who jumped to his feet and began to use his golfing words. All of them. Loudly. The reading of scripture stopped abruptly as the entire congregation turned toward him in astonishment.

"Holy smokes," said Meg, as mothers reached for their children, doing what they could to cover their ears. "He's speaking in unknown tongues!"

"I'd speak in unknown tongues too if a three pound pigeon hit *me* in the head," I said. "But, you're absolutely right to be upset. He's not supposed to speak in unknown tongues unless there's someone in the congregation to interpret." I paused. "I guess I could do it."

"I don't think anyone needs an interpretation," said Carol Sterling, who was sitting next to Meg. "We get the picture."

By now the rest of the birds, a mixture of doves and pigeons, had landed. Out of the eight, five managed to crash into unsuspecting parishioners. Three landed harmlessly in the aisle or on an empty seat. There was more screeching and general pandemonium, and several folks bolted for the door, not knowing how many other birds were likely to come crashing down on them. Two ushers finally appeared and began collecting the poor birds and putting them in a couple of men's hats. I didn't think the birds were hurt; they were certainly fluttering hard enough to break their falls, and as the furor subsided, we looked back up toward Father George. He was nowhere to be seen.

Georgia, one of the lay Eucharistic ministers, disappeared for a moment into the sacristy, then came back out, walked into the congregation and whispered something to Tony Brown, our retired priest. I could just imagine what *he* thought of the entire proceeding. Father Brown got up and followed Georgia into the sacristy. She came out a moment later and began the Creed.

"Apparently, we're not getting a sermon this morning," I said.

"I guess not," answered Meg, joining in with the congregation. "....Maker of heaven and earth. Of all that is, seen and unseen."

By the time the Nicene Creed was over, Father Brown had appeared in a robe and chasuble and offered the Prayers of the People. The rest of the service was comparatively uneventful.

"Whew," said Meg, during coffee hour. "That was one for the books. I'm always amazed at what we can come up with to celebrate God's Spirit with us. Has anyone heard from Father George?"

"He just walked out," said Bev. "Right in the middle of the service. Can you believe that? I called his house and left a message on his machine."

"Hey," said Georgia. "You don't think he's dead do you? The way things have been going around here for the last couple of years, he could be dead. Murdered in his office." She sounded hopeful.

"Nope," I said, as Billy Hixon walked up. "He's not dead."

"Who's not dead?" he asked.

"Father George."

"Oh," said Billy and changed the subject. "You're going to be here on Tuesday, right?"

"Yeah. I'll be here. Did you get hold of the bishop?"

"Not yet, but I've left several messages with his secretary."

I looked over at the cookie table and saw Moosey and Robert filling their pockets.

"What do you think about all this Satan stuff?" I heard Robert ask.

"Well, you know how Santa Claus turned out," answered Moosey. "It's probably just your dad."

After church, Meg and I headed out for our weekly picnic. Our lunch was on ice, securely in the trunk of Meg's Lexus, and consisted of cold lobster and dill sandwiches, Meg's special German potato salad and cheesecake for dessert. All this served with a Pinot Noir recommended by Bud.

"We're meeting on Tuesday at noon for our Bad Writing Circle," Meg said. "At the Bear and Brew."

"I'll be there. I'm not letting you three women gang up on me. Have you written any wonderfully bad sentences?"

Meg took a sip of her wine. "Maybe. I'm certainly working on it."

"Not as easy as you thought, is it?"

"No, but I'll get the hang of it. I picked up an old typewriter at the church. Elaine brought a couple up from the basement."

"You didn't want to use you mother's?"

"Nope. It's an Underwood, but not like yours. This one was probably made in the '50s. I had to put a new ribbon in it, but it works just fine. And you were right about one thing—it's much more fun than typing on a computer."

"I'll be there at noon," I said, "but I've got to keep it short. I have something at three."

"Oh, yes. The Blessing of the Racecar."

"I told Billy I'd be there. He's trying to get the bishop to come up for the service, but I think that's a pipedream."

"The bishop might come," Meg said, "if he finds out about the media coverage."

"What media coverage?"

"Well, Channel Four will be there. Then there are two TV stations from Charlotte, at least five newspapers, the NPR station from Asheville, and a crew from ESPN."

"Holy smokes!" I said. "I didn't know this was going to be such a big deal."

"Anyway," Meg continued. "I'm pretty sure that once the bishop finds out who's going to be here, he won't want to miss it. By the way, is there a liturgy for blessing a racecar?"

"I'm pretty sure there's not. Maybe Princess Foo-Foo can come up with one."

Chapter 5

I made my way into the Bear and Brew just in time to see Meg and Ruby join Elaine at a table near the back. The Bear and Brew had been an old feed store and still had the irregular pine floor boards and tin signs advertising Allis Chalmers tractor parts, Buckthorn Hogfeed, Columbia Steel Windmills and most everything else the farmer's supply stores at the turn of the century had to offer. Now, though, instead of the smell of fertilizer, leather harnesses and saddle soap, the permeating aroma was pizza—right out of the oven—with just a hint of beer. I took a big whiff and felt right at home.

"Afternoon, Hayden," Ruby said. "You're right on time. We haven't even looked at a menu yet."

"We thought you'd be late," said Elaine, "and we'd get a chance to order an artichoke and spinach pizza before you showed up."

"I like pizza so much, I'll even eat one covered with artichokes and spinach."

"Really?" said Meg. "It has Peruvian goat cheese on it."

I sighed. "Yes. Even with Peruvian goat cheese."

"Great," said Ruby. "Then we'll get a large one." She said this to Pauli Girl McCollough, whom I just noticed was standing by the table with an order pad in her hand.

"Pauli Girl! I didn't know you were working here," I said.

"Well, we just opened."

"Hey, that's great. Aren't you a little young to be serving beer?"

"Yeah. I'm not allowed to serve you beer. I can serve you pizza though and take your drink order, but the beer comes from the bar anyway, so Lisa will bring it to you."

"Fair enough. What do you have? Beer-wise?"

Pauli Girl smiled. ""I don't know. They won't tell me."

"Never mind. I'll just go on up to the bar. You ladies want anything?

"No, thanks," came the consensus from around the table. "We're all having raspberry tea," said Meg.

"Are you all donning red hats as well?" I grumbled as I went off to the bar. I returned shortly with a pint of Guinness.

"I've been looking at the Bulwer-Lytton website," said Elaine. "So I can get a feel for what they're looking for."

"I did the same thing," said Ruby. "I wasn't terribly impressed. I know that I haven't taught English for a number of years now, but it seems like the winners all tend to follow the same formula. The sentences are long; tightly constructed; mainly consisting of an elaborately over-inflated metaphor or simile that in the end is punctured by a ludicrously mundane or trivial final clause. We should be able to construct one of those by the numbers."

"Wow," I said. "I'm impressed. So, do you have a sentence to enter into the contest?"

"Nope," said Ruby, smiling. "Not yet."

"Me, neither," said Elaine.

"I almost had one," said Meg. "But it escaped at the last moment."

"Fine," I said. "Here's mine." I pulled a piece of paper out of my shirt pocket and read.

Lola, last evening's surprise winner of the Weehawken Symphony Competition, now hung grotesquely from the stage, her darkening features evoking the opening strains of her triumphant performance of Beethoven's 3rd piano concerto (opus 37 in c-minor), and her corpse swinging above the recently-tuned Bösendorfer like a giant meat-metronome set on andante or maybe piú lento, or even scherzo if anyone thought this was a musical joke and one bit funny.

"It's pretty good," Meg said thoughtfully. "And yet..."

"I don't get it," said Ruby. "A Bösendorfer is obviously a piano, but, not being a musician, I don't know what those other terms mean."

"Metronome?" I asked.

"No. The Italian. Tempos?"

"Yes," I explained. "Tempos. See, the metronome is set to different tempos to tell you how fast the music goes."

"Well, yes. I *know* that," said Ruby. "I just don't know what they mean."

"I got the first two," said Elaine. "Andante and pew something."

"Piú lento," I said. "It means very slowly."

"Yeah, I've heard of that one. But what was the third one?"

"Scherzo. That's what makes the whole thing funny," I said defensively. "A scherzo is a musical joke."

"Oh," said Meg. "So when you wrap it up with 'if anyone thought this was a musical joke and one bit funny,' that's part of the joke, because *scherzo* means musical joke."

"Yeah," I said, as the three women nodded in understanding. "Although when you take it apart like that, it's not quite so good."

"No, no," said Ruby. "It has several components that I really like. For example, *giant meat-metronome* is really clever. And I presume that Beethoven's 3rd piano concerto actually does have a dark and ominous beginning."

"Yes," I said. "Yes it does."

"All the better," said Meg. "But these are all details that we, as readers or better yet, judges, wouldn't know if we weren't musicians."

"So you guys think that the musical references are too obscure?" I asked.

The three women nodded.

"Or are you convinced that this entry is so good that none of you stand a chance and you're trying to put me off my game?"

The three women nodded.

And, just in time, the pizza arrived.

We walked out of the Bear and Brew, and the town square had been transformed. Pete, our stalwart mayor and never one to miss an opportunity, had told me yesterday about his plans. In the hour or so we spent eating pizza and discussing my shortcomings as an author, the news trucks had arrived, and the talent had begun to set up in Sterling Park across from St. Barnabas. Dave and Nancy had cordoned off Main Street on the west side of the square, and Junior Jameson's car was sitting on a trailer right in front of the church steps. Pete was directing a couple of city employees who were putting some red, white and blue bunting across the front of the church. Billy Hixon had the entire crew of Hixon Lawn Care out putting finishing touches on the park, and when he saw me, he shouted and waved me over. That is, I thought he might have shouted. His mouth moved, but I heard no sound above the din of a lawnmower, several weed-eaters and two leaf blowers.

"We're almost finished," Billy yelled as I walked up. "I wanted everything to look good."

"You guys just mowed this three days ago," I hollered back.

"WHAT?"

"YOU GUYS JUST MOWED THIS…"

The roar suddenly came to a halt as all the machines finished in astonishing synchronization.

"They all finish at the same time?" I bellowed.

"You don't have to yell," said Billy. "They're finished. And all at the same time."

"Oh yeah."

"Anyway, it looks good," said Billy, surveying the grounds as his crew loaded the bags of clippings and tools into the two pickup trucks displaying his logo. "We're gong to be on national news."

"Is the bishop going to be here?"

"Yep," said Billy. "He said he'd be here by two o'clock. I don't think I can get him to wear his cope and mitre even though I told him it'd make for better press."

"Just the purple shirt then?"

"I think so. And his big ol' cross. But what's the point of being the bishop if you won't wear the outfit?" Billy complained. "I think this is something we should find out before we elect them."

"I agree," said Pete, walking up to us. "It'd look a lot better on TV and in the paper if he was in full ecclesiastic regalia."

"You can still probably get a couple of acolytes out here in their robes with a couple of candles," I suggested.

"Already done," said Billy. "And Benny Dawkins is bringing the incense pot." He looked up toward the front of the church. "If we can get a couple of folks up on the steps in vestments, it'd help."

"Well, Bev's in the office," I said, "and Elaine will be here, right? We just finished having lunch."

"She's here now," said Pete. "I just saw her walk into church."

"I'll get her," Billy said. "Maybe Georgia's in there, too."

"You're married to Elaine," I said, "so you can probably talk her into it. Do you have anything on Georgia or Bev?"

"I'll appeal to their civic pride," said Billy, with a grin. "And they probably don't want to have to mow their *own* lawns for the rest of the summer."

Bishop O'Connell showed up at 2:50 pm. Billy was getting worried and had already given me a copy of the blessing just in case I had to preside. There wasn't much to it since everyone knew that the entire service wouldn't occupy more than a thirty-second bite on any of the networks, and newspapers would do well to get a photo and a caption out of the whole extravaganza.

It was a fact of life in the Episcopal Church that we didn't mind blessing all kinds of things, and Episcopal Bishops, in particular, knew that this was part and parcel of their ministry. Last year, during a "Blessing of the Animals" service on St. Francis' Day, Bishop O'Connell was photographed blessing a possum, so the St. Barnabas Racecar, dedicated to the glory of God, wasn't too far out of bounds. Since I didn't have any duties to attend to, I stood off to the side with Meg and Pete and enjoyed the show as well as the beautiful afternoon.

The clock at the top of the courthouse said three o'clock, but then again, that clock always said three o'clock. It had stopped thirty years ago and had never been fixed. The town council had decided that for what it would cost to fix the clock, it would be more economical to have the St. Germaine Town Clock tell the correct time exactly twice a day. It was no coincidence that almost all of our downtown events happened at three. I looked at the clock, then at my watch, and in precisely ten seconds, they lined up perfectly.

The church bell started ringing, the two front doors to the church opened and out walked the procession—two acolytes; Benny Dawkins swinging his thurible; Bishop O'Connell, Bev, Georgia and Elaine, all wearing cassocks; and finally, Billy Hixon, Lucille Murdock and Junior Jameson. Billy was grinning ear-to-ear. Lucille was clutching her purse with both white-gloved hands and blinking nervously behind her thick glasses. Junior waved to the crowd that now numbered close to two hundred. This was a good turnout for St. Germaine, but as I surveyed the crowd, I could tell that there were more out-of-towners than locals.

"Where'd all these people come from?" I asked Pete.

"I put an ad in the *Watauga Democrat*," admitted Pete. "Just a little one, but Junior Jameson is almost famous. If he starts winning races, we'll be set."

"Has he ever won?" I asked.

"Not a Winston Cup race," said Pete. "I don't think he's even had a top twenty finish."

"That's not too good, is it?" said Meg.

"Nope," answered Pete, "but that's all about to change."

Benny Dawkins started his walk-around. The car had been driven off the trailer and was now on Main Street at the bottom of the steps. The hood was up, but the doors and the trunk were closed.

"Shouldn't the doors be open, as well as the hood?" I asked. "For the blessing."

"They're welded shut," said Meg. I looked at her in astonishment.

"So?" she said, "I happen to like NASCAR racing. What about it?"

Benny walked around the car three times with his thurible, directing the fragrant smoke into and around the racecar, although the faint breeze blowing across the square whisked the fog away almost as soon as it appeared.

"Our help is in the name of the Lord," called out Bishop O'Connell.

"Who has made heaven and earth," answered the Blessing Party, consisting of those on the steps.

"The Lord be with you," said the bishop.

"And also with you," the Episcopalians in the crowd answered.

"This is a happy day in the life of St. Barnabas," said the bishop, beginning his homily. I knew it wasn't a happy day for the bishop. When St. Barnabas unexpectedly received a windfall of sixteen-million dollars, Bishop O'Connell was hoping that the diocese would receive its fair share. When we told him that the church had decided to sponsor a NASCAR racing team, he was not amused. But, as Billy put it, "It's our money. We'll do what we want." We looked at our beautiful car, sleek and obviously fast, deep purple with the St. Barnabas crest painted on the hood—a basic red and blue Episcopal shield with an olive branch blazoned across it. Across the doors on both sides were the words "St. Barnabas Episcopal Church, St. Germaine, NC." Painted on the roof was a huge gold cross with the number 17 outlined in black, and on the back of the car were the words "The wages of sin is death," and "Do you know where you'll spend eternity?" presumably there to inspire other drivers, sneaking up on Junior at 215 miles per hour, to reexamine their sordid lives—at least long enough for Junior to beat them to the finish line. It was quite a piece of art, let alone being a marvel of automotive mechanics.

Bishop O'Connell was finishing up, finally getting to the heart of the matter. Georgia moved up beside him with a bowl of water and a small branch taken from one of the sweet olive trees growing beside St. Barnabas. She held the bowl out in front of the bishop.

"Father, bless this water," Bishop O'Connell said, holding his hand over the water, "and let it be a reminder for us of our baptism. Help us to live as people of light, and to be blameless and worthy in your sight."

He then took the branch in his hand and walked toward the car with Georgia in tow, still holding the bowl of water aloft. He dipped the branch in the bowl, lifted it up, dripping, and used it as an asperge, flinging the Holy Water onto the car.

"Lend a willing ear, Lord God, to our prayers, and bless this racecar with Your holy right hand," said the bishop, finishing with the passenger side and walking around the back of the car. "Direct Your holy angels to accompany it, that they may free those who ride in it from all dangers, and always guard them." He dipped the branch into the bowl again and baptized the trunk, back bumper and any other parts that were within sprinkling distance. "And just as by your servant Philip, you gave faith and grace to the man of Ethiopia as he sat in his chariot reading the sacred Word, so point out to your servants the way of salvation." He walked around to the driver's side, and this time, after dunking the branch, reached inside the car and made sure the interior was suitably blessed. "Grant that those who witness the exploits of this car and driver, aided by your grace..." He moved to the front of the car. "...And with their hearts set on good works, they may, after all the joys and sorrows of this journey through life, merit to receive eternal joys, through Christ our Lord. Amen." He shook the remaining water off the branch.

"Hey," said Junior, joining Bishop O'Connell at the front of the car. "Let's put the rest of that Holy Water in the radiator."

From where I was standing, I could hear the bishop take a deep breath, but he nodded as the cameras clicked and whirred. Junior opened the radiator, and Bishop O'Connell took the bowl from Georgia and poured the remaining water into the radiator.

"Blessed are you, Lord God, king of the universe: you have made all things for your glory. Bless this engine and umm...radiator and grant that your servant Junior Jameson may use them in your service and for the good of this church and all your people. Amen."

"Great!" said Junior, clapping his hands and starting a round of applause. "That's that then. Thanks, yer Grace." He shook the bishop's hand. "Any of you reporters have any questions, I'll be back here at the car in just a minute."

The Blessing Party went back through the doors of the church and Junior Jameson reappeared a moment later, coming down to greet the mob of reporters gathered around the racecar.

"Did you have any idea there would be so much media coverage?" Meg asked.

"Nope," said Pete. "I guess with forty-seven cable news channels, they have to come up with something. I'm just mad that I didn't call them when we discovered the Immaculate Confection. I could have made some *real* money."

Chapter 6

I was feeling no adversarial pressure concerning our Bulwer-Lytton bet, and unless those three ladies were playing me like a Klezmer squeezebox, I figured that I had plenty of time to work on my detective story. Who knows? I might even come up with a couple of great sentences I could use. I put my fingers on the keys of the famous typewriter and started typing.

"Fishy Jim?" I said. "Everybody's heard of Fishy Jim. He's the lowest bass in three states."

"Yeah," Betsy sniffed. "Sometimes he sings right off the bottom of the piano, just to make me swoon."

"So, why do you think he's stepping out with another skirt?"

"I see all the signs," she sobbed. "Lipstick on his choir vestment, late night sectional rehearsals, love notes stuck in his hymnal."

I tossed the dead woodchuck into my salad and whistled for the waiter. Unless I was mistaken, I was being strung along by a gal who was as easy as a TV Guide crossword puzzle. No one puts love notes in a hymnal.

"What's his secret?" I asked.

"To attracting choir groupies?" she said, sarcastically.

"Nah," I answered. "I know what attracts choir groupies. All you need is a recording of Pachelbel's Canon and a bottle of Ripple. I'm talking about his low notes. I sure could use another octave."

"I can't tell you."

"C'mon, Toots. You can trust me." I handed the waiter my salad bowl and pointed to the hair peeking out from underneath a piece of arugula.

"You know how some singers have really good breath control?"

I nodded.

"Well, Fishy Jim has gills."

"He's gone," said Bev. "Father George is gone."

"*Gone,* gone?" I asked.

"Packed up and moved. I went by his house this morning because we hadn't heard anything from him since he disappeared on Sunday. Anyway, I knocked on the door. No answer. I looked in the front window and guess what? All the furniture is gone. So I went back to the church and got the key. It's empty. Everything gone. Furniture, appliances, clothes...everything."

"What about his wife? Is Suzanne gone as well?"

"Oh, she left about a month ago," Bev said, dismissively, "to look for a house and get settled." She shook her head. "But most of the furniture was still here. Now it's gone."

"His office?"

"He packed his office up last week, but he was supposed to stay through the end of June. Nope. I think he's gone for good."

"What are you going to do this Sunday?"

"Tony will be here. He'll take care of it. And we have an emergency vestry meeting tonight."

The Slab was bustling, and the breakfast crowd had picked up significantly in the past two weeks. Dave and Nancy were already eating when I joined them. Pete was standing behind the counter, making coffee. Collette was taking an order at one end of the restaurant, and Noylene Fabergé was busy at the other. Noylene, coffee pot in hand, came up to the table as soon as I sat down.

"Morning," she said, filling my cup without asking. "What can I get you?"

"I'll have an omelet. Bacon, mushroom and Swiss cheese."

"Toast?"

"That'd be great," I said. "Hey! I thought you were only going to work on Mondays and Tuesdays."

"Well, the Beautifery doesn't open until ten and Pete needs some help until he hires another waitress."

"And don't think I don't appreciate it," said Pete, walking up to the table. "We were getting swamped."

"Pull up a chair, Mr. Mayor," said Nancy.

"Thank you, I will," said Pete. He sat down and took one of Dave's biscuits. "Any nefarious or criminal activity afoot in our fair village?"

"I gave out two parking tickets yesterday," said Dave. "'Cause I'm a corporal now."

"I didn't have the productive day that Officer Snookie-Pie here had," said Nancy, "but the Gas and Go had a shoplifter. Or said they did. He was long gone by the time I got over there."

"What about that robbery at the Piggly Wiggly? You guys ever get that guy?" Pete asked, referring to a case that was now over a month old.

"Nope," I said. "He ran barefoot into the woods."

"What about the bloodhounds?" asked Pete. "What about the tracking dogs and the helicopter surveillance?"

"Well," said Nancy, "since we don't actually have a helicopter or bloodhounds and since he only got away with what Hannah had in the register, which was $23.45, and since he wasn't actually from Watauga County or someone would have recognized him from the pictures we got from the videotape, we decided to not waste too much time on it."

"It's the principle of the thing!" exclaimed Pete. "You just can't stick-up old ladies. We can't have folks committing felonies at the Piggly Wiggly and getting away with it! That's armed robbery!"

"Not armed, actually," said Nancy. "The guy threatened Hannah with a small stick. She just freaked out."

"Still..." said Pete.

"Listen," I said, "take comfort in the fact that all the checkout girls at the Piggly Wiggly are now packing 9mm automatics courtesy of Ken's Gun Emporium in Banner Elk. So shop with confidence, and, whatever you do, don't try to sneak through the ten-items-or-less line with a dozen donuts."

"Yikes," said Dave. "I almost always take a dozen donuts through the fast line."

"Here's some news," said Pete, ignoring him. "A friend of mine is visiting Appalachian State..."

"Yes," said Nancy. "That *is* news."

"Don't be snide, Lieutenant Parsky, or I'll bust you back down to dogcatcher. Don't forget. I'm the mayor."

Nancy snorted.

"As I was saying," continued Pete, "this friend of mine is a very famous scientist. She wasn't, of course, when I knew her. She was a hot doctoral student at the University of Maryland. Anyway, now she's in charge of the Gorilla Project on Interspecies Communication, and she's on tour with her gorilla."

"Kokomo?" asked Collette, overhearing Pete as she walked by the table.

"Umm, I think so," said Pete. "That sounds right. How did you know?"

"Kokomo's just about the most famous gorilla in the world!" said Collette. "He's got a little pet kitten, and he can talk with sign language. I saw him on the *Today Show*."

"Yeah, that's him," said Pete. "My friend Penny says we can come up and see him if y'all want to."

"Penny?" I asked.

"Well, Penelope. She prefers to be called Dr. Pelicane. Dr. P.A. Pelicane, PhD. But she'll always be 'Penny' to me."

"I'd *love* to go," squeaked Collette. "Dave wants to go, too."

We looked over at Dave, who had a mouthful of pancakes. He stopped chewing, returned our look, then shrugged and continued his breakfast.

"I want to see that gorilla," said Noylene. "And meet that woman. She must be a danged genius to teach him how to talk."

"Well, Noylene, I think you're a genius, too," Collette said. "Look how well your Beautifery has done."

Noylene blushed. "Nah. I ain't no genius. I just help folks find their inner beauty. A genius would be one of them guys like Norman Einstein." Noylene disappeared into the kitchen.

"Speaking of genius," said Pete, looking over at me, "I've got a new idea I want to run by you."

"Let's hear it," I said.

"I met this guy in Charlotte that has a cracker factory. It's called Pepperick Farms. Right now, they only sell around the state, but they're looking to go national. So we're having a couple of beers, and it turns out that he's a Methodist, and we got to talking about communion."

"Yeah," I said, "I've heard of Pepperick Farms." Noylene reappeared with my omelet and toast.

"So we're chatting away like old buds, and he's telling me that the Methodists have communion once a month."

"That's about right," I said. "Presbyterians and Methodists—once a month; Catholics, Episcopalians, Lutherans, Church of Christ, Disciples—every week; Baptists—once a quarter whether they need it or not."

"So there you go. All these churches are having communion, and most of them are eating these round things that taste like Styrofoam."

"Agreed," I said. Nancy and Dave nodded.

"So I'm thinking, why not market something to these churches that actually tastes good and has Christian symbolism at the same time?"

"That sounds like a fine idea," I said. "What's the gimmick?"

"It's no gimmick," Pete said. "This is serious. We're going to start marketing Pepperick Farms Communion Fish."

"Communion Fish?" said Nancy, not quite believing what she was hearing.

"Yep," said Pete, sitting proudly back in his chair. "Communion Fish in liturgical flavors. You see, the fish will be flavored, as well as coordinated with the correct color for the season."

"Dare I ask?" I said.

"You may," said Pete, a smile on his face. "We've come up with a few, but feel free to add some if you think of any. So far we've been thinking about *Angel-Nog* for Christmas, *Vinegar and Gall* for Holy Week, *Pillar O' Salty*, and *TestaMint*."

It was too much. Nancy and I burst out in laughter. Pete looked hurt.

"What? This is a *great* idea!"

"Oh, we agree," I said. "Will the fish crackers have little ichthus signs on them? You know, the Jesus fish?"

"Nah," said Pete. "Little crosses. We don't want to confuse anyone."

"That's really good," laughed Nancy. "How about *Tongues of Flame—Cajun Spicy*?"

Pete grabbed a napkin and pulled out a pen. "Yeah, that's a good one."

"How about *Paschal Lamb*?" I added. "For Easter. Or maybe *Ah Holy Cheeses*."

You're forgetting the best flavor of all," said Dave, who had finished his pancakes and was now taking an interest in our conversation. We looked across the table at him.

"*Barabba-que.*"

"Your fortune is as good as made," I snickered, as Pete scribbled away on his napkin. "I'm sure that many churches will want to participate. Anyway, not to change the subject, but I want to go and see that gorilla."

"Me, too," added Nancy. Dave nodded while Collette and Noylene stood by the counter, looking hopeful.

"Everyone's coming then," I said. "Better call Dr. P.A. Pelicane and set it up, Pete."

Unlike in the winter months, the days in early summer pass pretty quickly for us police-folk. There's always some problem to take care of, usually tourist-related as the locals and the reverse snowbirds know the routine, and, as irritating as the tourists can be, these folks are the life-blood of St. Germaine, and it pays to be nice. But nice, for me, wears thin after a while. I had just told Dave I was leaving and climbed behind the wheel of my truck when Bev Greene tapped on the windshield.

"Can I talk to you for a bit?" she asked.

"I've got to drive in to Boone," I said. "My chainsaw is fixed, and the repair shop closes in a half-hour. You want to ride with me?"

"Sure," answered Bev. She opened the passenger side door and climbed in. "Not too comfortable, is it?"

"These old trucks weren't built for comfort, but this one's working on 500,000 miles. Not too bad, I'd say." The Chevy rumbled to life and the sound of William Byrd's *Mass for Three Voices* came out of the speakers. I reached over and turned it down.

"Better roll your window down," I said. "No air-conditioning."

"I'm fine," replied Bev. "It's a hair thing. And anyway, it's a beautiful day."

She was right. We'd had more than our fair share of breathtaking weather during the month of May. It had stayed cool longer than any other year in recent memory, or so it seemed. The humidity was low and the mountain breezes just kept on coming. If you were out in the evening, it was a good idea to bring along a sweater. We drove out of St. Germaine and out to the Old Chambers Road, the winding, treacherous and very scenic alternate route to Boone.

"I thought you were in a hurry," Bev said.

"I have half an hour. We'll be fine. Anyway, this is a much nicer drive than taking the highway."

Bev nodded. "The vestry met last night. An emergency meeting. Remember? I think I told you about it."

"I remember."

"Billy finally got in touch with Father George. Apparently, the pigeon debacle at Pentecost was the straw that broke the rector's back. He packed up his stuff and had the movers come the next night. I didn't even know you could *get* movers to work at night."

"Well, that's that, then." I replied. "What's the plan?" I took a particularly sharp curve a little too fast, and Bev bounced against the truck door.

"Hey, where's the seatbelt?" she asked, looking for a shoulder belt and, not seeing one, checking the old bench seat for a lap belt.

"Doesn't have any. Too early. Seatbelts weren't even put in this model."

"Oh, that's just *great!* Then slow down will you?"

"Yeah. Sorry. Now, you were saying?"

"I've forgotten." She scrunched up her nose. "Oh yeah. The vestry got on a conference call with Gaylen Weatherall. You remember—she was teaching religious studies at Lenoir-Rhyne College last year."

I nodded.

"The vestry asked her if she'd like to come as an interim with an eye toward becoming our full-time priest if things worked out."

"Sort of a rent-with-option-to-buy deal," I said, with a smile. "A trial basis."

"Yep. We'd try her out, she'd try us out, and then we'd see what happens."

"I've seen other churches hire their interim, and sometimes it works out," I said, taking another curve, this time slower. "Generally, it's an interim priest that the church ends up liking while they're looking for someone else. They realize they already have what they're looking for and offer the interim priest the job. How long is the trial period?"

"Through the end of the year. Then we make a decision to either hire her full-time or look for another interim."

"That seems fair enough."

"Well, Gaylen seems very enthusiastic. She'll be here tomorrow to look around, and she'd really like to meet with *you*."

"Me? Why me?"

"Well...umm..." started Bev, not knowing how quite to broach the subject. "The vestry sort of told her that you were still the choir director, albeit on leave, and that you would be willing to come in and talk to her about resuming your duties."

"Did they?" I said, letting my irritation show. "Did they really?" I pushed down on the accelerator and took another curve. Bev slid all the way across the seat and banged up against me. She grabbed at the seat with both hands, but there was nothing to hold on to.

"It was Meg!" Bev blurted out. "She's the one who said it! Don't kill us!"

I slowed down again, rounding the next curve at a more leisurely pace. Bev crept back to her side of the seat.

"I almost think you did that on purpose," she said primly, straightening her blouse. "You sir, are a letch."

"I don't deny it," I said. "The letch part anyway. Have her give me a call. I'll be happy to meet with her. But I'm here to tell you, I've got some hard questions."

"I'm sure she has some as well."

Chapter 7

"I copied down your sentence about the 'bitter chalk of adolescence' and showed it to Mom," said Meg. "She liked it. Are you going to send it in?"

"I didn't even think about that one," I said. "But now that I look back on it, it has some real potential. How are you ladies doing with your entries?"

Meg sighed. "Mom's got another one, but it's not so good. I don't know how Elaine is doing, but I'm coming up blank. This shouldn't be that hard! I mean, they get over five thousand entries a year."

"Yes," I agreed. "But they're not all Bulwer-Lytton quality."

"That's the most oxymoronic thing I've ever heard."

So Fishy Jim had gills. The answer hit me like Vanna White thrown from the roof of a bowling alley. It was so simple. Why hadn't I seen it before? The extra large mouth; the olive-green hue that we'd attributed to too much time in the practice room; the unblinking orange eyes; the white, mottled belly and the two dorsal fins. I'd been in a couple of choirs with Fishy Jim. He had the lowest notes and the cleanest scales of anybody on the circuit, and now I knew why. His secret was out. He was a bass.

"Son of a clam!" I said.

"You won't tell anyone?" asked Betsy. "Don't we have some kind of detective/client privilege or something?"

"No such thing," I smirked. "But I won't tell."

Not yet, at least, I thought to myself. There was quite a hubbub going on in the church about being inclusive. Mixed marriages were one thing, but marrying outside your species was something else altogether.

I walked into St. Barnabas at exactly four o'clock, the precise time of my appointment with Rev. Dr. Gaylen Weatherall. I walked in through the Parish Hall doors, planning on getting a cup of coffee on my way to the meeting, and met Meg, Bev and Gaylen, all standing around the coffee pot with precisely the same idea.

"Hayden!" said Gaylen, walking over to me with an outstretched hand. "It's so good to finally meet you. I've heard such great things."

I smiled and shook her hand. "It's very nice to meet you, too."

"Why don't we go into the rector's office and chat," she said. "After you get a cup of coffee." She and Bev went down the hallway and disappeared from sight.

"She's clever, that one," I whispered, as they rounded the corner.

"What do you mean?" Meg whispered back.

"Did you notice how she said 'the rector's office' instead of '*my* office?'"

"That *is* clever," said Meg, her sarcasm apparent. "Oh, how will you ever cope with such a clever person? Now go on in and talk to her."

The rector's office was dominated by a massive oaken desk, left over from Father Barna's tenure, a former interim priest with a prodigious case of furniture envy. It was matched in size and ostentation by the overstuffed leather executive chair behind it. However, for this meeting, Gaylen had arranged four chairs in a comfortable pattern around the room.

"I hope you don't mind," Gaylen said. "I've asked Bev and Meg to join us. This is just an informal chat." She motioned for us all to be seated.

"That's fine with me," I said, taking the chair nearest the door.

"I've been talking with Bev, and she's explained the reason for your leave-of-absence."

"Actually, I was fired," I said.

"Yes, she mentioned that, too. Is there still a problem with any of the parishioners?"

"No. I don't think so. I've subbed a few times since then. Everything seems fine."

She nodded thoughtfully. "You've had a few problems with the clergy?"

"Well, let's see," I said. "Because of me, Loraine Ryan had to leave the priesthood for having an affair with the Senior Warden. Then Emil Barna's wife tried to kill me. And Father George gave me the sack. So the answer would be...yes."

"Bad apples," said Gaylen. "Tony Brown says you're the best organist in the state."

"Hardly," I said. "But I'm probably the best in town."

"How many are in town?" whispered Bev to Meg.

"Just one," answered Meg, "since Agnes Day got killed with the handbell."

"What would it take for you to come back?" Gaylen asked, finally getting to the heart of the matter. "A raise?"

"He's rich," said Bev. "I forgot to tell you that. He doesn't do it for the money."

"I've never taken a salary," I said. "But I've got a few questions for you."

"I'm at your disposal."

"How old are you?" I asked.

Bev and Meg gasped audibly.

"Fifty-five."

"Married?"

"Widowed. Three years ago."

"I'm sorry," I said. She nodded.

"How do you feel about re-naming the Trinity?" I asked.

"I presume you're referring to that Presbyterian clap-trap that happened at their National Assembly. Quite frankly, it's the best thing to happen to the Episcopal Church since those wacky Presbyterians came up with the 'Service of Milk and Honey' at the ReImagining conference in 1993. Lord knows, we've got plenty of problems we need to work out, and this should take the public eye off of us for a couple of months."

"So, I'm presuming you won't be renaming the Trinity in any of our liturgies."

"Nope. I stick pretty much to the Prayer Book. Those Presbyterians can call the Trinity 'Huey, Dewy and Louie' for all I care."

Meg giggled.

"What's your position on Clown Eucharists?" I asked.

"Kneeling in front of my statue of St. Genesius. Seriously, there certainly have been plenty of them, but I find them ridiculous." She looked thoughtful for a moment and then added "Pirate Eucharists as well."

"Someone's been telling tales," I said with a smile. "I read a couple of your books—*Engaging God: The Theology of Worship* and your memoir, *Beyond Bethel*. I enjoyed them both."

"I admit that I've enjoyed your writings as well. When I Googled you, a page came up entitled *The Usual Suspects*."

"Some of my best work," I said modestly.

"I didn't know he had any of her books," whispered Bev to Meg.

"I didn't know either," Meg whispered back.

"So," I said, "hypothetically speaking, if you were our priest, how would we address you? Mother Weatherall?

"Well, there is precedent for that, but I find it rather pretentious. If we're in a formal situation, 'Reverend or Doctor Weatherall' will do nicely. If not, I've always preferred 'Gaylen.'"

"What's your stance on sexual harassment?" I asked.

"I won't tolerate it," Gaylen said, smiling. "Oh, you may certainly compliment my hair or my outfit, and I'll do the same for you. You know, there's a video put out by the Diocese..."

"I've seen it," I interrupted. "I was particularly impressed by the stunning production values. But I meant Marilyn," I said, referring to our long-suffering church secretary. "If I come back, may I still sexually harass Marilyn?"

Gaylen look confused. "Did you before?"

"Kind of," I admitted, with a shrug.

"I'd rather that you didn't."

"Hmm. What about the altos? May I sexually harass the altos?"

"He doesn't actually harass us," said Meg. "Throw him a bone, will you?"

"Okay," said Gaylen. "You may sexually harass the altos. Up to a point. But if you tell anyone I said you could, I'll deny it."

"Ah, plausible deniability," I said. "But I have witnesses."

"No you don't," said Bev.

I looked over at Meg. She shook her head. "Nope."

"Fine," I shrugged.

"Now I have a couple of questions for *you*," Gaylen said. I looked at her in anticipation. She was quite an attractive woman, tall and slender with shoulder length white hair that rested gently on her shoulders, and an easy smile that lit her unlined face.

"Shoot," I said.

"Well, that's the first question. Do you actually keep a loaded pistol in the organ bench?"

"Yep. A Glock 9."

"May I ask why?"

"Well, I *am* a cop," I said. "Plus, there are rats in the choir loft, and I find it helps persuade the tenors to sing the right notes."

"Hmm," said Gaylen. "I can see where that might help. How about the psalms? Do you sing them or just say them?"

"We always sang them when I was here. I'm not quite sure what they do now."

"Well, I've gone over some of the bulletins from your tenure, and the music looked wonderful. If you decide to come back, I hope that you'll continue to provide the parish with that gift."

"No Hootnanny masses?" I asked. "No canned music?"

"No."

"Who picks the hymns?"

"You do."

"Who's going to fire the one-legged organist?"

"Bev is," said Gaylen, with another smile.

"Well, I'll certainly mull it over," I said, getting to my feet. "You've given me a lot to think about."

"I'll be here on Sunday," Gaylen said. "Tony will be celebrating, but I'll be helping out. The Sunday after that, it'll just be me. I hope you'll be back by then. Also, if you put copies of your detective stories in the choir folders, I expect one in my Prayerbook as well."

She stood and shook my hand. "It's been a real pleasure talking to you, Hayden."

"So, what do you think?" asked Meg. "C'mon. What do you think?"

"I think she's very clever," I said. "*Very* clever. Almost *too* clever."

74

"But you like her, right?"

"Yeah, I like her."

"So, you'll come back? I wouldn't ask you if I didn't think you'd enjoy yourself. And you just haven't been happy since you quit."

"I know," I said. "I do miss playing. I'll tell you what. I'll come back for a while, and we'll see how it goes."

I picked Moosey up at five-thirty in the morning. The sky was beginning to lighten, but the sun hadn't yet made its appearance. As I drove up to the McCollough trailer, my headlights swept across the porch and illuminated Moosey, sitting cross-legged, chewing happily on a candy bar, the coffee can full of worms next to him. I pulled up, and Moosey was into the truck before I had a chance to come to a full stop.

"Did you tell your Mom we were leaving?"

"She saw you through the window," Moosey said, pointing toward the living room. I looked over, but the curtains were drawn."

"You sure?"

"Yeah. She saw you drive up. Then she waved goodbye and everything."

I nodded. "Okay then. We'll be back by eight anyway."

We drove to the lake, carried our tackle down to Pete's boat, arranged ourselves and pushed off into the quiet water. It was one of those mornings that was dead still. I heard a few birds in the distance, but other than the sound of the oars in the water, the lake was as silent as the grave. The breeze that had welcomed us the first morning was nowhere to be found, and the fog rested on the surface of the lake like one of Ardine's quilts, making it tough to see the opposite shore even though it was a scant fifty yards away.

"You think we'll catch one today?" said Moosey. "I've never caught no fish before."

"Well, I hope so," I said. "Here, stick a worm on the end of that hook."

One thing I'll say for Moosey—he's never been squeamish when it comes to worms. We baited our hooks, clipped on the bobbers and

75

dropped our lines into the water. True anglers worried about casting close to the weeds, which lures would be most likely to work on any given day and making the plastic frog jump to look like something a fish would actually like to eat—but for me, fishing was mostly about dropping a worm in the lake and enjoying the morning. If some fish was stupid enough to eat it and get caught, that was his own dumb fault. I couldn't be blamed.

We'd sat there in silence for about thirty minutes, relaxing and switching worms when they either stopped wiggling, managed to escape, or were nibbled off our hooks by some smart fish. Then Moosey got a bite. And what a bite it was.

There was a big splash and a yell, and Moosey's pole bent almost double, the spinner having been locked to prevent a snarl. I was expecting that we might catch a brim or a blue-gill or, at the very most, a small bass, and locking the reel wouldn't have posed any problem. But what Moosey had was a monster.

"WhatdoIdoWhatdoIdo?" hollered Moosey, standing in the boat and hanging on to the fishing rod for dear life. I put my own rod down and stood behind him, putting my hands over his, helping him to hang on. The rod was bending at about a ninety-degree angle. I unlocked the spinner and the line sailed off the reel as the fish made a dash toward the middle of the lake.

"Wow!" I said. "Did you see him?"

"Just for a second," said Moosey excitedly. "When he came up for the worm."

"What did he look like?"

"He was darkish green and white! With some spikey fins on his back!"

"Not black? Like a catfish?"

"He ain't no catfish," Moosey declared. "I'll bet he's a big ol' bass."

I had to agree. I'd caught catfish in this little lake before, and I'd never seen a catfish take off like this fellow.

"Okay," I said. "Let's see if we can land him."

We began the traditional fisherman's dance, first pulling back on the pole, drawing the fish back toward the boat, then reeling in the excess line. We'd done this three times and were feeling pretty good about ourselves when the line went slack.

"He's heading back. Reel him in! Quick now!" I said.

Moosey reeled frantically and the spinner whirred, but just as almost all the line had been recovered, the fish changed direction again, bent the pole at another right angle and with a sickening 'pop,' the fishing line snapped.

"Aw, man!" said Moosey, disappointment clouding his face. "The line busted."

"Wow," I said. "That was a big one."

"He was as big as my arm," said Moosey, holding up his arm to show me.

"I don't know if he was that big," I said. "But I'll tell you what. We're going to get him before the summer's out."

"All right!" yelped Moosey. "Wait till I tell the guys."

"Nope," I said. "You can't tell anyone."

"Why not?"

"Because that's *your* fish, Moosey. If you tell anyone, pretty soon everybody will be down here trying to catch him. And we don't want that."

Moosey nodded thoughtfully. "I won't tell."

"That's good. 'Cause we're going to catch that rascal," I said with a smile. I was smiling because that fish snapped my twenty-five-pound-test fishing line like it was a piece of thread. If it *was* a bass, and I was pretty sure it was, he was one for the record books.

"How was the fishing?" asked Pete when I walked into the Slab.

"Well, we didn't catch anything," I said, truthfully.

"Get any bites?"

"Umm. Nope. Not a one."

"You're lying," said Pete with a grin. "You saw him, didn't you?"

"What are you talking about?"

Pete lowered his voice and leaned in close. "You saw Old Spiney. I can always tell." He grinned again, studying my face. "Yep. You saw him all right."

"Come sit down with me, Pete," I said gesturing to a booth, "and tell me all you know."

"I know two things," said Pete as he slid across the red Naugahyde bench. "That fish ain't never been caught, and he ain't likely to be."

"He's a largemouth?"

"Oh, yeah. I've hooked him about a dozen times over the years, but he's a cagey one. He'll run for the middle, then right back at the boat. He'll drag your line under a log, or throw it when he jumps up in the air. One time I had him look straight at me and just spit out the lure. How'd he get you?"

"Busted the line. How big do you think he is?"

"I wouldn't be surprised if he was up around eighteen pounds by now. He was big when I first hooked him about eight years ago. What test were you using?"

"Twenty-five."

"Did he snag it on something?"

Nope." I said. "Snapped it straight away."

"Whoa," said Pete. "Maybe he's bigger than I thought. You know, the Fish and Wildlife guys dumped a whole bunch or troutlings in that lake last year. Probably about a thousand."

"I'll bet they aren't there anymore," I said. "That fish probably went through those troutlings like a Sumo Wrestler at a Sushi Buffet and has graduated to eating the turtles. Moosey and I are going to get him, though."

"Well, good luck. If you get him, bring him on up here. We'll have a good old-fashioned fish fry. By the way," he said, changing the subject, "did you hear about Wormy? He's going to open a cemetery on Kenny's Frazier's old farm. Noylene was telling me about it."

"We need a cemetery?"

"Well, if you don't already have a plot at Mountainview, you're not likely to get one. It's full up, and they're not selling anymore."

"Well, it sure is pretty at the Old Frazier place," I said. "And he has about fifty acres, doesn't he?"

"That's about right," said Pete. "Wormy's going to demolish the house and the two barns. The house was a tear-down anyway."

"Has he sold any plots?" I asked.

"I don't think so, but he's going to start this next week. Planting begins in the fall."

I laughed. "Does this enterprise have a name yet?"

"Woodrow DuPont's Bellefontaine Cemetery."

"That's quite a beautiful and elegant appellation," I said in my best snooty accent, raising my cup of coffee in a mock-toast. "I shall look forward to being interred there, should the need arise."

"Well, 'Bellefontaine Cemetery' is the official name," said Pete. "But I'm calling it *Wormy Acres.*"

Chapter 8

"How's the story coming?" Meg asked. "Any bad sentences I can steal?"

"Nope. And I have to get serious about this detective story, now that I'm going to have a choir again."

Meg put her arms around me, bent down over my shoulder and put her face close to mine. "Listen," she said, blowing softly into my ear. "Do you think I might be allowed to use your magic typewriter sometime when you're not busy?"

My fingers hit seven keys at once. "Uh...I guess so."

"Really?" she whispered. "You wouldn't mind?"

"Yes...I mean no...I mean...umm...whatever you want."

"Thanks. And don't be too long. Supper's almost ready." Her fingers trailed through my hair as she walked out of the den.

"Hey, wait a minute," I called after her. "I was momentarily addled. What did I just agree to?"

The only answer was lilting laughter.

A bass, like any other singer, is only as good as his last solo. It's an axiom as old as Diane Bish's hairdo. Fishy Jim had never missed an entrance that I knew of, and I'd been around since Pavarotti was in Pampers.

I had a chat with the maitre d', got a voucher for two more free meals at the Chartreuse Chapeau, then went around back to retrieve my woodchuck out of the dumpster.

"Wow," said Betsy, standing waist deep in potato peels. "You really know how to show a gal a good time."

"Listen, Kitten," I said, looking at my watch. "I haven't got all night. And you couldn't very well boost ME into the dumpster. Not in THAT dress."

"Found it!" yelped Betsy. "Right here under these chicken skins!"

"Then hop out of there, throw it in the back seat, and let's paint the town red," I said.

"What are we going to sing on Wednesday?" Meg asked. "Do you have any great ideas yet?"

"Nope. I'll have to do some planning, I guess. How about Mozart's little d-minor mass?"

"I've never heard it. Is it good?" asked Meg, handing me a plate of pasta.

"Yeah, it is. A couple of violins, some nice little solos. Enchanting, really."

"Sounds like fun," Meg said, handing me a glass of red wine to go with my plate of noodles. "By the way, I'm tired of cooking every night. You're cooking the next three—no, make that four—times I come over."

"It'll be my pleasure, but you only come over for dinner a couple times a week. That's two weeks worth of cooking."

"Yep. And no take-out either. And no burgers or knockwurst. And *you* have to do the shopping."

"Sheesh," I said, tasting my pasta. "Is this what it's going to be like when we're married?"

"You wish!"

It was our plan to all meet at the biology department at Appalachian State. Pete had set up an "interview" with Dr. Pelicane and Kokomo the gorilla. We had quite a crew. There was Meg and myself; Moosey and his mother Ardine; Pete and his latest significant other, Molly Frazier; Dave, Collette and Nancy. Noylene was there, of course, and Wormy. Noylene had invited Brother Jimmy Kilroy, pastor of the New Fellowship Baptist Church, since she and Collette were members, and Brother Jimmy thought it would be fascinating to see a talking gorilla. He, in turn, had asked Rev. Francisco Garridos, a Baptist minister from Spain who was spending a month at NFBC studying church growth with Brother Jimmy. Kent Murphee, the coroner from Boone, made the two-block trek from his office at my invitation. I counted fourteen as we walked into the science building.

"Wow, there's quite a crew!" said a rather heavy-set, middle-aged woman wearing a white lab coat over a blouse and a pair of dark slacks. "I'm Dr. Pelicane."

"Hiya, Penny," Pete said. "We've all come to see your gorilla."

"Wonderful!" said Dr. Pelicane. "Great to see you again, Pete! Follow me this way and I'll give you the spiel."

"Kokomo has been with me for twenty-one years," said Dr. Pelicane, leading us down the hall. "I got him as a baby. He has a vocabulary of over a thousand words and can understand two-thousand words of spoken English."

"How does he talk?" asked Moosey, now walking beside Dr. Pelicane. "Can I ask him stuff?"

"He uses American Sign Language, but he's very selective about answering questions."

"I can talk in sign language!" said Moosey, excitedly. "I learned last year. We had a deaf kid in our class, and Mrs. Shields taught some of us sign language. I was the best at it though!"

"That's great," said Dr. Pelicane, still walking, with Moosey in close proximity, the rest of us doing our best to keep up and follow the conversation. "But he's very hard to understand. Some of his signs you'd recognize right away, but he uses different language patterns than we do. If he doesn't know a word, or if a word sounds a lot like one he *does* know, he might use that one. He often interchanges 'nipple' for 'people.'"

Moosey laughed. Apparently, Dr. Pelicane, in her ivory tower, didn't know that you can't say "nipple" to an eight year old.

"We call these 'sound-alikes,'" she continued. "In some other cases, he's decided to change the word completely. For example, for 'woman,' he would sign 'lip.' That's his word for woman."

"So a woman is a lip?" asked Pete. "He's a very perceptive gorilla."

"Oh yes," said Dr. Pelicane, completely missing Pete's joke. "He has an IQ of somewhere between 70 and 90. That's just slightly lower than an average human's. He'll even tell me a lie sometimes." She stopped in front of a door, took out a key, unlocked it and ushered us into a lab.

"It is an extremely interesting proposition," said Rev. Garridos in perfect English, but with a heavy Spanish accent. "In Spain, our governing party, what you would call the 'Socialists' I believe, is submitting a bill to grant human rights to four species of animals."

"Gorillas?" Dr. Pelicane asked.

"Yes, that is one," said Rev. Garridos. "Chimpanzees, bonobos, gorillas and orangutans; the *grandes simios*. Great apes."

"Well, you know that the great apes share 99.3 percent of their genetic material with humans," said Dr. Pelicane.

"Yes," said Rev. Garridos. "I find the entire exercise absurd, but champions of their rights say they have an emotional and cultural life, intelligence and moral qualities that are reminiscent of humans."

"I couldn't agree more," Dr. Pelicane said, leading us toward a door marked with a large, red exit sign. "Right through here. We could have gone the long way around, but this was easier."

We pushed open the door and walked out into a paved courtyard. In the center of the courtyard was a motor home—a big one, with the University of Maryland logo on the side.

"This is how we travel," Dr. Pelicane said. "Kokomo enjoys driving." She opened the door to the motor home, and we all piled inside. It was spacious, as motor homes go, thirty-nine feet long and eight and a half feet wide with a couple of slide-out walls that gave the occupants even more room. The air conditioner was on, and the temperature inside was rather cool. About two-thirds of the way back was a Plexiglas barrier, floor to ceiling, complete with a see-through door and several metal slotted disks inserted into the plastic for sound transmission.

"Hey, Cutie," Dr. Pelicane said loudly to Kokomo. "These are my friends. They've come to talk to you."

Kokomo moved her hands and pointed to Noylene's shirt.

"Yes, that red-pink," said Dr. Pelicane, then turned to us. "We were having a discussion about color earlier."

"Would that be all right with you?" she asked, speaking again to Kokomo, then turned to us and translated.

"She says, 'Fine hurry good.'"

I was watching Moosey during all this, and his eyes never left Kokomo's signing. He nodded when he heard "hurry good."

"That red," signed Kokomo, pointing at Dr. Pelicane's hair.

"No, Kokomo, that's black," corrected Dr. Pelicane.

"Black," signed Kokomo. "Candy give me."

"I will give you a treat when we're finished," said Dr. Pelicane. "but no candy."

Kokomo huffed and blew some air through his great lips. He wasn't a huge gorilla, but any gorilla is bigger than life in Boone, North Carolina. I had done some internet research before we left this morning—I was sure everyone else had as well—and found out that Kokomo was five-foot-eight-inches tall and weighed 480 pounds. He didn't look quite so big sitting down on the other side of the Plexiglas, but I didn't doubt these statistics. The gorilla site on the internet also pointed out that male gorillas are as strong as six to eight men. As tame as Kokomo was, I was glad of the barrier.

"Would any of you like to ask Kokomo a question?" asked Dr. Pelicane. "I can't guarantee he'll answer you. Sometimes he can be stubborn, but he seems to be in a good mood today."

"Can I ask him about his kitten?" asked Noylene. The doctor nodded.

"What is your kitten's name?" said Noylene very slowly and deliberately.

"Tiger," signed Kokomo.

"Tiger?" asked Moosey. "Did he say 'Tiger?'"

"He sure did," said Dr. Pelicane. "That's very good. Would you like to ask him a question?"

"Sure," said Moosey, thinking. "Do you like bananas?"

"Yes," signed Kokomo. "Kokomo like banana."

"He said 'Yes, he likes bananas!'" exclaimed Moosey, his excitement growing by the moment.

"Kokomo," said Pete, "how do you feel about our government's foreign policy? Specifically, the job our President is doing?"

"Pete..." hissed Meg. "Don't be rude."

"Like no little tree," signed Kokomo. "Candy give me."

"He wants some candy," blurted out Moosey. "Can I give him a treat when we're done?"

"Sure," said Dr. Pelicane. "Did you see what else he said?"

"He don't like no little trees," answered Moosey. "But I don't get it."

"Kokomo doesn't always have the vocabulary he needs, so sometimes he makes up words or puts words together."

I started laughing, and Pete caught on a moment later.

"That's great!" I said.

"That's one smart gorilla," said Pete, admiringly. "Although I think that he's been coached just a little."

"I assure you he has not," said Dr. Pelicane. "But I *will* tell you that he watches CNN for two hours almost every day. He has some very strong political opinions."

"What are you three talking about?" asked Meg.

"He doesn't like little trees," I said.

"So?"

"Bush," said Pete with a laugh. "He doesn't like Bush. What a hoot!"

"Wow," said Noylene.

After that, we all had questions, mostly about Kokomo's likes and dislikes, and Moosey was getting quite proficient at translating. About a third of the time, Kokomo's answers had more to do with the color of Noylene's shirt and when, if ever, he might get some candy. After about twenty minutes, though, it was pretty clear that Kokomo was getting tired of us.

"Hurry candy give me. You go."

"I think that's about it for this visit," said Dr. Pelicane. "Moosey, here's a plum you can give him. He likes plums. Just hold it up here." She unlatched the window and slid it open. "He won't hurt you. Gorillas are very gentle, but if they get excited, they'll use their arms to crash into things. If this barrier wasn't here and Kokomo got excited for some reason, it might be very dangerous."

"Does he have to stay behind the glass all the time?" asked Ardine.

"Oh, no," said Dr. Pelicane. "When I'm here alone with him, the door is open, and we interact freely."

"Thank you for letting us meet Kokomo," said Meg, and the rest of us offered our thanks as well.

"Can I ask one more question?" said Noylene.

"Sure," said Dr. Pelicane.

"Kokomo," said Noylene, putting her mouth close to one of the metal disks. "This is very important. Would you like to accept Jesus Christ as your personal Lord and Savior?"

The motor home became deathly quiet—the only sound, the hum of the air-conditioner. Thirteen people stood there looking at Noylene. There she was, witnessing to Kokomo, and none of us could move.

"Did you hear me Kokomo? Will you accept Jesus as your personal Lord and Savior?"

"Yes, Kokomo love hugs," Kokomo signed.

"Kokomo loves hugs," Moosey translated. "I guess he didn't understand."

"Oh, he understood," said Pete, looking over at me. I nodded.

"What?" said Meg, looking first at me, then over at Dr. Pelicane. The doctor looked puzzled, as if she was trying to figure out what Kokomo meant.

"Oh my," said Nancy, a look of understanding coming across her face. "Oh my. Not hugs..."

I whispered to Meg. "Remember the *Mouldy Cheese Madrigal*?"

"Sure."

"Kokomo just did the same thing." Everyone in the room was looking at me now. I felt as uncomfortable as Kokomo probably did on a daily basis. I looked around at the thirteen faces. The *Mouldy Cheese Madrigal* is this Christmas piece we sing that, for better or worse, rhymes 'Holy Jesus' with 'Mouldy Cheeses.' It started off as a joke, but it's a pretty good piece."

"No," smirked Meg. "No, it's not."

"So what are you saying?" said Kent. "That Kokomo is using a sound-alike? For what? Hugs?"

"Not hugs," said Dr. Pelicane, very quietly. "Squeezes."

"Yes...Kokomo...loves...squeezes," said Noylene, her voice approaching something akin to awe. "He loves Jesus," she whispered.

"Holy smokes," said Wormy. "That gorilla loves Jesus. He's done been saved!"

"Well...hallelujah...I guess," said Collette, quietly taking Dave's hand.

"Damn," whispered Molly.

I looked at Brother Jimmy Kilroy. His eyes were bright, and his face had a glow I hadn't noticed before.

"Well, Kokomo's been born again," said Pete, with a good-natured laugh. "This really opens a theological can of worms, don't it?"

86

"Well, what happens now?" said Collette.

"What do you mean?" I asked. After our visit to Appalachian State, Meg and I went back to the Slab for a piece of cake and a cup of coffee. Arriving there ahead of us, were Pete, Collette, Dave, Nancy, and Noylene. Pete and Collette were back at work, getting ready for the lunch crowd. That work included bringing the rest of us a piece of Red Velvet Cake and some of Pete's not-so-famous coffee.

"What about Kokomo? I mean now that he's been saved."

"This is an interesting conundrum," I said, "worthy of many interesting discussions."

"I don't see how there's anything to discuss," said Noylene. "If he's saved, he's saved. That's what the Bible says."

"I expect you'll get some debate on that," said Meg. "Hey Pete? Is Bud around? I need some advice."

"I'll get him," said Pete.

"Anyway, I'm glad Kokomo's not going to hell," said Collette. "He seems like a nice gorilla." She walked into the middle of the restaurant. "Dave and I have an announcement to make."

Everyone in the restaurant looked over at Collette.

"As you know, Dave and I got engaged and were going to get married in October."

"Do you think they broke up?" whispered Nancy to Meg. Meg shrugged.

"We've decided to move the wedding up to June! This month! We're so excited, aren't we Snookie-Pie?"

We all looked at Corporal Snookie-Pie for a verbal affirmation, but he had a mouth full of cake, so he just nodded, smiled and kept eating.

"Dave and I are getting married at New Fellowship Baptist Church. Brother Kilroy will be doing the service. You're all invited." She looked around the Slab and fixed her gaze on the ten or so customers populating the tables on the other side of the restaurant. "Y'all, too," she said with a smile. "All y'all are invited."

Bud came out of the kitchen and up to the table.

"Hi, Miss Farthing. Pete said you wanted to see me."

"Hi Bud. I wonder if you can suggest a couple of special wines that will go with whatever Hayden is planning on cooking for me." Meg looked over at me and gave me her nicest smile.

"Well, sure," said Bud. "What will you be having to eat?"

Meg's eyebrows went up. "Well, let's just find out, shall we?"

Yes," I said, "supper. I'm thinking that on Friday we'll probably begin with an onion tart, followed by an entree of seared scallops in a light tomato-plum sauce. I hadn't planned any dessert, but, now that I think about it, some baked D'Anjou pears would be nice."

I looked over at Meg and Nancy. Both their mouths were hanging open. I smiled at them and pulled out my pad to take notes. Bud was always thorough.

"Onions are really diverse and can be enjoyed with white and red wine," began Bud. "If you're using Vidalia onions you should choose a white with a more flinty tone like a Sauvignon Blanc from New Zealand. 'Cause Vidalias are sweeter. A Chardonnay from Washington or Central Coast would be just perfect. I would ordinarily choose a white over a red, but a Beaujolais Village from George Duboeuf or a Chianti Classico from Fonterutoli would also match very nice."

I nodded and jotted down this info. "Beaujolais Villoiage... George DuBoeuf...Chianti Classico."

"For the main course, if you're having a red with the appetizer, I'd go with a New Zealand Sauvinon Blanc or a light, crisp, clean Pinot Grigio."

"Got it," I said.

"Now for the pears." Bud stopped and thought for a moment. "Robert Mondavi is growing a delicious Moscato D'Oro. Also the vineyards from Martinelli are producing a tremendous Muscato. Those wines are rather powerful in acidity and have high levels of residual sugar. The flavors are full of pear, apricot, melon and honeysuckle. It would be a great match with this dessert. Also a sparkling wine or a glass of Champagne would be delicious."

"What do you think?" I asked Meg. "Champagne or a Moscato D'Oro?"

"I...uh..." said Meg, now at a loss for words. She hadn't planned on this. She'd been trying to catch me unprepared. I, on the other hand, had been planning for days.

"Champagne it is," I said, snapping my pad shut. "That settles it then. Thank you, Bud."

"No problem," said Bud. "I'm happy to help." He turned and walked back to the kitchen.

"That boy never fails to amaze," said Nancy. She looked at me. "You, too! Seared scallops in tomato-plum sauce? Where did you learn that?"

"Oh, here and there. I can be quite a cook when I get motivated."

"That's news to me," said Meg.

"News to us all," added Dave.

"Speaking of news," said Noylene. "I've got some news, as well."

"This morning is just getting better and better," I said.

"Y'all know that me and Wormy been seeing a lot of each other. Well, Wormy's going to open his cemetery in the fall, and I'm going to help him. I got some business experience since I opened the Beautifery—more'n Wormy anyway."

"That's great," said Meg. "I'm sure you both will do very well."

"Oh, that ain't the news," said Noylene, with a big smile. "The news is that Wormy and me's getting married, too. I'm keeping my professional name, but I may hyphenate for formal occasions. Noylene Faberge-DuPont."

"Umm, Noylene," Pete said. "Aren't you and Wormy first cousins?"

"Well, sure. Is that a problem?"

"Not in North Carolina," I said. "Not in North Carolina."

Chapter 9

Betsy was a good time waiting for a bus. We headed over to a dive I knew for some dancing and then to the Possum 'n Peasel for drinks. When I woke up the next morning, she was long gone—gone like the "Amens" on the end of some of those hymns, plagally content in their subdominant/dominant relationship until someone decided they weren't theologically accurate and dumped 'em as unceremoniously as I'd just been dumped by Betsy.

I peeled myself off the floor of the bar, staggered to my feet, looked around the P 'n P, brushed the cigar butts out of my hair, and decided that the next time a Methodist Minister challenged me to a vodka-drinking contest I wouldn't wear suede shoes. My head hurt the way your tongue hurts when you accidentally staple it to your tax return.

I headed back to the office. I still didn't know anything. I was supposed to find out who Fishy Jim was seeing on the sly, but this whole case stunk like a dead woodchuck wrapped in chicken skins lying in the backseat of a car. Which reminded me...

"This is very good writing," said Marjorie from the tenor section. "I'm glad you're still in fine form."

"Well, I need to keep in shape. I have a contest to win." I smiled over at Meg and Elaine.

This was my first choir rehearsal since before Christmas, not counting the couple of times I had subbed after Agnes Day died. Bev told me that Henrietta Burbank would no longer be showing up for services. I'd come up to the choir loft earlier in the day, set the organ back up the way I liked it, and spent a few hours reacquainting myself with the fine old instrument. It was soon apparent to me that I'd have to put in more than a few hours. As Paderewski, the famous pianist, once said, "If I don't practice for one day, I know it. If I don't practice for two days, the critics know it. If I don't practice for three days, everyone knows it." Granted, I wasn't in Paderewski's league, and I didn't practice every day anyway, but I'd been away long enough to notice a big difference. Still, I had some old standards under my fingers, and I'd rely on them until I was back in playing shape.

"Okay choir," I said. "I'm back. No more goofing off. And no more singing like pigs."

This brought snickers from the bass section. Sitting on the back row were the basses Fred, Bob, Mark and Phil. The tenors were a little thin, being anchored by Marjorie. Marjorie had been in the choir since God was a boy and had been singing in the men's section since 1972. "I'm a tenor, dammit!" was her answer to any organist brave enough to question her choice of seats. Marjorie also kept a flask in her hymnal rack. None of us dared check to see what it contained. The back row altos (or BRAs as they preferred to be known) were the rowdiest section. Rebecca Watts had made herself at home in this moderately militant feminist organization and sat next to Martha Hatteberg. Also gracing the alto section was Tiff, our unpaid summer intern from Appalachian State. The sopranos included Meg, Elaine, and Georgia. Bev, who had decided she could sing in the choir as well as be the Parish Administrator, was in the soprano section as well. Everyone included, I counted twenty-two folks.

"Are you saying we were singing like pigs?" asked Fred.

"Yes," I said. "Extremely porcinesque. They could hear the squealing all the way over at New Fellowship Baptist."

"Really?" said Elaine. "How could they hear us over their Electric Praise Team?"

"Okay," I said. "Let us not cast aspersions. We need to learn the Psalm, an offertory anthem, a communion anthem and a hymn descant. And that's just for *this* Sunday. Then we need to start looking ahead. We'll start with some easy stuff. Get out the Tallis *If Ye Love Me.*"

"May I be in this new story?" asked Elaine. "I want to be a Sultry Siren."

"I already have a Sultry Siren," I said.

"How about the Other Woman? Can I be the Other Woman?"

"No," I said. "Now, everyone, look at measure eight."

"I want to be in it, too," interrupted Marjorie. "I want to be the Hard-Drinking Bus Station Restroom Attendant With The Heart Of Gold."

Everyone laughed, and my shoulders slumped. "Fine," I said. "In the next one. If there *is* a next one."

"Dandy About Town," said Mark Wells from the bass section. "I want to be the Dandy About Town." There were more giggles from the sopranos. Dandy indeed. Mark hadn't taken his baseball cap off since Reagan was in office.

"I'll see what I can do."

The Ginger Cat has good food, if a bit too health-conscious for my tastes, though the coffee is always excellent and reason enough to be a steady patron. The Bear and Brew, St. Germaine's new pizza establishment and micro-brewery, has much to recommend it, including great pizza and many extraordinary beers on tap. But for theological discussion and Reuben sandwiches, there was only one place to go—The Slab Café.

There was quite a convocation gathering. Noylene, Collette and Pete were in attendance, of course. Nancy and Dave as well as Meg, Brother Jimmy Kilroy and Rev. Francisco Garridos.

"I think he's saved," said Noylene. "That's what the Bible says and I believe it."

"It's an interesting question," said Pete. "Because, in order to be saved, wouldn't Kokomo have to sin? He can't be born into sin since, not being human, he wasn't affected by the fall from grace. And he's a gorilla. Gorilla's can't sin."

"Gorillas can sin if they know it's wrong. Dr. Pelicane said that Kokomo tells lies sometimes. That's a sin."

"A sin for us, maybe," said Pete, "but I hardly think lying is a sin for a gorilla."

"What about lusting in his heart?" said Collette. "That's sure a sin. And while you guys were asking him questions, he was looking at Noylene in that pink shirt and lusting in his heart. I saw it! I just didn't want to say anything."

"Yes, I think we all saw it," said Meg, with a laugh. "It was kind of hard to miss. And I thought that Pete was being especially courteous not to mention it."

"What? I missed it?" said Pete. "Dagnabbit! That would have been hilarious!"

"What if he is saved?" said Nancy, weighing in. "Can a gorilla go to heaven? Are there any animals in heaven?"

"There are no animals in heaven," said Brother Kilroy, emphatically. "That's a fact."

"You mean I won't see my cat, Thumbelina, in heaven?" asked Collette. "I always thought I would."

"No pets," said Brother Kilroy. "The Word of God is very clear. No animals in heaven."

"Not regular animals," said Noylene. "But if Kokomo was saved, he could get in, I'll bet."

"What about the other gorillas? What happens to them?" said Dave. "He doesn't want to be the only gorilla in heaven. He'd have to hang around with the Seventh Day Adventists."

"I don't understand," said Rev. Garridos. "What are these Adventists?

"It's just one of Dave's bad jokes," said Nancy. "Pay no attention."

"Hey, I just thought of something," said Pete. "Shouldn't Kokomo get baptized? I thought you guys over at New Fellowship were big into baptizing?"

Noylene and Collette both nodded. "We've thought of that," said Noylene.

"I'm still praying about it," said Brother Kilroy. "I've been back to see Kokomo a couple of times. I'll admit that he is one amazing ape."

"If you decide to do it, you'll have to do it soon," said Pete. "Kokomo and Dr. P. are leaving the day after tomorrow."

"Maybe you could get another audience with Kokomo and give him a quick sprinkling," I suggested. "While he isn't looking."

"Sprinkling!" Brother Kilroy snorted. "What good would that do, other than get you wet? Sprinkling ain't nothin' but the devil's washtub."

Noylene traded glances with Collette but neither one said a word.

"Hey, Hayden! Did you hear about the race last Sunday?" Billy Hixon called to me from atop his riding mower as Moosey and I walked from Pete's boat back to my truck after another unsuccessful morning at the lake. Hixon's Lawn Care had the Mountainview Cemetery account and Billy spent a lot of time on the ten manicured acres.

"No, I didn't hear. How did our boy do?"

"He came in eighth. That's his first top-ten finish. He's very excited!"

"That's great, I guess. How will that affect us?"

"I imagine that we'll have a lot of tourists come up for the next blessing."

"What do you mean, the *next* blessing?"

"Junior wants to get the car blessed again. You know, drivers are very superstitious. He wants Benny Dawkins, too. He says 'the more Holy Smoke the better.'"

"Did anyone ask our new priest?"

"I haven't yet. I just talked to Junior's crew chief this morning, and they're on their way to Bristol so they're going to stop by tomorrow. I'm going to call Gaylen when I get finished here. By the way," he added, "did you catch him?"

"Catch who?" I asked.

"Old Spiney. I spent one whole summer after that fish. I saw him a couple of times. Never did get him though."

"You saw Old Spiney?" Moosey asked. "How big is he?"

"He's about this big," said Billy holding his hands shoulder width apart. "Probably weighs fifteen or twenty pounds by now. Good luck now, y'hear?" Billy started up his mower, engaged the blades and zipped down one of the rows of tombstones, grass clippings flying.

Chapter 10

Meg, Pete and I walked across the freshly-mown lawn of Sterling Park toward St. Barnabas. This was the first overcast day we'd had for several weeks, but the clouds hadn't dampened the spirits of the crowd gathered in front of the church. It was a repeat of the service two weeks ago, with a few exceptions. The bishop had been replaced by Rev. Weatherall (arrayed in her finest vestments), the number of television cameras had been cut by more than half (there were only two that I could see), and the crowd that numbered a couple of hundred at the first Blessing of the Racecar now looked to be closer to five hundred, most of them wearing purple with a whole lot of number 17s showing up on shirts and baseball caps.

"Where did all the people come from?" I asked Pete. "Did you put another ad in the paper?"

"No. They just all showed up. A top-ten finish will start bringing the fans out. They didn't care much about Junior Jameson a few weeks ago, but he's God's Messenger now."

We watched Benny walk around the car, his thurible dancing on its chains, the smoke billowing around the car.

"They came to watch the blessing?" asked Meg.

"Yep," answered Pete. "Then Junior will sign some autographs and head up to Bristol for the race. I'm thinking St. Barnabas is going to have quite a crowd on Sunday. The race isn't until three o'clock, and every hotel and B and B are full all weekend. These people are probably not going to Bristol until after church."

"Why not?" I asked.

"Why do sales of Tide go up every time No. 32 wins a race? Who knows? Maybe they want the whole St. Barnabas experience."

We looked at the racecar and Junior Jameson standing proudly on the steps with Billy, Bev and Georgia. Gaylen was walking around the car with the olive branch, giving the blessing and sprinkling the car as the bishop had done. She finished and started heading up the steps when Junior came down and whispered something to her. She nodded, went back to the car and, when Junior removed the radiator cap, poured the rest of the water into the radiator.

"Bless this car and grant that your servant Junior Jameson may use it in your service and for the good of this church and all your people. Amen," said Gaylen, wrapping up the blessing. "Go in peace to love and serve the Lord." She turned and went back into the church followed by Billy, Bev, Georgia, and Benny. Junior, this time, stayed down by the car and started signing autographs.

Pete's prediction was more than accurate. On Sunday morning, for the first time since Easter, St. Barnabas was packed. In fact, I didn't remember the ushers putting chairs in the aisles on Easter, but they were certainly doing their best to accommodate the crowd on this particular morning. The St. Barnabas members all showed up to hear Gaylen Weatherall's first sermon. The NASCAR crowd showed up to see what all the fuss was about and maybe pray Junior Jameson onto Victory Lane. Billy told me right before the service that he'd talked to Rev. Weatherall, and she'd agreed that, as long as racecar fever was raging, she'd be happy to include Junior Jameson and car number 17 in the Prayers of the People. "After all," said Gaylen, "It's our car. We might as well pray for it."

The only thing missing from the service was Benny Dawkins. We didn't usually have incense on a Sunday morning—not unless it was a feast day—but after church, it was decided that Benny would be invited to smoke up the church every Sunday for a while; at least until the crowds abated. Gaylen's sermon was very good, and the choir did well. There wasn't a Children's Moment, but the children were invited to process out behind the crucifer during the second hymn and go to Children's Church. They'd rejoin their families after the offertory just before communion. All things considered, it was a fine start. Many of the NASCAR fans stayed for coffee hour after church and expressed their appreciation and their intent to come back soon. At least as soon as Junior got the racecar blessed again.

"You should see the offering plates!" said Billy. "They were overflowing!"

"That may be true," said Carol Sterling, "but it's going to take a lot of full offering plates to add up to sixteen million dollars."

"There's a difference," said Billy. "This here's the Lord's money. Not the bank's."

"What are we going to do next week?" asked Bev. "I mean, if Junior wins the race in Bristol."

"Hardly much chance of that," said Meg. "He's never won a race yet. Last week was the best he's ever done."

"But now he has St. Barnabas on his side and Holy Water in the radiator," said Bev. "It's only a matter of time."

She was right. Junior Jameson won his first race that very afternoon.

"How are we doing?" I asked, using the royal "we." The Bad Writing Circle had decided to meet at the Bear and Brew, and all three ladies were looking glumly at their efforts when I arrived.

"I think we're all too good for this contest," said Elaine. "I can't seem to make the sentence bad enough."

"Maybe I can help," I said. "I'm not as good as you three."

Elaine sniffed. "Okay. Here's mine."

"Enid? Enid Pendulous?" Bernard called out into the waiting room, not for the first time regretting his occupation as a "glamour" photographer in the small town of Upchuck, Georgia; and, as he held the door open for his next appointment and watched, horrified, as his old Sunday School teacher walked in, dropped her robe, tousled her hair and settled, naked, onto the heart-shaped bed, he didn't wonder very long about what genetic make-up in her ancestry had been the origin of her strangely erotic surname.

"Hah!" I chuckled. "Okay. That one is pretty bad."

"Isn't that the point?" asked Elaine.

"I have one," said Meg.

Little Bunny Tinkletoes belied his name, being a stone-cold contract killer with a heart like a piece of granite and a face like an even cragglier piece of granite; the first piece being more of a regular piece--but as soon as he walked into the powder-puff pink boudoir and saw Cassandra Starlight laying wanly on her satin sheets, he knew that this assignment would be his last the way he knew that his mother gave him a better name than Little Bunny--Clarence, in fact--but not that much better.

"That one's great!" said Ruby. "It's bad in so many ways."

"Thanks, Mother. I wrote it on Hayden's magic typewriter."

"How come you get to use the magic typewriter?" asked Elaine.

"I just asked extra nicely," said Meg.

"Can I use it, too?"

"No," I said. "I'm very busy working on my detective story. And it's too late for you'se guys anyway. I have my final entry. It's perfect."

"Let's hear it," said Ruby. "I can't wait to hear what the master has come up with."

"Well, as you know," I said. "I already have my really good sentence about Lauren Bacall eating chalk..."

"Ah, yes," said Ruby. "I remember reading it. Meg brought me a copy of your latest choir missive."

"And my one about Lola, the meat-metronome," I continued, but this one may even be better."

Although Brandi had been named Valedictorian and the outfit for her speech carefully chosen to prove that beauty and brains could indeed mix, she suddenly regretted her choice of attire, her rain-soaked T-shirt now valiantly engaging in the titanic struggle between the tensile strength of cotton and Newton's first law of motion.

"It certainly is very good," agreed Meg. "A re-working from one of your earlier stories, is it not?"

"Not completely," I said. "But I did cobble together a few well chosen similes from previous efforts."

"Here's mine," said Ruby. "It's very poignant."

As he looked across the breakfast table at his aged, sickly wife slurping down a bowl of Wheateena, her teeth soaking in a glass that had once held her morning Mimosa, he remembered the woman he had once known—a vivacious, exciting beauty with a sense of adventure—and immediately wished he had married her instead.

"Bravo," said Meg, laughing. "Good work all around."

"Okay," I said. "Go to the Bulwer-Lytton website, get the address and send in your entries. You can e-mail them if you want."

"When's the deadline again?" asked Elaine.

"I think we can send them in through the end of June, but the official deadline is April 15th."

"So we're still okay?"

"I believe so. If we're too late this year, we'll have to try again, but we'll probably be all right."

"When do they decide the winners?" asked Ruby.

"The first week of July."

"And when do I have to take you all out to dinner?" Meg asked.

It was eight o'clock in the morning when Nancy called. I had finished showering, let Baxter out to chase the wild turkeys, put a deceased baby squirrel on Archimedes' sill, and settled down with a cup of coffee when the phone rang.

"Hayden Konig," I said, identifying myself, since I still hadn't bothered to get caller ID, and I had no idea who was calling.

"It's Nancy, Chief."

"What's up?"

"You'd better get on out to the New Fellowship Baptist Church. Dave just got a 911 call from Bootsie Watkins. She's the secretary. Something's going on."

"Are you there now?"

"I'm in Boone, but I'm on my way. I'll be there in about twenty minutes."

"That's about how long it'll take me," I said. "See you there."

New Fellowship Baptist Church was about two miles Northwest of town, and Nancy was waiting for me when I arrived. She hadn't been waiting long, I surmised, because she was just taking her helmet off and securing her Harley. The church had put up a new sanctuary about three years ago. It was a pre-fab metal building with a modicum of faux-stone around the edges to make it look more like a Baptist church and less like a warehouse. The large fiberglass steeple, frosted glass windows and drive-up covered portico completed the architectural facade. The appearance of a

99

frugal, monetarily conservative congregation disappeared, however, once Nancy and I stepped inside.

"Wow!" exclaimed Nancy. "I've never been in here before. What do you call this? A narthex?"

"A foyer, I think," I said, looking around. I was just as impressed as Nancy. "I doubt they'd know a narthex if it walked up, shook their hand and introduced itself. Maybe it's a lobby."

It was clear that whatever the church had saved on the shell of the building, they were happy to make up in furnishings and other accoutrements. We walked from the marble entryway onto a plush, deep purple carpet inset with dark red and gold runners. The lobby of the church reminded me of a very expensive hotel. There was gilded furniture strategically placed for decoration as well as to hold brochures on everything from the Three-Step Plan of Salvation to registration forms for the Iron Mike Men's Retreat. There were plants galore, a couple of small trees, rich draperies adorning the frosted windows and a chandelier with enough bangles to make ZsaZsa Gabor smack her grandma.

"Which way?" asked Nancy.

"I think Bootsie's office is this way." I started down the hall and heard Nancy's cell phone ring.

"Yeah," she said. "Yeah. Hang on a sec." She handed me her phone.

"Hayden here," I said.

"Hayden!" It was Kent Murphee on the phone. "Hayden, we need your help!"

"What do you need?" I asked.

"Kokomo is gone! Stolen! By that minister you guys brought over!"

"What? What are you talking about?"

"Penelope's over the edge. She's already called the University Police, the Boone Police and the FBI. The first two are on their way over to your minister's house."

"He's not *my* minister. Hey! Wait a minute. How do you know that the minister took him?"

"Penelope and I went out last night. She didn't want to go and leave Kokomo by himself. She said that when they're on the road, Kokomo gets upset if he's by himself for too long. Anyway, this Brother Kilroy has come to see the gorilla a couple of times over the past few days, and they get along fine together. Real friendly. So when I ask Penelope out, he volunteers to stay with Kokomo. He says don't worry about it; the wife's out of town, stay out as late as we want. So we did."

"When did you get in?"

"Umm, about 7:30 this morning. We lost track of the time."

"And when you got back?" I didn't even bother to needle him about his date.

The gorilla was nowhere to be found. He's gone and so is Kilroy."

"Get Penelope, tell her to bring her dart gun or whatever she uses in case of an emergency, and come over to the New Fellowship Baptist Church. I'm afraid I know what's happened."

"What?"

"I'll tell you when you get here. Call the police too, and send them over here. A five hundred pound gorilla is nothing to mess with."

Bootsie Watkins was standing by her desk under the most impressive beehive hair-do it has ever been my pleasure to witness. She was wringing her hands. Actually wringing them. It was the first time I'd ever actually seen a person do such a thing.

"You've got to come with me," she said. "Something is terribly, terribly wrong."

We followed her bouncing beehive down another purple and gold-carpeted hallway.

"I got here at eight. I always get here at eight. Mr. Shipley had an appointment with Brother Kilroy at eight, and he was here as well."

"Mr. Shipley?" Nancy asked, writing in her pad while we walked down the hall. We heard a crash come from somewhere close.

"Bennett Shipley. He's the head deacon. He's still waiting outside Brother Kilroy's office. We've been banging on the door, but he doesn't answer. All we heard were crashing sounds and some kind of shrieking."

We turned one more corner and came to an alcove outside a heavy wooden door with a stained glass window in the center about a foot square. Mr. Shipley was pounding his fist heavily on the jamb.

He was middle-aged, about five-foot-eight and in good shape. His hair, dark brown with a premature white stripe running through it, swooped back away from his face, and was held in place with an inordinate amount of hairspray. He saw us and stopped.

"It's locked," he said. "From the inside. I'm pretty sure it's going to take a key to open it."

"Do you have a key?" I asked Bootsie. She shook her head.

"Brother Kilroy had the only key. He brought this door from his grandfather's old church. His grandfather was a preacher, too. It has an old-fashioned lock. Once it's locked, you need a key. Or a locksmith."

"We could break it down," said Nancy.

I shook my head. "Look at the size of that door. It's solid wood. We might break the jamb, but it's just as likely we'll break a shoulder. Just shoot the lock off, will you?"

Nancy put her pad away and was reaching for her gun when we heard another shriek come from inside the office.

"Wait a second," said Mr. Shipley, "before you do that." He picked up a hymnal from a side table and smashed the stained glass. Then he reached through the opening and found the lock.

"The key's in it," he said, fumbling for a moment longer. Then we heard a distinct click and the door swung open onto a startling and terrible sight.

Brother Jimmy Kilroy's huge office had been a tribute to his expansive ego. Bootsie Watkins told me later that his wife, Mona, had taken complete charge of the decorating. It had been a study in extravagant opulence. The seating area at one end of the room incorporated a gas fireplace, a leather sofa and two armchairs. In the center of the office was a desk that would have put Father Barna's monstrosity at St. Barnabas to shame. It was constructed of black walnut and matched the built-in bookcases that surrounded the room. I recognized Amish craftsmanship when I saw it. There were a few Persian rugs lying on the hardwood floors. On the other side of the room was a grand piano. It might have been a beautiful office except for one thing. All the furniture had been smashed to kindling.

The sofa had been ripped open, and the cushions (which had

been down-filled) were empty, the feathers now spread across the room. The heavy oak frame of the sofa had been crushed, broken in half and thrown up against the fireplace. The chairs had fared no better. Across the entire room were pieces of books, yanked from the shelves, torn apart and scattered across the officescape.

The desk had managed better than the sofa with the minor exception that it was now in two pieces. It looked as though a wrecking ball had been dropped directly in the center, smashing through the top and breaking it exactly in half. There were pieces of a computer on the desk—at least I suspected it was a computer.

The grand piano was lying on its side, the top torn from the hinges, piano wire snarling around the soundboard and three of the four legs snapped off. I looked around and saw one of these legs protruding lewdly from one of the bookcases.

What was left of the rugs was strewn across the wreckage of the furniture. Behind the upended piano were double doors standing open and looking in on a bathroom spa that would be the envy of any five-star establishment in the Carolinas. Nancy and I both pulled our guns and picked our way through the debris toward the bathroom.

We peered into a room almost as large as the office itself and then moved gingerly across the marble tile. To our right was a vanity with two sinks and gold-plated fixtures—to our left, an open Roman shower, also with golden fixtures. Straight ahead of us, dropping into the floor, was an expansive, ten-foot-sqare, built-in tub. Behind the tub stood a marble modesty wall, five feet tall, but it was the tub that interested us now. It was full of brownish water and contained—along with a torn chair cushion, a telephone, and several books—Brother Jimmy Kilroy, floating face down. Bootsie screamed from the doorway.

"Is that Kilroy?" Nancy asked. "I can't tell."

"Yes. I think so," Bootsie sobbed.

"Go outside and wait for the rest of the police," I said to Bootsie. "They'll be here in a couple of minutes." She nodded and left. Mr. Shipley stood silently at the door of the bathroom, wiped his eyes with a handkerchief, and followed Bootsie out of the office.

Nancy and I inched around the tub, both of us holding our weapons in front of us, and headed toward the wall, determined to look in the last place left to us. When we came around the side, our leveled guns were pointed directly at Kokomo, sitting on the toilet.

He knew we were there, of course—we hadn't intended to surprise him—but when he saw us, he leapt off the toilet with a roar that shivered every hair on my head. The floor shook and tiles broke when he landed—four hundred eighty pounds of pissed-off gorilla—and then he roared again, stretched to his full five-foot-eight-inches, showed me fangs that made my blood run cold, and pounded his hands on his massive chest just like every King-Kong movie I've ever seen. Nancy and I both froze. We were still twelve feet away, but twelve feet wasn't nearly enough.

"This little gun isn't going to stop this gorilla," I whispered to Nancy. "If he gets it in his mind to eat us, I mean."

"Nope," agreed Nancy, also in a whisper. "Did you just wet your pants, too?"

"Yep. Can we agree that Jimmy Kilroy is dead?"

"Oh, yeah," whispered Nancy.

"Then let's just back out of the room and wait for Dr. Pelicane."

"That's a plan," said Nancy.

Chapter 11

Dr. Pelicane and Kent Murphee arrived thirty minutes after I'd spoken with Kent on the phone. The two officers from the Boone P.D. were already on their way to Jimmy Kilroy's house and beat them by fifteen minutes. I knew them both. The older fellow, a sergeant, was an experienced officer named Todd McKay. The other one, a new recruit named Burt Coley, had sung in the St. Barnabas choir when he'd been a student at ASU.

"Hayden," he laughed, "did you know your pants are wet? What'd you do, spill some coffee?" Nancy had taken off her jacket and tied it around her waist, but I didn't have the luxury.

"One more crack out of you, and I'm sending you in there to get the monkey," I snarled, not at all amused.

"Sheesh, if it's just a monkey, I'll go get it," said Burt. "Gimme a net or something."

I looked at him, then at Todd.

"I haven't told him yet," said Todd, grinning. "Go ahead and give him a net."

"Let's just wait on Kent and the handler," I said. "The pastor's not going anywhere."

When Dr. Pelicane arrived, she was in a state of near panic. Kent had her by the arm, or she would have raced right past us and into the church.

"Where is Kokomo? What has that *idiot* done with him?" Her voice was high pitched and frantic.

"Calm down," I said. "The gorilla is fine, but we have to figure out what to do next."

"What do you mean, 'what to do next?' Give me my gorilla! *This instant!*"

"I understand your concern," I said. "But take a few deep breaths and calm down."

"Hey," said Kent, looking at my pants, "did you..."

A look from me shut him up.

"Did you bring a tranquillizer gun or something?" I asked.

"I don't use them." Dr. Pelicane spat out the words. "There's no need. Kokomo is very gentle."

"There's a need now," said Nancy. "That gorilla is madder than a wet badger, and the minister is dead."

"What?" exclaimed Dr. Pelicane, panic once again rising in her voice.

I nodded. "He's dead, and the place looks like a tornado hit it."

"Two tornados," added Nancy.

"Give...me...back...my...gorilla!" said Dr. Pelicane, slowly, with emphasis on every word of her demand.

"It's not that easy now," said Sergeant McKay. "If that gorilla's killed someone, he's got to be quarantined and destroyed. That's the law."

"What?!" yelled Dr. Pelicane, her voice rising close to hysteria. "He didn't do it. I'm sure he didn't. And if he did, there's a perfectly logical reason. You can't just kill an intelligent animal!" She looked in desperation to Kent and then to me.

"Look," I said. "One problem at a time. We've got to get Kokomo out of there and somewhere safe."

"He can come back with me," said Dr. Pelicane, desperation evident in her voice. "I can lock him in the motor home."

"That's not an option," said Sergeant McKay. "No offense ma'am, but if he's killed someone, he's got to be under the control of the Fish and Game Commission until he's put down."

"I'm sure it wasn't his fault!" cried Dr. Pelicane. "I've had him for twenty years! He's never harmed anyone!"

"We've got a dart gun in the trunk," Burt offered. "We use it for black bears, but it should take down a gorilla. How big is he? I can set the dosage by his weight."

"Five hundred pounds," I said. "You still want that net?"

Burt smiled, shook his head and went over to the trunk of the squad car.

"Let me talk to Kokomo!" demanded Dr. Pelicane. "He'll listen to me!"

Sergeant McCay ignored her. "The Fish and Game Commission has an office in Greensboro. I'll call over there and find out what they want us to do."

I nodded glumly and turned to Dr. Pelicane. "Even if Kokomo did listen, he wouldn't be allowed to go with you. You understand that, right? He'd have to go with the Fish and Game Commission, and I'm not sure that he'd be too keen on that right now."

"*Do something!*" Dr. Pelicane yelled at Kent.

"Penelope...I..." Kent was at a loss.

"First things, first," I said. "Look, if we can't get him tranquillized and out safely, he's likely to have to be shot, so why don't you sit down over there, and let these officers do what they have to do. The dart won't hurt him, and we'll be able to move him safely. Then we can get Kilroy's body out of there and figure out what to do next."

Kokomo was sitting in the corner of the bathroom spa with his eyes closed when the two Boone officers, Nancy and I inched our way back into the room. I could see that the officers were as stunned by the carnage as we had been. Sergeant McCay had the dart gun loaded. Nancy, Burt and I had our service pistols drawn and ready in case we had need of them.

"You're going to have to hit him where he can't reach it and pull it out," I said.

"And where's that?" asked McCay.

"I have no idea. Take your best guess."

McCay's dart went into Kokomo's arm. I expected that he'd yank it out, but he just grunted, kept his eyes closed and didn't move. After ten minutes of watching him, we walked up toward what we hoped was a sleeping gorilla. It was.

We called Dr. Pelicane and Kent into the spa. She saw the sleeping form in the far corner and ran across the tile, ignoring the body, still floating face down in the water.

"Is he okay?" she said.

"He's fine, I think," said Sergeant McCay. "Just sleeping."

"What's the word from Greensboro?" asked Nancy.

"They said the animal has to be quarantined for seventy-two hours to see if it shows any signs of being infected. Then, if the death was an accident, like maybe getting kicked in the head by a horse, there's some leeway. But if it was an attack, like a pit-bull or a bear attack, the animal is destroyed."

"Oh *no!*" said Dr. Pelicane. "This can't be happening."

"But it may be," said Sergeant McCoy, "that if the family of the victim doesn't want to see the gorilla destroyed, we can talk to Raleigh and see what they say. This is a famous gorilla, after all."

"Really?" said Dr. Pelicane, a modicum of hope retuning to her voice. "With whom do I have to speak?"

"I guess that Mrs. Kilroy would be a good place to start," I said.

"So," Nancy said, "where do we quarantine this gorilla?"

"Fish and Game said to take him to the nearest animal facility. That'd be up here, I guess. Doesn't St. Germaine have an animal shelter?"

I nodded. "Behind Gwen Jackson's veterinary practice. There are several big enclosures. She's kept black bears back there occasionally."

"Then let's take him over there," said McCay. "It's only for a few days."

"And I'm going to want to be there as well," said Dr. Pelicane. "I presume that there's somewhere I can park the motor home."

"We'll ask Dr. Jackson," I said. "But I can't imagine that there'd be a problem."

"I'll just ask Kokomo what happened when he wakes up," said Dr. Pelicane. "He'll explain everything."

"Huh?" said Burt.

"Oh, yeah," I said. "This is a talking gorilla."

"That gorilla can talk?" exclaimed Burt. "Holy Moses!"

With Kokomo asleep, I went over to the pool, fished the body to the side, spun him over in the water and looked down on the face of Brother Jimmy Kilroy.

"It's Kilroy, all right," I said. "I was pretty sure already, but, yeah. That's him."

Todd McCay and I pulled him out of the tepid water and laid him out on the cold tile.

"Looks like his neck is broken," said Kent. "But I'll still have to do a work-up."

I nodded. "You're the best coroner around. Do it as quickly as you can."

"I'll get to work as soon as I get the body to the lab. Did you call the ambulance?"

"Already done," said Nancy.

The ambulance drove up to the church, lights blazing and siren wailing. The two EMTs on duty were Mike and Joe. Nancy had been dating Mike, off and on, for about a year, and she adjusted the jacket around her waist when she saw him.

"Hi, Nance," he called, as he and Joe got the gurney out of the back of the truck. "No hurry on this one, I guess. I heard he was going to Kent's office."

"Yeah," said Nancy. "The vic's inside. And when you're finished, we need some help carrying the gorilla."

"What gorilla?" asked Joe.

"The one that's asleep in the bathroom."

"You know, Nancy," said Mike, "I love it up here in St. Germaine."

It took all six of us to put Kokomo in the back of my truck. Nancy called Gwen Jackson, found out there was a cage available and told her we were on our way. Kent and Dr. Pelicane drove back to Boone to pack up the motor home and bring it over. When they left, Nancy and I got into my truck. Sergeant McCay and Burt Coley were going to follow us to Dr. Jackson's to help unload Kokomo.

"Hey boss," said Nancy, once we'd pulled out of the parking lot. "Where does a five hundred pound gorilla sleep?"

"We've gotta change our pants," I answered.

Chapter 12

After we dropped a still sleeping Kokomo at Dr. Jackson's place, I called the Slab and made arrangements for Noylene and Collette to meet me down at the station. I figured they knew what was going on and, if they weren't directly involved, could at the very least give us some idea of what Brother Kilroy was up to. I had to drive Nancy back to the New Fellowship Baptist Church to pick up her motorcycle.

"What a morning," I said. "Why don't you go home, change your clothes and then come on back here and see if you can find anything that might be helpful. Go over what's left of the crime scene."

"It seems pretty cut and dried to me."

"Yeah, it does, but check it out anyway. That's why they pay us the big bucks. Let's get in there before any church folks start going through his papers. Who knows what secrets Brother Kilroy was privy to?"

"Will do."

I met Noylene and Collette at the station, both of them as pale as Casper's bedsheet. The grapevine in St. Germaine was as fast and effective as any other small town, and both women had already heard the news.

"C'mon in," I said, motioning them into my office. "I'll bet you two can fill me in on a few missing details."

"I jes' can't believe it," said Collette, barely containing her tears. "Brother Kilroy...gone."

"He was a good man," said Noylene, dabbing at one eye with a handkerchief.

"Sure," I said. "Now tell me what happened. And don't pretend you don't know. I saw you two swapping glances the other afternoon."

The two women looked at each other for a long moment.

"Well," began Noylene finally. She stopped talking, then sighed and finally continued. "Well, Brother Kilroy and Rev. Garridos have been arguing about that gorilla for days. I never should have asked Kokomo if he loved Jesus."

"It warn't your fault," sniffed Collette. "You was jes' trying to help that poor dumb creature."

"So Brother Kilroy felt..." I waited for Noylene to finish the sentence.

"That Kokomo was intelligent, and if he accepted Jesus, he deserved to be saved," finished Noylene. "But Rev. Garridos said that it was foolishness. That God's grace was for humans and not for monkeys."

"So where is Rev. Garridos?"

"He went back to Spain yesterday afternoon. His month was up."

"Okay. So tell me what happened."

"I don't know for sure," continued Noylene. "But I do know that Brother Kilroy had been going over to see Kokomo. Three or four times I think, I went with him once. He kept feeding Kokomo Milk Duds that he'd sneak in to the trailer."

"Did Brother Kilroy say anything to Kokomo while you were there with them?"

"Well, sure. Brother Kilroy kept talking to him about Jesus. You know, turning away from sin and keeping love in your heart."

"Okay," I said. "What happened last night?"

Noylene looked over at Collette, and the younger girl broke down.

"Oh, why? Why? Why? Why?" Collette blubbered.

"I don't know what happened for sure," said Noylene. "Are we in trouble?"

"Not yet," I said, impatience creeping into my voice. "But you both may be soon if I don't get some answers!"

"Waahhhh," sobbed Collette. "Brother Kilroy took Kokomo to baptize him," she blurted out. "He said Kokomo deserved all of God's Grace, and he couldn't have it unless he was baptized a new creature in the Lord."

"So he went over to baby-sit Kokomo..." I said, once again leading the witness.

Collette sniveled. "And when Dr. Pelicane went out, he took Kokomo out to his car and drove him over to the church. He said it would only take about an hour. The water was already in the pool, and all Brother Kilroy had to do was lead Kokomo into the pool and dunk him under the water."

"And the gorilla didn't want to be dunked."

"I guess not," Collette sniffed. "And now Brother Kilroy's dead. Gone straight to heaven and into the waiting arms of Jesus."

"Did either of you have anything to do with taking the gorilla?" I asked. Both women shook their heads.

"Brother Kilroy didn't want any help. He said he could do this all by himself," said Noylene. "I guess it was a good thing we weren't there. That gorilla would have killed us all."

It was late in the afternoon before I made it over to Kent Murphee's office. We didn't have a coroner in St. Germaine, and Kent covered all of Watauga County. He was sitting at his desk when I walked in, filling out reports, a pen in one hand and his pipe clenched tightly between his teeth. Kent was dressed in his usual attire—tweed jacket, vest and tie.

"How about a drink?" asked Kent. "It's been a long day."

"Yeah, okay," I said, slumping into the chair opposite him. "Anything to report on the Kilroy case?"

Kent pushed my drink across his desk. "Well, I can tell you the cause of death. He drowned."

"He drowned?"

"That's what killed him. Of course, he also had a broken neck, a four-inch laceration on his scalp and a subdural hematoma."

"So let me get this straight. He got whacked in the head, then broke his neck and laid in the water till he drowned?"

"I'm pretty sure, although the order could have been different. There's no real way to tell. He could have had his neck broken, then been whacked, and then drowned."

"But the drowning killed him?"

"Yeah. He had water in his lungs."

"Wouldn't the broken neck kill him?" I asked.

Kent shook his head. "Not necessarily. I doubt that he was conscious though. The shot to his head was a doozy. It would have knocked him cold. That is to say, if his neck wasn't already broken when it happened."

"So, it looks as though the gorilla is responsible."

"It's not for me to say, but it appears to be the case. There weren't any bruises on the body though. Just the one head injury and the broken neck."

"How's Penelope doing?" I asked.

"Not very well. She's been on the phone all day explaining to her department head why the world's most famous gorilla is now at the St. Germaine animal shelter."

"Has she moved her motor home over there yet?

"She's on the way, I think. I talked to her about an hour ago."

"I'll go by and check on her when I get back to town."

"I'd appreciate that," said Kent. "You know, gorillas usually don't have a problem with water like chimps do. Kilroy probably would have been fine if he hadn't tried to hold him under."

"No kidding."

I got back in my truck and put a Muddy Waters CD into the changer. This had been a day I wouldn't soon forget, and I was ready to listen to the blues. Not the blues written by a guy named Chad who's girl-friend, Jennifer, died during a liposuction treatment, but the real thing—and Muddy was as real as it got.

The meanest woman I most ever seen
I asked for water. She brought me gasoline.

By the time I had gotten back to St. Germaine, I felt a whole lot better. The Blues will do that for you. Meg and Pete were waiting for me at the Slab when I walked in. Meg had ordered me a burger, and it was delivered just as I sat down at the table.

"What a deal!" I said. "I guess I missed lunch, but now supper is served. And no waiting, either."

"I called Kent," said Meg, "and he said you were on your way back. So I went ahead and ordered for you."

"Great," I said, sitting down and picking up my burger with both hands. I took a big bite.

"Wait a minute," said Pete. "Aren't you going to tell us what happened at the Baptist Church? You've been running around all day, and all we have are rumors and conjecture. We need some answers."

"Yeah," added Meg. "Answers."

"Mggrumph," I said, swallowing hard. "Can't talk...eating..."

"Oh, you'll talk, all right," said Meg. "Or I'll take that plate straight to the dishwasher."

"Okay, okay." I grabbed another quick bite and chewed quickly. "Here's what I know. Or what I assume, anyway."

"Brother Jimmy Kilroy is dead," I started. "We found him this morning lying, face down, in the pool in his office."

"His pool?" said Pete.

"It's a pool, sure enough," I said. "Maybe more like a spa. It was in his bathroom. You guys wouldn't believe that place."

"We heard about it from Nancy," Meg said. "She said she'd never seen anything like it."

"That's for sure. Not in a church anyway," I said. "Could I maybe have one of these French fries while I'm talking? Anyway, here's how I figure it."

"Brother Kilroy decides that he needs to baptize Kokomo because he's given his life to Jesus. Rev. Garridos disagrees, but he's heading back to Spain so Brother Kilroy decides that the time is right. He's been over to Penelope Pelicane's trailer a few times since we visited, and Kokomo likes him, probably because he's been sneaking him Milk Duds. Anyway, Dr. Pelicane's getting ready to head down to South Carolina—USC, I think—and time's running out. Still with me?"

Meg and Pete both nodded. I ate another French fry.

"So Brother Kilroy is over at the trailer visiting Kokomo—probably loading him up with Milk Duds on the sly—when Kent calls up and asks Penelope to go out. She says that she can't go—that she has to stay and watch the gorilla, and this is the opening that Brother Kilroy's been waiting for. He volunteers to babysit Kokomo for the evening. He tells Penelope that his wife's out of town and to stay out as late as she likes. He's going to take this opportunity to baptize Kokomo, and no one will be the wiser. This is more than a fortuitous event. This is Divine Intervention."

I grabbed another bite of my burger and continued.

"Now, if Brother Kilroy's a Presbyterian or a Methodist, a Lutheran or an Episcopalian, there's no problem. If Kokomo needs to get baptized, Brother Kilroy could do it with a squirt gun if he had to. But he's not. He's a Baptist, and you're not born again unless you go under for the count."

"Is that true?" asked Pete. "Sprinkling doesn't count?"

"Of course it counts," said Meg. "For us, anyway. Baptists just think a little differently." She looked back at me. "Continue, please."

I nodded. "So, Brother Kilroy figures he can do the baptism and get back to the trailer in a little over an hour. It should be pretty easy. It's a twenty-minute drive to the New Fellowship Baptist Church, the baptism should only take a couple of minutes, and twenty minutes back. Penelope and Kent return after their night out, Kokomo is saved, and no one is the wiser."

"So he stole Kokomo and took him to the church?" asked Pete.

"Yep. And he did it by himself. He told Noylene that he didn't want anyone else involved. There's a big baptismal pool in the sanctuary, but Brother Kilroy decided that he'd rather do the baptism in the smaller pool in his office. The spa. He'd already filled it up so he wouldn't have to wait once they'd arrived. The minister and the gorilla got to the church, went into his office and went back to the bathroom where the spa is. Then something went wrong."

"Kokomo didn't want to be dunked," said Meg.

"That could have been it." I shrugged. "But normally, gorillas have no problem with water. So I'm thinking that something else might have triggered the rampage. Whatever it was, Kokomo went crazy, and a crazy five-hundred-pound gorilla is nothing to mess with. I'm telling you, the place was torn apart. Busted furniture, the piano, books...everything. Brother Kilroy was face down in the pool when we got there this morning. Kent says his neck was broken and he was knocked pretty hard in the head, but it was drowning that finished him off."

"So the gorilla killed him?" asked Pete.

"It looks like it. The strange thing is that there were no other marks, no defensive bruises...nothing."

"But Nancy said that when you got there the door was locked," said Meg.

"From the inside. Not only that, the key was still in the lock. It looks like an open and shut case. I don't know what Mona Kilroy is going to say, but I don't think that Kokomo has much of a prayer. It's a shame all the way around."

"Yeah," said Pete. "And we're going to get some really bad publicity. We were doing pretty well with this racecar thing, too.

By the way," he added, changing the subject." "How did that dinner you were cooking turn out?"

"It was delicious," answered Meg. "Amazing. Onion tart, scallops and baked pears."

I tried to look humble. "It was nothing, really."

"I can hardly wait to see what he's going to serve tonight."

"Huh?" I said, startled. "Tonight?"

"Yes, dear, it's Tuesday," said Meg, with a smile. "Fridays and Tuesdays. Don't fret too much. We'll have a late supper. See you around nine?" She gave me a quick kiss and disappeared out the door.

"So, what're you having tonight?" asked Pete, with a grin.

"What have you got in the walk-in? Any leftovers?"

"I can give you a couple of marinated steaks and some twice-baked potatoes you can heat up." Pete thought for a moment. "Some salad, bleu-cheese dressing, and a couple of pieces of strawberry short cake. You'll have to grill the steaks and come up with your own wine, though."

"I can do that. Thanks, Pete! You're a life saver!"

"No problem. I'm just glad to help another bachelor in trouble."

"How's your Communion Fish venture going?"

"It's going great. The plant has the machinery retooled and the recipes finished. We should have some prototypes ready to go within a couple of weeks. You think your new priest will try 'em one Sunday?"

"She's pretty much a traditionalist," I said, "but I'll ask her. Can we get *Barabba-que*?"

"Now, Hayden, you know that wouldn't be appropriate. Holy Week is over. Let's start you off with *Tongues of Fire—Cajun Spicy*."

"Send over a couple bags," I said. "If we don't use them for communion, we can always munch on them during choir practice."

"Marilyn," I barked, "hustle your duck-pins in here. You're supposed to be my secretary. Where've you been for the past two days?"

"I told you," Marilyn said. "I went to a feminist empowerment weekend."

"I didn't pay for that, did I?" I didn't remember authorizing such an expense--not on my bread and water salary--but then I remembered that Marilyn kept the books.

"You paid for it all right."

Marilyn smiled; her lips, two red worms lying together on the cracked sidewalk of her countenance, first stretching out to take advantage of the early morning warmth, but then, later in the afternoon, writhing on the hot cement before finally turning brown and curling up at the ends--it was a cruel smile and annelidical.

"And now that I'm empowered, you can't tell me to hustle my duck-pins in here anymore."

"Sheesh, Marilyn," I said. "You know I think of you as the sister I never had."

"But, you have a sister. You have three sisters."

"I think of you as the sister I NEVER had. Not the ones I DO have. Now get me a cup of java, will you? And hold the castor oil."

I settled back in my chair, the shadows playing with the Venetian blinds like a bad tailor sewing a burlap suit. I didn't know what was going on yet, but I knew one thing: somebody was trawling for information, and Fishy Jim was the bait, Betsy was the hook, Marilyn was one of those red and white bobber thingys and I was the sinker.

Something was about to happen. I could tell. I'm a detective.

I clattered to a stop, wrapping up another successful venture into the world of bad detective fiction. Meg was due any time and supper, sans steaks, was on the table. The steaks would only take a few minutes, and I'd be off the alimentary hook for another few days. Baxter, as usual, had ascertained a steak supper was imminent and assumed a supine position under the table, waiting for any spare scraps that happened to be thrown his way. I hadn't seen Archimedes since last night, but he'd be back around before too long.

I headed into the kitchen whistling a Bach toccata, took the steaks out to the grill and laid them on the fire just as Meg walked up.

"Hey, Honeybunch," she said sweetly, giving me a kiss. "What are we having for dinner?"

"Honeybunch, eh?"

"Would you prefer 'Pookie-Bear?'"

"No thank you. As you can plainly see, we're having grilled steaks. Also twice-baked potatoes, tossed salad with home-made bleu-cheese dressing and strawberry shortcake for dessert. Are you impressed?"

"Very impressed. It sounds suspiciously like the Tuesday night special from Pete's walk-in."

"Yeah? Well...I'll have you know I'm working very hard on this dinner. I have to grill the steaks. It counts."

"Oh, I didn't say it didn't count. It smells delicious. By the way, I talked with Noylene after I left the Slab. She said that Wormy is ready to start selling plots over at his Bellefontaine Cemetery. He's got the house and the barns down and the roads pushed in by the bulldozers."

"Great," I said. "Should we go ahead and get ours? I think the side by side His 'n Hers would be a good choice."

"Not yet. We don't need to rush. There's plenty of room. It won't fill up for a hundred years or so."

Chapter 13

I was on my second stogy and third drink when the door flew open and a couple of ginks wedged themselves through the opening.

"Hello boys," I snarled through the cigar smoke. "I wondered when you'd show up." I recognized them right away. The big one was called Ray, the little one was Reef --a couple of sharks from downtown. I knew mussel when I saw it.

"What'd you do with Marilyn?"

"Locked her in the filing cabinet," said Reef. "Under Y for 'yap.'" He laughed, showing three rows of yellow pointed teeth. "She wouldn't clam up."

"So, what's the grift?"

"Dis got squid to do wid you," said Ray, shaking a limpet off his arm. "You oyster stay out of it."

"Too late for that," I said. "I've already been hired."

"We know all about it. She won't be needing your services no more. What's da matter? You hard of herring?"

"Who are you remoras working for?" I asked, lighting another stogy. "You're not the brains of this operation. You boys ain't smart enough to find your own dorsals with a map and a one cheek head start."

"Let's just say we're in the fish business," said Reef, pulling out his gat and leveling it at me. "And you're about to go swimming with them."

I would have been worried, but I'd tried to lock Marilyn in the filing cabinet once before. It just made her mad. Ray never saw her coming, and she clobbered the big guy with my hard-bound copy of the Bach Orgelbüchlein. He dropped to his knees like a monkfish at vespers. When Reef turned to see what happened, I pulled out my roscoe and plugged him like a bad hair replacement.

"You shot him," said Marilyn. "I was only going to beat him till he squealed."

"That one's still alive," I said. "He's all yours."

"You might want to leave the room," Marilyn said, pulling a claw-cracker and an oyster-shucker out of her purse. "That is, if you're squeamish."

Dr. P.A. Pelicane's motor home was parked behind the vet's office when I drove up the next morning. Dr. Pelicane was beside the cage, sitting in a lawn chair, and talking to Gwen Jackson. She was obviously agitated. I'd been here many times. This was where Dr. Jackson kept quarantined animals or wild animals awaiting relocation. There were two enclosures, both big enough to accommodate a good-sized bear, constructed of heavy chain link over an iron frame. Kokomo's was locked with a key as well as with a chain sporting a big padlock.

"Morning," said Gwen, as I walked up.

"Good morning," I said.

"I can't see what's good about it," answered Dr. Pelicane. "Kokomo is locked up, accused of homicide, and he won't talk to me. He just sits in the corner, rocking."

"Did you call Mona Kilroy and talk to her about Kokomo?"

"I called and left about a dozen messages. I left my cell number, but she hasn't called me back."

"Well, she's probably busy with funeral arrangements and such. I'll go by her house this morning and see if I can find her."

"No need," said Gwen, looking over my shoulder. "Here she comes now."

Walking up the path in a fury was Mona Kilroy, followed closely by two rangers. One of the men was carrying a rifle—a .30-06.

"Mona, I'm really sorry..." I started, but she stormed past me and headed to the door of the cage.

"There it is!" she spat. "There's the thing that killed my husband."

"It wasn't his fault," pleaded Dr. Pelicane. "Your husband should have never taken him. If I could just have a couple of minutes to talk to you..."

"Officers," commanded Mona. "Do your duty and shoot that animal!"

Dr. Pelicane gasped. "No!"

"Hang on," I said, holding up my new badge identifying me as the Chief of Police. "There's not going to be any shooting today. Do you have a warrant to destroy this animal?" I sincerely hoped that they didn't, but I was pretty sure that Mona hadn't managed to get one this quickly.

"We weren't told we needed one," said Ranger One, the one with the rifle. "Fish and Game called us and told us there was an animal that needed to be destroyed. They told us to meet Mrs. Kilroy and she'd show us where it was."

"You certainly do need a warrant," I said. "Mrs. Kilroy can apply for one from the state, and the animal will remain here until she has one. That is..." I looked over at Mona. "Unless Mrs. Kilroy decides that destroying the gorilla isn't necessary and that her husband's actions actually precipitated his own death." I tried to sound hopeful, but Mona wasn't having any of it.

"It bloody well *is* necessary!" spat Mona, venom dripping from her lips. "That beast killed my husband! I'll see it shot if it's the last thing I do on this earth!"

"Please!" pleaded Dr. Pelicane. "Please don't do this. It wasn't his fault!"

"Gorilla?" said Ranger Two. "Nobody told us it was a gorilla."

Mona turned to the rangers. "Where do I get a warrant?"

Ranger One shrugged and looked over at me.

"You have to apply to the state," I said. "Call the Fish and Game Commission. They'll help you fill out the papers."

"How long does it take?"

"A couple of days," I answered.

"And that animal stays locked up until then?"

"That's the law," I said.

"I'll be back in two days! I have to go and bury my husband." Mona spun on her heel and marched back down the path. The two rangers walked over to the cage and looked in.

"I'll be a horn-toad," said Ranger One. "It *is* a gorilla."

"Sure is," said Ranger Two. "I've never even seen a live one before. Seems a shame to shoot it."

I heard a stifled sob come from Dr. Pelicane.

"I guess we'll see you in a couple of days," Ranger Two said to me. He tipped his hat, and they both headed back to their SUV.

"Is there anything we can do?" asked Dr. Pelicane.

"I don't think so. The law is pretty clear on this one. I can put in a call to the governor's office."

"Do you think it'll do any good?" asked Gwen.

"I'll give it a try. Kokomo's pretty famous, and the circumstances are unusual to say the least. Try to get him to talk, will you? He's a witness. Maybe he can tell us something that we don't know yet."

"Junior's coming back through town," said Billy Hixon.

"What for?" asked Meg. We were sitting in the park, enjoying a mid-morning coffee as Billy drove up on his golf cart. Billy spent most of the summer driving all over the downtown area, checking on his landscaping crew.

"He won last Sunday!"

"Yeah, we heard," said Meg. "What? Does he need another blessing?"

"Indeed he does," answered Billy. "You know how these guys are. Superstitious. If something's working for them, they're not about to change anything until it stops working. I know one guy who always wears one red sock and keeps an old fingernail from his dead crew chief in his pocket."

"Eeeww," said Meg.

"You think that's bad," continued Billy, now enjoying his role as purveyor of disgusting trivia, "there's this other guy..."

"Enough!" said Meg.

"Okay, okay," laughed Billy. "I'm just sayin' that once these guys latch onto something, it's going to be hard to get them to give up on it."

"So, anyway," I interrupted, "Junior's coming back in today?"

"This afternoon. He's just stopping for a few minutes. He's got to get down to Darlington, South Carolina, for the next race."

"Did you tell Gaylen?"

"Yeah. She's fine with it, although she's not going to get all gussied up. Just a simple cassock. She says she'll come out and bless it on the trailer. Give it a splash, pour the Holy Water in the radiator and say the blessing. There'll be some media here, too. This is a big story for them."

"I'm glad she agreed to do it," said Meg. I nodded in agreement.

"He won last week, so Sunday's service should be full. That's the way it works. There's no business like show business!"

We were finishing up our coffee, and I was seriously contemplating going in to practice the organ for a couple of hours when I saw Wormy DuPont sitting at a card table outside of Noylene's Beautifery.

"This bears investigation," I told Meg. "Maybe *Wormy Acres* is up and running."

"I'd better come with you. I don't want you buying anything and putting *my* name on it."

"Why Pookie-Bear, don't you want to rest beside me for all eternity?"

"I haven't decided yet," she said. "I may not want to be buried. What are my other options?"

"We could cremate you," I said, "and sprinkle your ashes into the organ pipes. Then, little by little, you'd be spread all over the church."

"Nope."

"You could be in an urn on the mantle."

"No. I have an unnatural fear of urns."

"How about a vase?" I suggested. "Or a coffee can? You like coffee, don't you?"

"What about that diamond thing that we saw on CNN?" asked Meg.

"Oh, yeah. That was interesting. They take your ashes, put them under incredible pressure and compress you into a diamond."

"That's nice. I think I'd like that."

"It's not without problems," I said.

"What problems?"

"Let's just say that you're a diamond," I began. "One of the hardest known substances in the world and virtually indestructible, and you leave yourself to the church to be set into a silver chalice to serve communion."

"Yes," said Meg, with a wistful smile. "That's what I want to do. A beautiful chalice."

"And then, one dark night, the church is broken into by vandals, and they steal the chalice. They take it down to the Pawn Shop in Boone and Two-Fingered Larry gives them fifty bucks for it."

"Fifty bucks?"

"Yep. Then Two-Fingered Larry pries the diamond out of the setting and takes it down to Atlanta to see what he can get for it. It's a big one—three carats—and the fence down in Atlanta gives him two grand and then turns around and sells it to a dealer in Los Angeles for six."

Meg looked horrified.

"Then," I continued, "a boutique in Beverly Hills purchases it, puts a stud on the back and Britney Spears wanders in and purchases you to ornament her belly-button. Or worse! And if that wasn't humiliation enough, she decides to feature you in her new video, *Brokeback Booty*."

"That slut!"

"There you go," I said, shrugging my shoulders. "It could easily happen. Better the worms should get you than Britney Spears."

"You're not kidding!"

"Hi, Wormy," I said as we walked up, not noticing that he was talking on his cell phone. He was sitting in a folding chair at his card table, papers scattered across the top, a half-full cup of coffee holding them down. He waved at us and motioned for us to pull up the two folding chairs opposite his own.

"Be right with you folks," he said, his thumb discreetly over the mouthpiece of his phone. Then he got up and walked a few steps away from the table. Meg and I sat down.

"How's your cell service?" Meg asked me. "Mine was okay all winter, but now it's spotty at best. I may have to switch carriers."

"I don't think you'll do much better with another carrier," I said. "The reception in winter's better up here because there aren't any leaves on the trees. In summer, we have to do the best we can. They're putting up towers as quick as shopping malls though, so it won't be too long before we're covered coast-to-coast."

"How're y'all doing?" said Wormy, coming back to the table and sticking out his hand. "Woodrow DuPont's the name. Eternal rest is my game. I'd like to welcome you to the sales office of Woodrow DuPont's Bellefontaine Cemetery."

"We already know you," said Meg, hesitation clouding her voice. "Remember?"

"Sure," said Wormy. "I'se just practicin'." He smiled his best salesman smile. "Y'all need a buryin' plot?"

"Maybe," I said. "If the price was right. What do you have in a XXL?"

"Hmm," said Wormy, studying a plot of the farm. "I've got these two nice plots here in section D." He spun the paper around and pointed to a couple of numbers in the lower right corner. "These is right nice."

"I don't know," I said. "I'd want to make sure we're buried in the right section. You know, with *our* type of people."

"Hayden!" hissed Meg. "What are you saying? I'm so embarrassed!"

"That's all right m'am," said Wormy. He looked back at me. "I knows exactly what you mean." He made a show of looking right and left before leaning in and speaking in a hushed voice.

"This here section—Section D—that's for white folks only."

Meg was horrified.

"White folks?" I said. "No, you misunderstand. I want a plot in the No-Smoking section."

"No-Smoking?"

"Oh, yeah," I said. "Make no mistake—I do enjoy the occassional cigar. But if I'm going to be dead and underneath the ground, I sure don't want to be in the Smoking section, if you know what I mean."

"I see," said Wormy, thoughtfully. He sat back in his chair and nodded. "I see. I hadn't given no thought to a No-Smokin' section, but now that you mention it, I can see the advantages."

"So, you can accommodate us?" I asked.

"I feels sure that I can." Wormy was smiling again. "Now let me tell you about our special music program."

"You have an special music program?" asked Meg. "Do tell."

"This is getting better and better," I said.

"Here's how it works," said Wormy. "It's called *Eternizak*. We've got cable run out there, and we've subscribed to a music service. When y'all buys a plot, we puts in a wire from the main building and when you're buried, we stick a speaker right in your casket. All we have to do is drill a little hole, feed the wire through, and seal it back up with silicone."

"Very nice," I said and looked over at Meg. She was spccchlcss.

"We've got about two hundred channels of music. We can pipe any kind of music into your casket for as long as you want. And it's only $19 a month."

"So I can listen to Palestrina for all eternity? Or at least until my credit card expires?"

"I never heard of that group, but I guess so. Sure!"

"Here's an idea," I said. "Let's just say that my friend Pete was killed in a horrible toaster-related accident..."

Wormy nodded, now wearing his serious, bereavement face.

"Toaster-related?" said Meg. *"Toaster-related?"*

"It could happen. He's always sticking a butter knife into that thing. It's going to kill him some day. Anyway..." I turned my attention back to Wormy. "Let's say that he was buried out at your place. Could I offer to pay for his *Eternizak*?"

"Why, sure. That'd be a nice gesture."

"So I could arrange, let's just say for example, for *Eternizak* to play *The Carpenters Greatest Hits* for a few years? Then switch to accordion music? Maybe some Lawrence Welk polkas?"

"Of course," said Wormy. "No problem at all."

"You *wouldn't!*" said Meg.

"Wormy," I said, standing up and thrusting out my hand. "You are a genius. I'll be in touch!"

"Thanks! Here. You folks take a brochure and a map. I'll let you know about that No-Smokin' section right soon."

"I'd appreciate it, Wormy. Thanks."

"By the way," said Wormy. "Y'all know that Noylene and me is gettin' hitched?"

"We heard," said Meg. "Congratulations."

"What's all the racket?" asked Nancy, looking out the front window of the Police Department.

"I guess it's Junior Jameson back for another blessing," I said. "Billy told me he was going to swing by on his way to Darlington."

"Should I head out there? It looks like quite a crowd."

"It wouldn't hurt. I'll go with you."

The crowd was gathering. Even though Junior was stopping just long enough to get the car blessed and refilled with Holy Water, his fans had heard he was on the way, and some had driven all the way up from South Carolina just to get a glimpse of the service.

"If he keeps winning, or is even close," Nancy said grimly, "this is only going to get worse. I sort of preferred a nice, quiet little town."

"Wait a minute," I said, looking across the park lawn. "Those aren't NASCAR fans."

"Oh Lord, what now?" said Nancy.

We studied the fifty or so people at the far end of the park.

They were gathering separately from the racecar fans. Then I saw a placard come up in the hand of a familiar face.

"Oh, no," I said. "This isn't going to be good."

Dr. P.A. Pelicane had found out about the Blessing of the Racecar, rallied her forces, and was leading them across the park. I heard the shouting and saw the rest of the signs go up.

"Free Kokomo now! Free Kokomo now!" the crowd chanted.

I looked up at Gaylen Weatherall in her cassock, standing at the top of the steps with Junior Jameson. She hadn't begun the blessing, and they both stared at the group coming toward them, trying to make some sense of it. The rest of the two hundred people, who had come to cheer Junior's car on to greater glory, also turned to watch the approaching mob. They were joined by one CNN camera and a news crew from Darlington that had been sent to get footage of the blessing of Car 17. As long as Junior was winning, the news crews would be in attendance, and Dr. Pelicane had figured out that publicity would be Kokomo's best ally.

"Free Kokomo now! Shoot Baptists, not gorillas!" shouted the crowd, echoing the slogans on their signs waving above their heads.

"What're we going to do?" asked Nancy.

"Well, I'm not sure that fifty animal rights activists are going to be able to take two hundred NASCAR fans. And that's if the fight is fair."

"I've never known a NASCAR fan to fight fair," Nancy said.

"You go tell Gaylen what's happening. I'll talk to Dr. Pelicane."

"Hang on," I said, standing in front of the crowd with my hand out, my badge clearly visible. "This is a private religious service."

"Out of our way!" said a man in the front of the pack. "You can't stop us from demonstrating in a public park."

"Do you have a permit?" I asked.

"Don't need one," said the front man. "I checked your local ordinances. I'm a lawyer."

I tried a different tact. "If you interrupt them, those NASCAR fans will beat you half to death," I said. "You guys aren't PETA are you?"

"Yeah, what's it *to* you?" shouted a pimply-faced young man wearing a tie-died t-shirt, jeans and sandals. "You gonna arrest us?"

"No, just hang on a minute," I said. "The news people will still be here when the car leaves. You can talk to them then."

"Shoot Baptists, not gorillas!" shouted the pimply man into my face. "Free Kokomo now!" The rest of the protesters took up the mantra, and they marched past me. I turned and watched them head toward the steps of St. Barnabas.

"What's going on?" said a voice behind me. I turned around and saw Moosey standing there, watching the crowd.

"They're trying to save Kokomo," I said, "because he killed that minister by accident."

"Are you going to arrest them?"

"I guess I will as soon as someone actually breaks the law. I'm going to have to arrest a whole bunch of people. Listen, Moosey, you go on over to the other side of the park and find somewhere to watch. I don't want you getting hurt." Moosey nodded.

I followed the mob across the park, jogging my way around the outside of the phalanx. I could see Nancy, and she was talking to Gaylen and Junior. They were nodding at her. Gaylen, apparently deciding to get the blessing over and done with, carried her branch and the bowl of water down the steps and walked up to the car. I arrived at the front steps just as the protesters came up behind the NASCAR fans.

"Free Kokomo now!" the group shouted.

"Hey," yelled Junior. "Y'all shut up, dammit! We're trying to pray here!"

"Shoot Baptists, not gorillas!"

"Hey, that's about enough!" Junior hollered back. "*I'm* a Baptist! Hell, we're *all* Baptists! And I'm telling you for the last time! We're *trying* to pray!"

By this time, I was on the top step next to Junior. "Let's just all be quiet for a minute, and we'll work this out," I yelled. It was no use. No one could hear me over fifty animal rights activists chanting at the top of their lungs. I saw one unfortunate protester, obviously carried away in the heat of the moment, swing his sign at the head

of one of the NASCAR fans. The protester was a tall man and thin—
a vegan, perhaps. I noticed his pallor wasn't nearly as ruddy as that
of his target—a 280 pound carnivore wearing a baseball cap that
said "Beer—It's Not Just For Breakfast Anymore," and a sleeveless
t-shirt showing off his Special Forces tattoo. I saw the sign bounce
harmlessly off his cap, watched him turn around, grab the protester
by his shirt and lift him off the ground with a roar. I saw his fist
draw back, but lost sight of them as both sides weighed in.

I ran down the steps, grabbed hold of Gaylen's arm and pointed
her toward the doors of the church. She took the hint. Nancy was at
my side in a matter of moments.

"What do we do now?" she said, looking out over the melee that
had begun in a matter of seconds.

I surveyed a scene that would later be described by the TV
newscaster as "a one-sided donnybrook with Junior Jameson's
fans in the driver's seat." The animal rights people may have been
used to protesting in California, where people chat for a while, wave
a sign, throw a bucket of paint on a fur coat, and then go out for
some Brie and a nice Merlot, but that wasn't happening here. They
had angered the wrong folks. From my vantage point, I saw at least
ten of the PETA protesters lying on the ground. The PETA women
weren't faring much better than the men, because, although a male
NASCAR fan isn't likely to hit a woman that he's not married to, a
female NASCAR fan has no such problem, and the ladies were taking
advantage of easy pickin's. The PETA women probably didn't even
realize that brass-knuckles came in designer colors. Junior Jameson,
never one to walk away from a good brawl, was in the middle of it,
snatching up protesters by the scruff of the neck, punching them
once, and tossing them aside like rag dolls, all the while yelling at the
top of his lungs, "Y'all shut the hell up! We're trying to pray!"

I let out a big breath. "Give me your gun," I said to Nancy.

"You gonna shoot one?" asked Nancy, unholstering her .357
Magnum and handing to me.

"Hope not." I raise the gun over my head, cocked the hammer
back and fired one shot into the air. It was like a cannon had gone
off. Everyone stopped dead in mid-punch.

"Now," I hollered, "don't make me shoot you, 'cause I will!
I'm crazy. Ask anyone." I fired one more shot into the air for good
measure.

"You PETA folks gather up your wounded and head on over to the police station. You're all under arrest."

The protesters started make some noise, so I fired another shot into the air.

"I wish you'd tell me when you're going to do that," said Nancy, under her breath. "You're killing my ear-drums."

"I've got three shots left," I muttered.

"Whad's da chahge?" hollered the PETA attorney, using a handkerchief to stem the blood coming out of his broken nose.

"Disturbing the peace, assault, and PISSING ME OFF!" I shouted back.

"Pissig you off id dot agaid da law," the lawyer sputtered. "Oh, by dose!"

"Mr. Mayor?" I said, now noticing Pete standing on the steps beside me.

"Oh, yes it is," said Pete. "The town Council passed that law about three years ago. You can look it up!"

"Id wod hold up id court," said the lawyer. "We'll sue."

"And you might win," said Nancy. "But for now, you're all under arrest. Now march over to the police station. You know the drill!"

"What about them?" whined the pimply-faced boy, one of his arms hanging loosely at his side. "I think my arm is broken."

"You started it," I said. "Now get on over there." I pointed across Sterling Park toward the police station. They turned dejectedly and started walking.

The NASCAR fans were in a fine mood, Junior included. There were high-fives all around and a general consensus that with the Blessing of the Racecar coupled with a good ol' fashioned brawl—all caught on video-tape, it had been a fine afternoon.

"Go get Gaylen and let's get this blessing finished," I said to Pete. He nodded and disappeared inside the front doors of the church.

Pete and Meg were already at a table when I walked into the Slab Café later that afternoon. Collette was putting two pieces of Black Forest Cake in front of them.

"Did you really arrest them all?" asked Meg. "That's a whole lot of work isn't it—charging and fingerprinting fifty people? Not to mention the fact that you'd have to find somewhere to put them until they're arraigned. And think of the paperwork."

"I did," I said, sitting down and borrowing Meg's fork. "That's why I let them all go." Meg pushed her slice of cake in front of me in resignation.

"I figured," said Pete. "What did Dr. Pelicane have to say about the whole thing?"

"She wasn't there. I think she vamoosed after the trouble started. Great cake, by the way."

"Did all the protesters go home?" asked Meg.

"I don't think so. I heard some talk about heading out to the animal shelter to have a candlelight vigil tonight and then another protest tomorrow morning. Hey, Meg, you should try some of this cake."

"Did you call Gwen?" asked Pete. "You should probably give her a heads up."

"Already done," I said. "She's waiting for them."

"Here you are Hon," said Collette as she put another piece of cake in front of Meg. "Can I ask you something, Hayden?"

"Sure."

"You know that Dave and me were supposed to get married in a couple weeks."

"Yep. We're all looking forward to the ceremony."

"That's just it," said Collette, with a muffled sob. "We can't get married. Brother Kilroy is dead!"

"I'm sure another minister will do the service," said Meg. "Has New Fellowship Baptist arranged for an interim?"

"A what?" sniffled Collette.

"An interim minister," said Meg. "A sub."

"I don't think so. At least, I haven't heard of anyone. I thought maybe Hayden could do it."

"I'm not actually ordained," I said. "Sorry."

"Why don't you call Bootsie Watkins and ask her," suggested Pete. "She'd know if New Fellowship was getting a minister."

"I will. I'll ask Noylene, too," said Collette. "She and Wormy are supposed to get married. Maybe she's found someone to do the ceremony."

"Maybe," said Pete. "And maybe you could bring us some coffee."

"Coming up."

"Let me get this straight," said Meg, once Collette had made for the coffee pot. "Noylene and Wormy are cousins, but it's legal for them to get married?"

"Of course," said Pete. "North Carolina is an equal opportunity state."

"First cousins? Isn't that creepy?" Meg said.

"Nah," Pete answered. "There's lots of precedent. Edgar Allen Poe married his cousin. Charles Darwin, Albert Einstein..."

"Queen Victoria," I added, happy to add to the list. "J.S. Bach. Even Mary and Joseph.

"What? Mary and Joseph were not cousins!"

"Oh, yes they were," I said. "Check your New Testament genealogy. But seriously, it was very common for cousins to get married until well into the twentieth century."

"I still think it's creepy."

"Well, maybe they won't be having any children," Pete said. "Noylene's got to be what? Forty-five? Fifty?"

"I wouldn't hazard a guess," I said, "but if I did, it wouldn't be that high. Maybe early forties. Her son's got to be twenty-five at least."

"D'Artagnan's twenty-four," said Meg. "And Noylene is thirty-eight. She had him when she was fourteen. She could easily have some more kids."

"How old is Wormy?" I asked.

"I don't know," answered Meg, "but I'll bet he hasn't seen forty-five yet."

I sighed. "They sure start life early up here in the hills."

"You might want to leave the room," Marilyn said again, for the benefit of those readers who had forgotten where we were in the story. She pulled a crab-leg cracker and an oyster-shucker out of her purse.

"That is, if you're squeamish," she added.

I was squeamish enough. I went out for a hot cup of joe, and when I got back an hour later, Marilyn was sitting primly at her desk, typing titillatingly on her tidy typewriter. I glanced into my office. The two goons were nowhere to be seen.

"It's a good thing for you I'm empowered," said Marilyn. "Or you'd be swimming with the fishes."

"Speaking of fishes, where are the boys?"

"I showed them out."

"Did Ray have anything to say?"

"Oh, yes. He was very talkative."

"Spill it, Sweetheart."

"It's a guy named Moby Mel. He's behind the whole deal. He's been buying up all the fish markets all over the city."

"What for?"

"He's got his hooks into the bishop. If Moby Mel can get the clergy to okay his new 'Fish on Friday' agenda, Moby Mel's fortune is made."

Yeah, it all made sense now. A "Fish on Friday" edict would give Moby Mel a share of all the food served in the city, and that was a whole lot of sushi.

"Another brilliant installment," said Georgia as she looked over my latest offering at choir practice. "I can't say you're getting better, but I don't think you're getting any worse."

"I notice that I'm not in the story yet," huffed Marjorie.

"I haven't had time to work in the Hard-Drinking Bus Station Restroom Attendant With The Heart Of Gold just yet," I said. "I've been terribly busy."

"Gaylen said that she'd like one of these in her prayer book on Sunday morning," said Bev. "I'll take care of it. She just wants to keep up."

"Then I'll be careful what I write," I said. "Okay, time to rehearse. Let's take out the Charles Wood piece. Start at measure twelve. And sing it like you mean it!"

Chapter 14

It was a Thursday—a sticky Thursday morning with summer beginning to bear down on us. It was a day I was not looking forward to. I figured that if the boys from the Fish and Wildlife Commission had gotten their warrant to destroy Kokomo, they'd get an early start, so by seven o'clock, I'd showered, shaved, fed Baxter and Archimedes and was on my way into town. I was expecting a fax from the North Carolina Attorney General that I thought might help diffuse the situation.

I had enough time to stop by the Ginger Cat and get a cup of coffee, get to the Police Department, settle into my chair, and read two pages of the *Watauga Democrat* when the phone rang.

"Hayden Konig," I said, identifying myself.

"Hayden, you'd better get out here." I recognized Gwen Jackson's voice right away.

"Why? What's going on?"

"I let those protesters camp out in front of the office, but now they want to come in and wave their signs in front of my patients. I just won't have it."

"Any sign of the Fish and Wildlife rangers?"

"Not yet. It's been two days though."

"Yeah, that's what I'm thinking, too. Is the gorilla locked up?"

"Yep. I haven't checked on him yet, but his cage is in a locked enclosure. The PETA crew can't get back there. They'd have to come through the clinic because the gate is locked, and I'm not opening the doors until you get here."

"What about Dr. Pelicane?" I asked.

"She's with them. I'm not letting her in either, and she's screaming bloody murder."

"I'll be there in ten minutes."

It was closer to twenty minutes by the time I'd gotten the fax I needed, found the ammunition for my gun (it was in the bottom drawer of my desk), shanghaied Nancy from her breakfast repast at the Slab and made the drive out to the veterinary clinic. I pulled up onto the sidewalk in front of the building, forcing a number of protesters to move away from the doors where they'd gathered. Dr. Pelicane was the first to meet me as I exited the truck.

"The vet won't let me in!"

"Well, you sort of opened a can of worms here," I said.

Dr. Pelicane shrugged. "I just wanted the publicity. I figured that the public outcry would be enough to get Kokomo released."

"It might still. Why don't you sneak away and meet me around back? I'll get you in, but don't bring any of these people with you."

"Okay, I'll try."

The crowd was quite a bit smaller than the one that attacked the NASCAR fans. I counted about twenty. Nancy, who had tried to disperse the people in front of the glass double doors, was now being threatened by a rather mousy looking woman.

"I've been shot at by Russian whalers!" she screamed into Nancy's face. "I'm not scared of your Nazi storm-trooper tactics!"

I sighed and called to Nancy. "Go ahead and arrest her if it'll make you feel any better."

"Yeah," answered Nancy, "as a matter of fact, it would."

I watched as Nancy grabbed the woman by the ear, spun her around and zipped a nylon wrist restraint around both her hands. Then Nancy picked her up and threw her into the back of my pick-up.

"Owwwww," the woman wailed. "My ear! Police brutality! You all saw it!"

"Who's next?" said Nancy.

"You can't do that!" yelled another young man that I recognized from the day before. He reached out and grabbed Nancy by the arm. "Hey...wait a minute...Yowww!"

He landed with a thud in the back of the truck next to the mousy woman, his hands secured tightly behind his back.

"I've got about a hundred of these restraints," announced Nancy. "Anyone else?"

"Now just one moment, young lady..." said the PETA lawyer.

"How about this one, Hayden?" Nancy called.

"He's a big one," I answered. "And he's definitely trespassing. Five bucks says you can't throw him over the side."

"Ooomph," went the lawyer as he landed on top of the young man.

"I've been working out," said Nancy, "and you owe me five bucks. Now, who's next?"

She didn't have any takers.

Gwen and I walked through the clinic to the back and opened the lock on the fence surrounding the compound. Dr. Pelicane was alone and waiting just outside the gate.

"C'mon in," said Gwen, a sour note in her voice. "I just want you to know that I don't appreciate this at all."

"I'm sorry," said Dr. Pelicane. "I didn't know it would get out of hand. Is Kokomo doing all right?"

"As far as I can tell."

"Hey," called Nancy from the gate. "I thought you should know that the rangers just drove up. They've got Mona and another guy with them."

"Better bring them around back," I said.

"No!" screamed Dr. Pelicane. "Don't let them come back here!"

"It's okay," I said. "I think I can help. At least temporarily." I called back to Nancy. "Go ahead and bring them back."

"Where is that animal?" hissed Mona. She stomped back to the cages with a paper clenched tightly in her hand. Following hot on her heels was Bennett Shipley, the head deacon of New Fellowship Baptist Church. The two rangers were right behind him—Ranger One still carrying the rifle, Ranger Two carrying a clipboard with a sheaf of papers attached.

"I have the warrant right here," Mona said. "All legal. We've come to see that animal shot!"

"Hang on," I said. "I need to see that warrant, if you don't mind."

Mona shoved her crumpled paper at me. I took it, opened it and read it over carefully. It was all legal, signed and sealed.

"Everything seems to be in order," I said. "But I have a fax here from the attorney general granting a stay until the governor has a chance to review the case and make a final decision. You understand that this is a very special animal."

"We got the word from Raleigh that this might be coming," said Ranger Two, taking the fax and looking it over. "Mrs. Kilroy insisted on dragging us out here anyway. I think she figured you might not have heard yet."

"Of all the *despicable...*" started Dr. Pelicane.

"That's okay," I said, cutting her off. "No harm done."

"I heard that was a talking gorilla," said Bennett Shipley. "Is that right?"

"He's not talking now," said Dr. Pelicane. "He hasn't said a word since the...umm...accident."

"Well, I don't care if he does talk! We'll see that monkey dead if it's the last thing we do!" spat Bennett Shipley. "Jimmy Kilroy was my best friend, and I'll have that gorilla head hanging on my wall!"

"The governor promised a decision by Monday," I said. "I'll see you then. Right now, I have to get these protesters back to the station."

Chapter 15

I headed back over to Betsy's. I'd told her I was a Renaissance man and now she was playing me like a crumhorn or maybe a hurdy-gurdy, and I wasn't happy about it. She had another agenda and it didn't include Fishy Jim stepping out on her. Fishy Jim was like every other bass—he always headed upstream to spawn—and if Betsy wasn't used to it by now, she never would be. No, there was more to Betsy than a woman scorned. She had a reason to put me on to Fishy Jim. She wanted him watched and kept as close as Brigham Young's underwear.

I knocked on her door and heard a gruff voice answer.

"Yeah, waddaya want?"

"I'm looking for Betsy.

"She ain't here."

I smelled crab cakes and onion pie. Something was definitely up.

"I'll come back," I said. Which I did—precisely five seconds later. The latch on the door had about as much chance as a Little Debbie on Ted Kennedy's nightstand.

"Drop that basting brush!" I yelled to a couple of fry boys standing over a hot rotisserie. "And get up against the wall!" I moved across the floor like an octopus with seven wooden legs. I was too late. I recognized Fishy Jim right away. He was a little green around the gills, but he'd been kept on ice for a couple of days. Now he was stretched out on the charcoal with a little paprika, some olive oil, garlic, and a sprig of rosemary.

Basso alla Capricia. What a way to go.

I'd been avoiding the dreaded church staff meeting for several weeks, but Gaylen had moved it to Thursday afternoon. I'd begged off of Tuesdays, the traditional time for such meetings, due to my very hectic police schedule. Finally, she pigeon-holed me and asked when I thought I *might* be able to make it.

"Every fourth Thursday afternoon?" I suggested.

"Thursday afternoons sound good," Gaylen said. "About 3:30?"

"Yes," I said. "Every *fourth* Thursday. Once a month."

"How about three Thursdays a month? You pick."

"Too many. I'll come every *other* Thursday."

"Deal." She spit on her hand and stuck it out to me.

I'd spit on mine in the time-honored tradition of mountain folk everywhere and sealed the pact, but now, of course, I found myself actually having to attend.

I stopped by the Ginger Cat on my way to St. Barnabas and fortified myself with a large cup of coffee containing two shots of espresso. I went into the library and greeted Marilyn, the church secretary.

"You're early," Marilyn said.

"A little. Sorry. I didn't bring you any coffee."

"Too late in the day for me."

Gaylen came in next, followed by Bev, Georgia, Brenda Marshall, Joyce Cooper and Billy Hixon.

"What're you doing here?" I asked Billy.

"We've got to figure something out. There's too many people coming to church on Sunday. We don't have enough ushers, folks are sitting in my pew...it's a real mess."

"Okay, then," said Gaylen. "We've got quite an agenda to get through, so let's get started. Billy, would you open the meeting with a prayer?"

"Huh?" said Billy. "Do what?"

"Open the meeting with a prayer," she repeated, closing her eyes and folding her hands in front of her, a smile playing on her lips. We all bowed our heads as well.

I'd never heard Billy pray in public before. Oh, I'd heard him ask the Lord, in no uncertain terms, to smite a few of his clients and to cast Holy Wrath upon eighty-year-old bad drivers, but that was a hop and a skip from praying in front of clergy.

"Uh..." started Billy. "Hey God. This here's Billy. Billy Hixon. Umm...if you could do something about those fire ants on the front lawn, we'd all appreciate it. Also, bless this meeting and the hands that fixed it."

"Amen," said Gaylen.

"Amen," we echoed.

"First order of business," said Gaylen, looking down at her notes. "Who orders the coffee around here? It's awful!"

"We've got about forty pounds of coffee that Father George got us," said Georgia. "It's in the kitchen. He said that if we ordered it in bulk, we'd get a better price."

"It's virtually undrinkable. Let's throw it out," said Gaylen, "and get back on the Community Coffee delivery plan. All in favor?"

"Aye," came the answer.

"All opposed?"

"I don't think you should throw it out," started Brenda, aka Princess Foo-Foo. "What a waste of money! Don't you think..."

"Doesn't matter," said Gaylen, sweetly. "Motion carried and approved. Second order of business, the crowds on Sunday. Billy?"

"It's gettin' really bad," Billy said. "There's just too many folks. I mean, it's a good thing, but what's going to happen if we keep on?"

"How many did we have last Sunday?" I asked.

"Four hundred and thirty-three," said Billy. "We're putting chairs up everywhere. And we're running out of cookies at coffee hour after the service."

"How many can we seat comfortably?" asked Gaylen.

"About three hundred," said Billy.

"I'll take care of the cookie problem," said Joyce. "But how long do we expect that racecar driver to keep winning?"

"I've got no idea," said Billy. "That Holy Water is really doing the trick. I'm thinking we should bottle it, bless it and sell it on the NASCAR circuit."

"Sorry," said Gaylen. "My blessings aren't for sale. This isn't a Catholic church, you know. With that many people, we need to hire another sexton." She turned to Bev. "Do we have the money?"

"Sure," said Bev. "I'll put an ad in the paper."

"What about a second service?" said Georgia. "We could have it at 8:30. You know, before Sunday School. At least for the summer."

"It's something to think about," said Gaylen. "Let's not announce it just yet. Maybe the furor will calm down a little. But if we're still at capacity in July, we'll start another service. All in favor?"

"Aye," came the answers from around the table.

"But don't you think we should form a committee to look at the long range..." began Princess Foo-Foo.

"Sorry. The motion has been carried," said Gaylen. "Now, what about some new service music for the Eucharist?" She looked over at me. "Can we come up with something different? I like the stuff in the hymnal, but we've been singing it for twenty years."

"I'll see what I can come up with," I said.

"Great!" she said, making another check on her pad. "You'll have to teach it to the congregation. I don't want to be the only one singing. Item four. Vacation Bible School. Brenda, what are our plans?"

"I...uh...I don't have any actual plans yet..." said Brenda. "Father George and I decided that it was better to concentrate on our Sunday School program."

"I see," said Gaylen. "Okay, what do you have planned for our Sunday School program?"

"Well...Father George and I were working on it, but then he left. I really don't have anything."

"Tell you what," said Gaylen. "Let's have a Vacation Bible School for the kids. A one-afternoon event. Let's say a week from Saturday, noon to four. Marilyn, you put it in the newsletter and print up some flyers." Marilyn nodded and jotted some notes on her pad.

"Brenda, you go ahead and plan it. I'll expect you to have some ideas on my desk Monday morning. Okay?" She looked around the table. "That's it then. Let us pray."

We all bowed our heads, and I snuck a look at my watch. It was 3:43.

"Grant, O Lord, that we may follow the example of your faithful servant Barnabas, who, seeking not his own renown but the well-being of your Church, gave generously of his life and substance for the relief of the poor and the spread of the Gospel; through Jesus Christ our Lord, who lives and reigns with you and the Holy Spirit, one God, for ever and ever. Amen."

"Amen," we all repeated.

"Wow!" said Georgia, after we'd all dispersed. "I think that was the most efficient church meeting I've ever attended."

"I didn't mind that at all," I said. "But somehow—and I don't remember exactly how it happened—I volunteered to find some new service music and teach it to the congregation."

"Yeah," said Georgia. "She's got me heading a task force to start a Habitat for Humanity house. She invited me for a cup of coffee and that's the last thing I remember till the North Carolina Habitat office called me the next day." Georgia smiled. "Maybe she's a witch."

"Hey, wait a minute," I said. "Did I agree to playing for a second service on Sunday mornings?"

"Yep. I think so."

"She's a witch."

"I like her though."

"Yeah," I said. "Me, too."

Chapter 16

It was 8:30 by the time Moosey and I got to the lake—a late start to be sure, but I was hopeful.

"We're gonna get Ol' Spikey today, aren't we?" said Moosey.

"Old Spiney," I corrected. "I think his name is Old Spiney. Anyway, yeah, I'm hoping we'll get him."

We got our gear squared away in Pete's rowboat, put our life jackets on and shoved off into the still water.

"Did you fix dinner for Miss Farthing last night?" asked Moosey, as I pulled on the oars, propelling us into the middle of the lake.

"Yep. I did. Now I'm off the hook for a while."

"Off the hook," chuckled Moosey. "That's funny. 'Cause we're fishin'. What did you fix anyway?"

"Some kebobs and a salad."

"I like macaroni," said Moosey. "You know how to cook that?"

"Nope. I could read the directions, I suppose."

"I can cook it myself, but I like it better when Mama does it. When I eat it, I pretend that it's cheesy worms!" Moosey laughed.

"Here," I said, handing Moosey his pole. "Put a cheesy worm on that hook and let's get it in the water. Maybe Old Spiney will like it as much as you like macaroni."

I decided to go with a lure that Pete suggested called a Walking Worm. It had worked twice for him, but the fish snapped the line both times. With this in mind, I'd also ordered some new 20 lb. test microfilament line that, according to the manufacturer, was a lot less likely to break. I had my line in the water and was just starting to relax when I heard a roar overhead.

"Look at that!" exclaimed Moosey. "Its an old-timey airplane!"

"It's Five-Dollar Frank," I said, "He'll give you a ride for five dollars. And that's called a biplane. Look. It has two wings on each side—one on top of the other." We looked up at the bright yellow plane glinting in the sun. "He does crop-dusting sometimes. Wave at him. Maybe he'll wave back."

Moosey put down his pole, stood up in the boat and waved and hollered for all he was worth. Frank brought the plane in low over the lake and waggled his wings in reply.

"He did it! He waved at us!" said Moosey. "Hey, what's that behind the plane?"

"He's got a banner behind it," I said. "That's what he's up to. He's advertising for someone. Can you read it?"

"Naw. He's comin' straight at us. Wait. Now I can. It says 'We Got Worms.' What's that mean?"

I laughed. "He's advertising for Uncle Jerry's Bait Shop in Boone. That's what their big sign says on the highway. 'We Got Worms.'"

"Maybe we should get some worms from Uncle Jerry. I mean, they might be *professional* worms."

I chuckled. "Let's see how we do today before we bring in the professional worms."

"What do you think's going to happen to Kokomo?" asked Moosey, once our lines were back in the water. Moosey was letting his pole rest over the side of the boat, but I'd cast my lure about thirty yards toward the shallows and was reeling it slowly in.

"I hope he'll be okay," I said. "Maybe the governor will let him go since it was an accident."

"That's good. When will y'all find out?"

"The governor said he'd call on Monday."

"You know the governor? That's cool!"

"I've met him a couple of...Hey! I've got a bite!" I yanked hard on my line to set the hook. My Walking Worm had done its job and the line cut a furrow in the surface of the water as the big fish took off toward the middle of the lake. I let some line out with a heavy drag to slow him down and wear him out.

"You got him! You got him!" shouted Moosey, dropping his own pole and grabbing the back of my shirt. "Reel him in! Don't let him get away!"

I felt the line go slack, but I wasn't buying it. I'd set the hook pretty well and I suspected that the fish was heading back toward the rowboat. I started to reel in the line, trying to keep pace with him, but he was fast. Too fast.

"He's coming back toward us," I said. "He's a smart one, and he's got a plan."

"But you're reeling him in," said Moosey. "He'll be at the boat in a second."

I nodded and wound the line back onto the spinner as fast as I could. We watched as the line cut back across the water toward the boat, but by the time I'd caught up with him, he was directly underneath us.

"He's right under us!" exclaimed Moosey. "We've got him now! That's for sure!"

I reeled in the line as far as I could and felt the tension as the end of the pole dipped toward the lake.

"I think he's foxed us again," I said. "See this? He's not moving. He went underneath our boat and wrapped the line around a stump or something."

"Can't you just pull him up?" asked Moosey, disappointment evident in every word.

"Nope," I answered. "See? Look here. I'm pulling on the line as as hard as I can. The end of the pole is almost in the water. He's caught the line on something, and he's just waiting for me to cut it."

"What if you don't cut it?" Moosey asked.

"We can't stay out here forever," I said. "And anyway, we'll get another chance at him. I'm going to think of a plan to catch that smart old fish. You'd better cut him loose for now."

"Won't that line get caught on a tree or something while he's swimming around?"

"It might, but I don't think so. And there's a good chance he'll work that hook out eventually. Cut it down as low as you can reach."

Moosey reached over the side with a pair of snips and, with an audible sigh, cut the line.

"Dadburn fish!" he said.

"Junior got the pole position at Darlington," Billy said with a grin. "He's driving like a maniac!"

"Is that good?" asked Elaine.

"Heck, yeah!" exclaimed Billy. "That means he's got the fastest car out there right now. By the way, I found four more ushers for this morning."

"Great," I said. There was still an hour until the service started, and I told the choir that we'd have to practice beforehand. These big crowds were beginning to wear on all of us. "If this keeps up, I'm going to want a pay raise."

"Fine," said Billy. "We'll double your money. No, we'll triple it."

"You understand that even though I give my salary back, my check goes into the music fund, right?"

"Really? Okay then, never mind."

The church was filling up, even as we rehearsed. We went over the service music, the Psalm and the hymns, but the anthem was falling flat. Being a highly-trained professional, I immediately hit on the problem.

"Where are all the stupid tenors?" I asked.

"Hey!" said Marjorie. "I'm not *that* stupid."

"I mean the ones that aren't here."

Marjorie shook her head in despair. "I don't know. This is like Easter every Sunday. Or Christmas Eve. I'm not sure I can take the pressure to perform."

"I'm sure you'll manage just fine," said Meg. "But you'll have to sing a solo this morning. You look like the only tenor."

"This is what I'm talking about!" wailed Marjorie. "The stress is too much!"

"Don't panic," I said. "Everyone look in the back of your folders and pull out Emergency Anthem number one. *Come Thou Fount of Every Blessing*. It's two part and you all know it."

"But it's not what's listed in the bulletin," said Fred.

"Let's just see how many people notice," I said with a smile.

"I need a drink," said Marjorie, reaching for her flask.

"Where's our latest installment of *The Bass Wore Scales*?" asked Martha.

"It's on the back of the Psalm," said Meg, answering Martha's query. "I begged him not to do it."

"Did you give Gaylen one?" asked Rebecca.

"I put one in her prayer book," said Bev. "I just hope it doesn't get mixed in with her sermon."

After church, at Meg's behest, a group of us headed over to her house to watch the race. Ruby had fixed lunch for us as well as an abundance of snacks. I wasn't really a race fan, but I really liked snacks and, as they say, when you have a dog in the hunt, it makes it a lot more interesting. We were crowded into Meg's living room—Billy and Elaine, Pete, Georgia, Noylene and Wormy, Molly and Nancy. Meg didn't have a big screen TV, but we all managed to find a seat with a view.

We weren't in our seats two hours later, though, when Junior Jameson won his second race in a row. It was a close and exciting race. On the last lap, Junior just managed to edge out the second place car after he'd nudged the leader into the wall. The announcers were getting ready to replay the unfortunate bump, all the while debating whether the officials would let the victory stand, when Junior Jameson decided to show off with a double-donut at the end of his victory lap. He spun around the first time with a squeal of tires, smoke billowing from the rear of his car. He should have stopped there and headed into Victory Lane, but Junior was riding high on adrenaline and Holy Water. We watched in horror as the second donut took him into the wall in front of the grandstand. As a wreck, it didn't look that bad. But it was.

And now Junior Jameson was dead.

When I arrived at the office on Monday, Nancy was waiting for me with a cup of coffee in both hands.

"Here's your coffee, Chief. We've got to go to Boone and see Kent Murphee."

"What's up?"

"He says he wants us in the coroner's office ASAP. Something about the Kilroy killing."

"You want me to drive?" I asked.

"Unless you want to ride on the back of the motorcycle."

"I'll drive. I'll play some Medieval music for you on the way. I've got a new recording of a bladder-pipe ensemble."

"Oh goody."

We wandered into Kent's office about a half an hour later, and he was sitting at his desk reading a *Playboy* magazine from the 1970s.

"Reading the articles?" Nancy asked as we both sat down in the armchairs opposite his desk.

"As a matter of fact, yes. Did you know, for instance, that there have only been two instances ever reported of gorillas in the wild using tools? That is, an object to help perform a specific task?"

"I didn't know that," I said. "Is that in the *Playboy* article?"

"Nah," said Kent, putting the magazine down on his desk. "I was just looking at Miss November. I dated her in graduate school, you know." He lovingly patted the top of the magazine. "I talked with Penelope. She said that Kokomo uses tools all the time, but he's picked it up from watching and living with people. He can use a nutcracker, for instance, and will, on occasion, eat with a fork."

"That's very interesting," said Nancy, stifling a yawn. "Is that why we're here?"

"Yep. I finished the autopsy. I had a devil of a time convincing Mrs. Kilroy to let me do it. Since the death was listed as an accident of sorts, she had the last word on whether the autopsy should be performed."

"And you talked her into it?" I said.

"Nah. I lied. I told her that in all cases of animal homicide in North Carolina, an autopsy was required."

"And she agreed?"

"I just pushed the paper across the desk, and she signed off. That was last Friday."

"You could be fired, you know," said Nancy.

"Doesn't matter," said Kent, with a smile. "I'm crazy, and everyone knows it. Anyway, I doubt I'll be fired." He handed Nancy and me each a copy of his report.

"There wasn't any DNA evidence. He'd been floating in the water too long, and it was full of chlorine. I'm guessing that Kilroy threw a tablet in when he filled it." Kent picked up his own copy. "Of course, he had a broken neck—that was obvious. And it seems," he continued, "the blow to Jimmy Kilroy's head was substantial. It caused a four-inch gash that bled profusely. The blow was also responsible for an acute subdural hematoma—that is, a blood collection below the inner layer of the dura but external to the brain itself and the arachnoid membrane."

"Arachnoid membrane?" said Nancy. "I've got spiders in my brain?"

"Most definitely," I said. "They crawl out your ears sometimes."

"Same root word," said Kent. "The membrane's like a spider-web forming the middle of the three coverings of the brain and the spinal cord. Anyway, the indentation on Kilroy's skull was caused by a cylindrical iron object. Like an old pipe, for instance. I found traces of rust deep inside the wound. I would never have seen them without the autopsy—there was too much blood. Also, when I x-rayed the skull, I could see the indentation of the pipe. Again, not apparent to the naked eye. So I would say the weapon was an iron pipe, two-inches in diameter."

"Kokomo hit him with a pipe?" asked Nancy.

"Could be," said Kent. "But here's the thing. If Kokomo got mad and hit him with a pipe, Kilroy would have been unconscious. I can't see him breaking Kilroy's neck just for spite. And, if he broke his neck first, then why come back and whack him with a pipe? Now, I know this is a gorilla, and I have no idea what his thought process might be, but it just doesn't make sense."

"Hmm," said Nancy.

"I don't think Kokomo did it," said Kent. "I can't prove it, of course, and I'll admit I'm biased since I really like Penelope, but it just doesn't add up. Oh, I think the gorilla tore the office up, that's for sure. There aren't many people capable of throwing a grand piano across a room. But his tantrum, if we can call it that, may have been a reaction to the killing. I just don't know."

"Here's another question," I added. "If, as we surmised, Kokomo was in the pool with Kilroy to be baptized, why would he be holding a pipe?"

"Did you find one at the scene?" asked Kent.

"No," admitted Nancy. "But the place looked like a tornado hit it. And we didn't know what we were looking for."

"Have they cleaned everything up?" asked Kent.

"Yeah," I said. "But it's all sitting in a dumpster around the back of the church. I don't think the disposal company has picked it up yet."

"You'd better get back to work then," said Kent with a grin. He picked up his *Playboy*. "Here's the other thing. You've got a witness. A talking gorilla."

Nancy was silent on the drive back to St. Germaine, a sure sign that she was thinking—or maybe just enjoying the bladder-pipe music. We arrived at the New Fellowship Baptist church just in time to see a flat-bed truck with "New River Dumpster Service" written on the side pull into the parking lot. I walked up to the driver, showed him my badge, told him he wouldn't need to pick this dumpster up for a few days, and asked if he could bring us another one the same size.

"That one's twenty feet long, and it's just a little more than half-full. What're you gonna do with another one?" he asked.

"We need to empty all this trash out and go through it piece by piece," I said. "If you'd put it right next to that one, it'd be a big help."

"I can't get back here till tomorrow morning," the driver said. "I'm booked up today."

"What's the weather supposed to do?" I asked Nancy, knowing she always checked the weather before taking her motorcycle out.

"I think we're fine—until Friday anyway," said Nancy.

"Tomorrow will be fine," I said. "First thing, right?"

"First thing," said the driver. "Should I have it billed to the church?"

"No, bill it to the St. Germaine Police Department."

"Will do."

We watched the truck pull away. "Call Dave," I said to Nancy, "and get him to bring a tarp down here and cover up that dumpster just in case the weatherman's wrong. Then let's go in and take another look at the office."

Chapter 17

"Can I help you?" asked Bootsie Watkins, when we walked into her office.

"We need to see Brother Kilroy's office, if you don't mind," I said.

"We've had a couple of men from the church working on cleaning it up, off and on, for the past couple of days. Ever since the insurance adjustor gave us the okay."

"Can we have the key?"

"It's open," said Bootsie, "but here's the key. It's the only one. We're going to change that old lock and get a new door. There's no reason to keep that one since Brother Kilroy is de...uh...no longer with us. It came out of his grandfather's old church."

I looked at the key that she handed me. It was a skeleton key, dark with age, the once sharp edges worn down over decades of use.

"Thanks," I said. "I'll check back with you when we're finished."

Nancy and I walked down the hall to Kilroy's office. We reached the heavy wooden door, and Nancy reached for the knob.

"Hang on a second," I said. "Before you open it. Let's think about this."

Nancy pulled her hand back and looked at the door. "The window's still broken," she said.

"Yep. But, here's the thing. When we got here, the door was locked. Remember? Locked from the inside."

"I remember. The key was still in the lock."

"Right. The door couldn't have been locked simply by pulling it closed. It's not that kind of lock. So, if there was another person in there—someone who hit Kilroy in the head with a pipe—how did he get out?"

"Window?" said Nancy.

"I don't remember one," I said. "But maybe we missed it."

"Chimney?"

"There's a fireplace, but it's gas if I remember correctly. Probably unvented, so there wouldn't be a chimney, but let's check."

"Secret passage?" said Nancy, with a smile. "Like the pope?"

"Not as outlandish as you might think," I said. "I know several churches that have less than conspicuous means of egress for the clergy. Sometimes they want to get out of the building without anyone seeing them. And these entrances aren't always obvious."

"Should we ask Bootsie?"

"Let's see if we can find something first," I suggested.

We opened the door to the office and went in. The office was bare. The desk was gone—presumably in the dumpster outside—along with the piano, books, computer, rugs, chairs and sofas. The built-in bookcases were the only furniture remaining."

"I guess the insurance company gave them a total loss on the furnishings," Nancy said.

"From what I remember, it *was* a total loss."

Nancy nodded in agreement and walked into to the bathroom.

"Nothing in here either," she said. "If there was an iron pipe, and it was still here, it's probably in the dumpster. But I'm not betting on it."

"I don't think it's there either," I said. "But we'll have to go through everything anyway. Any windows in the bathroom?"

"Nope."

"There aren't any in here either. And no chimney."

"Then, supposing there was a killer, how did he get out?"

"Check everything. Make sure there's not another way out of the bathroom. I'll do the same in here."

"Will do," said Nancy.

Ten minutes later, we were convinced that there was only one entrance to the office.

"We'll check around the outside of the building on the way out, but it looks like the door is the only way in or out," I said. "Let's ask the secretary just to be sure."

We closed the door to the office behind us and walked back down the hall to Bootsie's office.

"No," she said, surprised at our question. "Wait a minute. I have the blueprints to the building." She walked over to a filing cabinet, rummaged for a moment and brought us a big file containing a set of folded blueprints. "Take them with you if you want."

"Thanks," I said. "Here's the key to the office. We'll bring these blueprints back in a few days."

Nancy and I went into the Slab Café for another cup of coffee and some breakfast. Dave was waiting for us at a table.

"Did you see the race yesterday?" he asked.

"Yeah, I did," I said, taking a seat. "It's hard to believe."

Collette walked up and set down some mugs. "He was just showing off," she said. "That's why he died. Micah 6:8 tells us to walk humbly with our God. James 4:10 says 'Humble yourselves in the presence of the Lord and He will exalt you.' Junior Jameson wasn't humble. He was a show-off, and that's why he's dead."

"Kind of a harsh sentence," said Nancy. She held up her mug for Collette to fill.

"It don't do to mock God," sniffed Collette, as she walked away.

"Does she have the whole Bible memorized?" Nancy asked Dave.

"It seems like it," said Dave with a sigh. "She quotes scripture at me almost all day long. I thought it would slow down a little once Brother Kilroy was killed, but it's just gotten worse. I tell you, it's wearing me out."

"I'm sorry," said Nancy.

I looked over at her, waiting for her to take the shot I knew was coming, but she just took a sip of her coffee.

"Thanks," said Dave. "Anyway, what did Kent Murphee say?"

We went over Kent's findings with him, Nancy filling her pad with notes as we talked. Then we discussed the crime scene and what needed to be done.

"You mean someone's got to go through all that trash?" asked Dave.

"Not just anyone, Dave," said Nancy. "Someone with the rank of corporal."

"Me?"

"You," said Nancy, with a smile.

"I think it'll go faster if there's a lieutenant involved as well," I added. "Tomorrow morning. First thing."

"Oh, man..." said Nancy.

"Here's your breakfast," said Pete. "Did you hear anything from the governor?"

"The governor?" I said.

"Kokomo? Amnesty? The governor? Remember?"

"Ah. I'm sorry. There's a lot going on today," I said. "I haven't heard anything. I'll call Raleigh as soon as we're finished. We may have some new information on the Kilroy case."

"What's up?"

"Kent doesn't think that Kokomo did it. Quite frankly, I'm having doubts as well."

"Really? Then the governor will have to hold off."

"We don't have any proof yet. We're working on it. I'll call right after breakfast."

Dave, Nancy and I were on our way back to the Police Department when Billy yelled to me from across the park.

"Hayden! Come over here for a second."

"You guys go on," I said to Nancy and Dave. "I've got to talk to Billy. I'll be there shortly."

"I've been calling Junior Jameson's office all morning. I finally got through," said Billy, as I walked up.

"What did they say?"

"No comment."

"You can't tell me?"

"No. They said 'no comment.' So then I called the crew chief. I have his cell number," Billy added.

"And?"

"And he said he was talking with Kimmy Jo Jameson—you know, Junior's wife. They want to have the funeral here in St.

Germaine. Kimmy Jo said that it's what Junior wanted. They're going to let us know about the final plans, but it's going to be on Thursday afternoon."

"I'll put it on my calendar."

"You're darn right you will. The choir is singing," laughed Billy.

"What are we singing?" I asked.

" Kimmy Jo's going to fax everything to the church. There's something else, too."

"What?"

"St. Barnabas is getting most of its money back. Our contract was with Junior. He was the driver and owned the racing team. Since he's dead, the contract is null and void. We get 15.1 million dollars."

"So we've got to go through the whole thing again?" I asked.

"Nope," said Billy. "Gaylen Weatherall's in charge now. I have a feeling this won't be a problem."

"What did the governor's office say?" asked Nancy when I put down the phone.

"They're not going to intervene."

"Did you tell them about the new evidence?"

"I did, but it doesn't matter. They asked if we had any concrete evidence. Until we have proof that Kokomo didn't do it, he did."

"What about 'innocent until proven guilty?'"

"It doesn't apply to animals," I said, with a shake of my head.

"Dave and I could go out and find the pipe tonight," Nancy offered. "If it's there."

"Even if you found it, all we could prove is that we had a pipe that was used to hit Kilroy in the head. Until we did some DNA or fingerprint analysis on it, it wouldn't give us any new information."

"So the warrant stands?"

"It looks like it. I'll call and have Gwen give Dr. Pelicane the bad news. I guess I've also got to be there tomorrow morning when the rangers show up."

"Want me to go?"

"Yeah," I said. "You and Dave meet me out there just in case those PETA folks get out of hand. Then go and find that pipe if it's there."

"I've been thinking," said Nancy. "That office was really a mess when we got there. Is it possible that the killer was still there? Maybe he was as scared as we were and was hiding under the busted up piano or a rug or something."

"You think so?" I asked.

"Nah," said Nancy. "It was just a thought."

Chapter 18

All of a sudden a chill went down my spine like two-dozen mice running from my hat into my shorts; mice that had their claws dipped in something really, really cold, like liquid nitrogen or maybe frozen yogurt.

"Where are Fishy Jim's scales?" I asked, poking at one of the fry-boys with my heater. "You cleaned him. Where are they?"

"Who wants to know?"

"Sorry, no questions," I said. Then I shot him.

"I'll talk! I'll talk!" shouted the other one. "The Minimalist was up here. He paid us. Then he took the lot."

"The Minimalist? He took all of them?"

"Yeah," said the fry-boy, shaking like a Frenchman in a white-flag factory. "All of them."

"All three forms of the minor?" Fry-boy nodded.

"He got 'em all," Fry-boy wailed. "He said nobody would be needing them anymore. Please let me go."

I waved him to the door with my gun hand. "Get lost," I said, "and don't let me catch you snuffling around here again."

It all made sense. This had nothing to do with Fish on Friday. That was just a smoke screen. The Minimalist was back--my archenemy--and now he had scales. I didn't think he knew how to use them yet. His gang only used four notes, over and over, until you wanted to take a shotgun and blow your own brains out. Oh, they had devotees, to be sure, and I'd hear of a John Tavener anthem sneaking into the liturgy now and again. But if The Minimalist figured out how to use all the scales, it'd be a disaster. He'd turn minimalism into a few trite praise choruses, stick 'em on a big screen in front of the church, buy a tambourine, hire a worship-team, and I'd be out of business. He had to be stopped.

I moved to the door, but then I realized three things. There wasn't any big rush, I was hungry, and Fishy Jim was looking pretty good.

"This is kind of funny," said Meg, putting down my missive and taking a sip of her iced tea. "Although, this supper reminds me of Fishy Jim. I don't know if I can eat him." She looked at the broiled fish on the plate in front of her.

"But the couscous is almost done," I argued. "Look. You said four meals, so this is your last chance at supper, and, as they say in the culinary arts, 'it is medium-well with my sole.'"

"Oh. That's okay, then."

Dr. P.A. Pelicane and Kent Murphee met me outside the Police Station at 7:30 the next morning.

"Gwen Jackson made me move the motor home," said Dr. Pelicane. "She said it was in the way and causing too much of a distraction. She also had a copy of the warrant that was faxed over to her by the Fish and Wildlife Commission. It said that I shouldn't be allowed to visit Kokomo without an officer of the court present. That's you, right? You're an officer of the court?"

"That's me. Let's drive on out there."

Dr. Pelicane and Kent slid into my truck, and we headed out toward the animal shelter. We were silent most of the way, but finally, I had to ask a couple of questions. I looked at Kent to see if he'd told her about our suspicions. He recognized the look and gave a slight shake his head. I agreed with him. It would just make it harder on Dr. Pelicane if she knew what we thought might have happened.

"Penelope, did Kokomo sign anything to you in the last few days? Since the killing took place?"

"He hasn't said anything," said Dr. Pelicane sadly. "This happened once before. When his first kitten died, he wouldn't talk for a month. He just sat in the corner of his enclosure."

"So he might not be able to tell us anything for weeks," I said, "and even then, it'd be guesswork on our part as to what he meant. I mean, nothing he tells us is going to stand up in any courtroom."

"That's true," said Kent.

"I guess it won't matter soon," said Dr. Pelicane, resignation apparent in every word. "Kokomo killed him, of course, but it was that stupid preacher's own damn fault."

We pulled up to Gwen Jackson's Veterinary Clinic, and the protesters were out in force. It wasn't quite eight o'clock by my watch, and I didn't see Gwen's SUV in the parking lot, but the clinic didn't open until eight, and I figured there wasn't any reason to be early this morning and plenty of reasons not to. The PETA people were gathered on one side of the parking lot. On the other side were the two rangers, Mona Kilroy and Bennett Shipley. Nancy was in the middle, glaring at the protesters, daring one of them to make an illegal move. Dave was beside her, looking slightly more nervous than I thought a corporal should. Nancy had obviously told the rangers, Mrs. Kilroy and Mr. Shipley to wait on the other side of the lot until Gwen Jackson arrived. Ranger One was cradling a rifle. They were standing there, calmly eyeing the scene as I walked over to them.

"Sorry we gotta do this," Ranger One said. "I hate this kind of stuff."

I nodded and took the warrant that he offered me. I glanced over it quickly. It was a copy of the same one that I had in my pocket—faxed to the Police Department yesterday afternoon. I looked at my watch again. It was eight o'clock, and, as if on cue, Gwen drove her Explorer into the parking lot and around the side of the building toward the back. The protesters, realizing the time had come, started yelling and moving toward the front glass doors.

"Gwen's going around. She won't open the front doors until you're finished," I said. "Let's go to the back gate. Nancy and Dave can handle this out here." I said it and hoped that it was true.

"Fine!" spat Mona. "Let's get this over with."

We walked in silent procession except for the occasional sob from Dr. Pelicane. Kent has his arm around her, and she was leaning heavily on him. Gwen was at the back gate, unlocking the padlock, when we walked up. She nodded at me, sadly, and led the way back to the pens.

"Please don't do this," said Dr. Pelicane to Mona in a desperate voice. "You can stop it."

"Shut your mouth!" hissed Mona. "It'll be my pleasure to watch that beast take its last breath."

Dr. Pelicane sobbed again and sagged against Kent, but we kept walking. There was one more lock, another padlock, that Gwen opened from her ring of keys. She then stepped back away from the gate, and the two rangers walked forward.

"Y'all stand back. We can't have you within twenty yards," said Ranger Two. "And put your fingers in your ears. This rifle's plenty loud."

The two men walked past the first enclosure to the second cage that was Kokomo's last habitat. The rest of us gritted our teeth, not willing to put our fingers into our ears until the rifle came up. They stood in front of the cage for a moment and then called back to us.

"Hey! What's the deal?"

"What's up?" I called back.

"That gorilla," Ranger One said, slinging his rifle back onto his shoulder. "He's gone."

We all rushed to the cage.

"What did you do with him?" Mona Kilroy was livid and screaming at Dr. Pelicane. "You took him! I know you did!"

I looked at Penelope. She seemed to be as surprised as the rest of us.

Gwen had the lock in her hand and gave it a yank. It dropped open. "No, she didn't," Gwen said. "She couldn't have. All the gates were locked when I came in. I have the only keys."

"Might you have forgotten to lock the cage back after you fed him yesterday evening?" I asked.

"I don't think so, but if I did, I doubt that Kokomo would have bothered to put the lock back on once he'd escaped."

"I doubt it, too," I said. "So someone came in..." I looked around. "...Over the fence?"

"That barbed wire on the top of the fence is pretty hairy," Gwen said, pointing at the coils of wire atop the chain-link fence that surrounded the back of the clinic. "It would take a very determined person to pick his way over that fence."

"How about getting out?" Ranger Two said.

"Same thing," said Kent.

"Then there's the matter of getting the lock opened," Ranger One said.

"Well, the gorilla's gone," I said. "Why don't you send my two deputies back here on your way out."

"Will do," said Ranger Two. They both shook my hand and headed back to the gate.

"We are not having this!" said a furious Bennett Shipley. "We have a warrant to destroy that animal. I'm putting a bounty on that gorilla. I'll pay five thousand!"

"Five thousand?" said Kent. "Dollars?"

"To whoever kills that animal. And I'm going to do my best to see that I don't have to pay anyone by shooting it myself." Bennett Shipley and Mona stomped off just as Nancy and Dave walked up.

We heard a cheer come up from the protesters, and I figured that the rangers had just given them the news of Kokomo's escape. Nancy and I went to the cage to give it a once-over. Dave and Gwen started walking the fence, checking for something out of the ordinary.

"Look at this," said Nancy, holding up the lock for me to examine. "Around the shackle. Look at the scratches."

"Somebody picked it?"

"Looks like it to me. I'm going to take it with us and see how long it'd take me."

"You know how to pick a lock?" I asked.

"It's pretty easy if you have the right tools." She turned the lock over in her hands. "With a hairpin, I'll bet that it'll take me maybe two minutes."

"Two minutes?"

"Well, I'm out of practice. It's an old Masterlock—single latch with four pins that are so sloppy that it makes a great lock for learning how to pick. If you have a set of shims, you could open this in ten seconds. With a pick, a minute, tops. Hairpin, two minutes."

"Do *you* have a set of padlock shims?"

"Of course. I'm a policewoman."

I went into the cage and looked around. It had been cleaned yesterday, and there was fresh straw on the floor. In the corner was half a head of cabbage, a few carrots and a banana peel. I stepped on something that crackled under my foot. I looked down, picked it up and stuck it in my pocket.

"I know someone else with a set of padlock shims," I said to Nancy.

"Yeah," said Nancy. "Me, too."

Nancy and I went into the Slab and sat down at a table. Kent and Penelope had driven back with me, but headed directly back to Boone to report to the University. Dave and Gwen hadn't found any anomalies around the perimeter of the fence, and Dave had headed out to the Baptist church to start sorting through the trash. Nancy told him she'd join him as soon as she could.

"Two questions," said Pete, as he pulled up a chair. "Did the Fish and Game Commission do its duty, and how about some waffles?"

"We're not here for breakfast," I said. "I need to talk to Bud."

"He's not here. What's up?"

"Kokomo got away," said Nancy.

"No kidding?" said Pete.

"I thought that Bud was working here this summer," I said.

"Oh, he is. But he's off this week. He got a gig as a roadie for a rockabilly band while they do a swing through the Carolinas. The Carburetors. Ever heard them play?"

"I have, actually. Meg and I saw them over at the Eagles Nest in Banner Elk."

"Well, Bud's gone for the whole week. He left yesterday morning. You need a sommelier?"

"Not right now," I said. "You remember when we had that rash of wine thefts about three years ago."

"Yeah. Nancy caught Bud red-handed. Hey, wait a minute. He's not doing it again, is he?"

"No," I said. "But the lock was picked on Kokomo's cage. Those scratches sure look familiar."

"Oh, yeah?" said Pete. "Well, it wasn't Bud. Not if it happened last night. He's not even in town."

"Bennett Shipley has put a bounty on Kokomo's head," said Nancy. "Five thousand dollars."

"Wow! Five grand! That's a lot of money up here in the hills. There's going to be quite a stampede. How're you going to handle it?"

"I don't know yet," I said.

162

"Well, I do," said Pete. "We'll sell a gorilla hunting license for $80 and tell the hunters that if they don't have a license and they shoot that gorilla, they'll spend three months in the county lock-up. That'll weed out most of them. At least you won't have six hundred hunters walking around the mountains with high powered rifles."

"It might work," I said. "It won't stop all of them, but it might make them think twice."

"And the city will make a pile of money!" said Pete. "Now, how about those waffles?"

Chapter 19

"Thanks for coming over," said Gaylen. She was sitting on a bench in the garden in back of the church. She had been reading her prayer book as I walked up, and now she set it on the bench beside her and stood to greet me.

"No problem. Is this about the funeral?"

"Partly. I think it's going to be quite a show. But there's something else I need to talk to you about."

I nodded.

"The main reason I asked you in is to tell you that Princess Foo-Foo is no longer with us."

"Princess Foo-Foo?"

Gaylen laughed. "Meg told me what she called her. Princess Foo-Foo is pretty apt. Anyway, Brenda was supposed to have a Bible School plan for me yesterday morning. She called in sick yesterday and resigned this morning."

"My, but you do have a way about you," I said, with a smile. "By the way, any thoughts about what St. Barnabas will do with fifteen million dollars?"

"Oh, I have lots of thoughts. For now, it's going into a money market account. Meg thinks that, even in this market, we can realize seven or eight percent."

"Wow," I said. "That's a little over a million dollars a year in interest."

"Meg pointed that out. If we leave it alone for a year, the church will have the entire sixteen million back and we can spend a million a year on outreach, camp improvements, Habitat houses, music and art festivals or whatever we decide without ever touching the principle. That's a whole lot of money."

"I'll miss seeing our name on that racecar, though. What about Lucille Murdock? She's the one who decided that the money should go to Junior Jameson—coincidentally, her favorite nephew."

"I've spoken with Lucille. She's understandably upset about Junior's demise, and she's declined to be involved in the decision again."

"It sounds as though you have everything under control."

"I still have Bible School to worry about. I guess I never should have had Marilyn print up those flyers."

"It's this Saturday, right?"

"Yes."

"If you want to drive up to Sugar Grove, I've got a friend who puts food baskets together every Saturday. People start coming out of the hills and down to the Good Shepherd Food Pantry at about one o'clock. He could use the help, and it might be good for the kids."

"How far is Sugar Grove from here?"

"Half an hour drive," I said.

"That's perfect!" said Gaylen. "I'll put together a little lesson, we'll help at the Good Shepherd Food Pantry and then stop for pizza on the way home."

"Sounds like a plan," I said. "I'll give him a call this afternoon."

It was creeping up on lunchtime, and I decided to be a good boss for a change and take some vittles out to the New Fellowship Baptist Church for Nancy and Dave. They'd been rooting around in the dumpster for a couple of hours, and I figured they could use a break. I called the Bear and Brew and arranged to pick up a large deep-dish "Heart Attack" pizza with garlic crust and three bottles of Sierra Nevada Pale Ale. I was feeling pretty good about my leadership attributes as I hopped in my truck, set the pizza in beside me, put on a CD of Bach's *Orchestral Suite No. 1* and headed out of town to the sounds of a merry gavotte.

It was a warm day, to be sure, and I had the windows down. I decided to take the scenic route out to the church, the drive taking me three miles out of the way, but through a couple of passes that were awash in rhododendron, the rich pink and purple flowers that covered the mountain's lower ridges. High above the rhododendron, white clusters of the mountain laurel blooms were still visible and dotting the roadside were clusters of wild geraniums. I was rethinking my lack of appreciation for the month of June.

I turned off the music as I pulled into the parking lot. I'd already parked by the front door before I remembered that Nancy and Dave were around back by the dumpsters. By then, I'd turned off the truck and decided to hoof it around the big metal building with the pizza and refreshments. I turned the corner at the back of the church and saw the two twenty-foot long, red dumpsters sitting side by side—each of them six feet tall and about twelve feet wide. I didn't see Nancy or Dave and thought they might be inside the church taking a break. I set down the pizza and the three brews in the shade and walked over to the newly delivered dumpster to check on the progress that Nancy and Dave had made in the last couple of hours. I grabbed the edge of the dumpster, stepped up onto a metal ledge and hoisted myself up.

"Hey, you two," I said, barely able to keep the laughter out of my voice. "Get off that piano. You're both out of uniform!"

"You missed a button," I said to Nancy, when she and Dave climbed out of the dumpster. "That one, right there."

"Yeah...well...we...uh..." stuttered Nancy, fumbling with her shirt.

"Uh...I...that is...we...umm..." added Dave. "You see..."

"I see, exactly," I said. "And I brought pizza and beer to celebrate!"

"I am *so* embarrassed!" said Nancy.

"You should be. I mean *really!* Snookie-Pie Dumpster Love? What if one of the Baptists had come out here?"

"Not much chance of that," said Dave. "We couldn't even get anyone to answer the door. The church is locked up."

"Bootsie's probably at lunch."

"Oh...yeah," said Dave.

"This certainly is an interesting turn of events," I said, offering pizza all around. "Is this serious? What are you going to tell Collette?"

"I can't marry her. She's too holy. She just wears me out."

"Well, you'd better tell her soon," I said. "Because you're supposed to get married next week."

"I think we've postponed it," said Dave. "But I don't know for sure. We're still waiting to hear if our apostle can make it over to perform the wedding."

"You have an apostle?" Nancy asked.

"Well...the church has one. Apostle Jerome. He's from somewhere down in Georgia. He comes up twice a year for revivals, but whether he can come up next week or not, I'm not getting married."

"Because of...umm...this?" asked Nancy.

"Not entirely," said Dave, smiling. "But mostly."

My piece of pizza disappeared with a smack, and I got to my feet. "Well, I'll leave you two alone. Finish lunch and then see if you can manage to go through the dumpster before dark. Let me know if you find anything."

"I need to talk to Bootsie Watkins," I said to Pete later that afternoon, over a piece of pecan pie.

"Good idea. The church secretary always knows more than she's telling. That's one of the first things they teach you in detective school."

"Exactly. If Jimmy Kilroy was killed, she might have some insight. Mona's personality isn't exactly peaches and cream."

"Yeah, she's quite a piece of work," said Pete.

"On the other hand, her husband's just been killed, and she has no reason to believe that he wasn't killed by the gorilla. I can see where she'd want it destroyed."

"But if there were doin's afoot at New Fellowship Baptist Church, Bootsie would know," said Pete.

"Doin's?"

"Yep. Doin's. Like if Brother Kilroy was having an affair with the piano player and her husband found out and threatened to kill Kilroy if he didn't stop. Those would be *doin's*."

"Those would indeed be *doin's*."

The bell on the door of the Slab jingled, announcing Dave and Nancy's entrance. They came up to the table carrying a black plastic bag and sat down in the two empty chairs.

"Found it," said Nancy.

"Really?" I was genuinely shocked. "I didn't expect that."

"Me neither," said Dave. "We tossed almost everything from one dumpster into the other, and then Nancy saw it."

"It's a piece of pipe, just like we thought," said Nancy, holding up the bag. "There's still some blood on one end of it."

"It was wedged in the grand piano between the big iron plate and the big piece of wood," said Dave. "Kokomo broke the board in half. That's why Nancy was able to see it."

"In between the harp and the sounding board."

"I guess," said Dave. "There were quite a few holes in the metal piece. Big enough to slide the pipe in and wedge it against the side."

"Yeah. The iron plate holds the strings and the holes make it a lot lighter without sacrificing any of the strength. There's a lot of tension there. Wow! We never would have found it if Kokomo hadn't broken the piano."

"But we did," said Nancy, with a small smile.

"Let's get it over to Boone and see if we can get any prints or maybe a DNA sample."

Nancy nodded and got to her feet.

"I'll take it over there now." She looked over at Dave. "You want to come?"

"No thanks. I've got to talk to Collette."

"Now, Snookie-Pie?" asked Nancy.

"No time like the present. I've got to tell her the wedding is off. Is she here?" he asked Pete.

Pete looked confused, but interested. "In the kitchen. Feel free."

"What are you going to tell her?" asked Nancy.

"The truth, I guess.

"I'm outta here," said Nancy.

The bell jingled again, and Meg exchanged a brief hello with Nancy as they passed each other in the doorway.

"What's up?" Meg asked, taking Nancy's seat. "You guys are staring at the kitchen like a couple of foxes watching a henhouse."

"Shhh," said Pete. "Dave's going to break up with Collette."

"What?" whispered Meg. "Right now?"

"In the kitchen," Pete added.

"What brought that on?"

"I'll tell you later," I said.

Suddenly a plate broke in the kitchen. Then another one.

"Oh, man," said Pete, "she's breaking the dishes."

"What do you mean you want to break up?!" Collette wailed, her voice carrying from the kitchen into the dining room. "What do you mean you can't marry me?!"

We didn't hear anything for another few seconds, then another scream.

"Whaaaaat? You did *what?* With *her?* In the *dumpster?*"

"Ooo," I said, with a grimace. "I don't believe I'd have told her *that.*"

"The dumpster, eh?" chuckled Pete. "With who? Nancy?"

Collette slammed open the door of the kitchen, grabbed two dirty plates from off of the counter, spun on her heel and threw them back into the kitchen, presumably at an unapologetic Dave. We heard one crash immediately, but the other brought a yelp with the sound of the breaking china. Collette looked around the restaurant in a fury. The only other plates that were handy held our half-eaten pieces of pecan pie. Collette swiped them up in a single pass, kicked the kitchen door open and heaved them, one at a time, at the hapless Dave.

"Aw," said Pete, "that was the last piece, too."

"She's got a good arm," said Meg.

"This is *your* fault!" Collette screamed, turning her fury toward me. "*You're* the one that sent them to the dumpster!" She saw a rack of coffee cups behind the counter and moved toward them with murder in her eyes.

"Let's get you out of here!" I said, grabbing Meg's hand. "I'll be back in a second, Pete." I ducked as a cup whizzed by my head and crashed into the wall behind the table. Meg and I made it to the front door before the second cup broke on the jamb. We managed to get outside, where we turned and viewed the rampage from a safe distance.

"Collette!" bellowed Pete, "stop throwing stuff!"

"You all sit there every day!" shrieked Collette, coffee mugs flying from her hands and smashing into the walls. "You sit there every day and make jokes, and all the while my fiancée is planning on breaking up with me! *And you all knew it!*" Collette found the glass coffee pots and both of them flew toward Pete.

"Yooow," hollered Pete. He ducked under the table, but the pots crashed on the top, splattering him with hot coffee. "Collette! We didn't know anything. And you're fired!"

"I'll fire *you!*" She picked up the Belgian waffle iron and threw it against the pie case. Glass exploded in all directions. Dave peeked out of the kitchen, and Collette saw him out of the corner of her eye. She grabbed a glass sugar shaker from off the counter and whipped it toward the kitchen door. Dave never saw it coming and it caught him right above the eye. He dropped to the floor like a hundred and sixty pounds of wet sand.

"That's enough of that," I said, going back through the front door. "Collette, put it down!"

She turned toward me, grabbed a saltshaker off a table and threw it at my head. I ducked the missile, flipped a table on its side and dropped in behind it.

"Collette, you're under arrest!" I yelled.

"You have the right to remain silent!" added Pete from under his table.

"Ahhhrrrr," howled Collette, and I saw a butcher-knife fly by the table.

"She's into the knives!" I called to Pete. "Stay down!"

"No kidding!"

An iron frying pan whizzed across the restaurant and crashed through one of the front, plate-glass windows.

"Dammit!" yelled Pete. "Collette! Quit it!"

Her answer was another carving knife, this one sticking an inch into the wall—an unlikely but startling result, and one due to luck rather than any knife-throwing skill. Still, it was disconcerting.

"Don't throw any more knives! I'll shoot you, Collette. I swear I will," I yelled. "I've got my gun out, and I'll shoot you right in the leg!"

"Me, too!" hollered Pete.

"You don't got no gun!" screeched Collette, sending one of Pete's two toasters crashing into an empty booth. "Neither of you!"

After a long minute of howling and breaking glass, an eerie stillness fell over the Slab, and I ventured a look past the edge of the table. Collette had sunk to the floor—her rage finally spent—and sat amidst shards of glass, food and other debris, her face in her hands, silent sobs wracking her body. Meg, being outside and having a better view than either Pete or I did, came back in, walked past my upturned table and over to Collette. She put her arms around her and helped her to her feet.

"C'mon, honey," Meg said. "I know..."

I was about to say something, but a look from Meg closed my mouth. This was a look that I'd seen before. Pete crawled out from under his table, and we watched as Meg led a sobbing Collette out the front door and down the street.

"You want me to go arrest her?" I asked.

"No, I guess not," said Pete, with a sigh. "Look at this place, though. I'll have to close for a couple days just to clean up."

"Let's check on Dave. He's not moving."

We kicked our way through the wreckage and over to the kitchen door. Dave let out a moan and opened one eye.

"Is she gone yet?" he whispered.

"Yeah, Corporal Snookie-Pie," said Pete. "She's gone. What did you tell her, anyway? She was as mad as a bag of weasels."

Dave sat up, brushed pieces of glass from his hair and blinked his eyes like a toad in a hailstorm. "I told her the truth. That I couldn't marry her. That I was in love with Nancy and that Chief Konig caught us...umm..."

"*In flagrante delicto*?" Pete said.

"Yeah. That. In the dumpster behind the Baptist church."

"Why on earth did you tell her that?" I asked.

"It was bound to come out," Dave said. "I thought it would be better coming from me."

"Dave, think for a minute. Why was it bound to come out?"

"You wouldn't have told anyone? Not even Meg?"

"Well, I might have told Meg. But she wouldn't have told anyone. Except maybe her mother. And maybe...hmm...I see your point."

"Oh well," said Dave, glumly. He rubbed a huge knot just above his right eye. "It's out now."

I left Pete to clean up. On the way back to the office, I went by Noylene's and explained the situation to her. The Beautifery was having a slow day, and Noylene volunteered to go over to the Slab Café and help Pete.

"I'd get Wormy to come with me, but he's busy getting the cemetery ready."

"Ready for what?"

"That racecar driver. He's going to be buried in the Bellefontaine Cemetery."

"Junior Jameson?"

"That's the one," Noylene said. "He'll be the first one infirmed."

"Interred," I gently corrected.

"Right. Buried. That's why he's gettin' a discount."

"This is on Saturday, right?"

"Yeah. Saturday."

I nodded and turned to leave. "Thanks for helping Pete. It's a real mess over there."

"Oh, by the way," said Noylene. "Junior's bein' buried in his car. They've hired a crane to lower him into the grave, racecar and all."

"You're kidding!"

"No, I'm not. And Wormy's going to pipe in *Eternizak Country* and *Eternizak Gospel* through the car radio—at least for the first five years. That's all they've paid for."

My truck pulled up at Ardine McCollough's trailer just as the sun was beginning to drop below the tree-line. There were still a couple of hours of sunlight left, but the shadows of the hardwoods crisscrossed the driveway like a Japanese art print. Pauli Girl was sitting on the front porch in a pair of cut-offs and a t-shirt, drinking a can of Cheerwine, and looking for all the world like Daisy May, the poster-girl for Fleetside Mobile Homes. She waved to me as I slammed the door of the pick-up.

"Hey there, Hayden."

"You're not working today?"

"Naw. Them gummint boys—those ones from Fish and Wildlife—they came in for a pizza and found me out. I'm really not even old enough to wait tables."

"Ah, sorry."

"That's okay. I didn't really like working anyway."

"Spoken like a true fourteen-year-old."

She laughed. "I guess. You want to see Mama? She's not home yet."

"I was hoping to see Moosey."

Pauli Girl furrowed her brow. "I saw him a little while ago. I think he was running through the kitchen. He might be out back in the woods."

"Thanks. I'll see if I can find him."

"Moosey!" I called. "Moosey! Can you hear me?"

The McCollough's trailer backed up to the Pisgah National Forest, half a million acres of beautiful and rugged mountain scenery that covered a large portion of the western edge of the state. Moosey was probably well acquainted with a couple hundred of them. If he wanted to play hide and seek, I'd have a hard time finding him without a couple of bloodhounds.

"Moosey! I know you can hear me. I'll wait up at your house. Don't be too long."

I turned and walked back to the trailer.

Ten minutes later, a breathless Moosey banged in the back door. I was sitting with Ardine and Pauli Girl in the living room, admiring Ardine's latest quilt. Ardine made and sold three or four a year to supplement her meager income at the Pine Valley Christmas Tree Farm.

"Hey Mom," said Moosey. "Did you just get home?"

"Yes. Just now. I think Hayden wants to talk with you."

I saw a worried look cross Moosey's visage just for an instant. Then his happy-go-lucky demeanor was back front and center.

"Okay. What's up?"

"Let's go out on the porch," I said.

"Sure."

We went out on the porch and sat down, our legs hanging off the edge, my feet planted firmly on the ground—Moosey's dangling above the dirt, swinging back and forth. I looked at him. He was nervously chewing the inside of his cheek.

"You know," I started. "I was out at Dr. Jackson's this morning. Someone stole Kokomo from his cage."

"Hmm," said Moosey.

"Whoever got him out used a set of padlock shims. Do you know what those are?"

"Hmm," said Moosey.

"You know, Bud had a set of those. Remember when Nancy caught him a couple of years ago breaking into houses? Have you seen those shims?"

"Hmm," said Moosey.

"You know what else? When I was looking around the cage, I found this." I pulled a Milky Way wrapper out of my pocket and showed it to Moosey. "I wonder if I could get any fingerprints off this?"

"I don't think so," said Moosey. "I'll throw it away for you if you want me to."

"Now listen to me, young man. I don't know where you put Kokomo, but you cannot be around him for a while. There are going to be hunters all over town tomorrow and out in these woods, too. You're coming with me. I'll pick you up at seven in the morning. Understand?"

Moosey nodded.

"Is Kokomo locked up?"

Moosey shook his head. "He said he didn't want to be."

"He's talking to you?"

"Yeah."

"How did you get into the fence?" I asked.

There's a loose place in the back. You can undo the wires and pull the fence away from the pole. That's how I always get in."

"You've been in before?"

Moosey nodded. "Sometimes I go in to look at the bears. Then, when I leave, I just hook the wires back."

"How did Kokomo get out?"

"Sheesh!" said Moosey. "You should have seen him. He just climbed right over that fence like it wasn't even there."

"What about the razor wire on the top?"

Moosey shrugged. "Don't know. He just went right over it."

"Did you see any cuts on him?"

"Nope. He's fine."

"Is he in the woods?"

"There's an old school bus..." Moosey pointed to the woods behind the trailer. "Back there. About a mile down the holler. Some boys used to use it for camping, but no one's been in it for a couple of years. You can't even see it unless you know where it is."

"Did you leave him some food?"

"Yeah. Lots."

"Not candy," I said.

"Not candy."

"Did he say anything else?"

"I asked him what happened."

"You did?"

"Well, sure. He said 'Kokomo scared. Tiger bad.' I don't know what that means."

"Wasn't Tiger the name of his kitten?"

"Yeah," said Moosey, with a nod. "Kokomo didn't kill that man, though. That's why I rescued him."

"I know. And I think you're right about Kokomo. He didn't kill Brother Kilroy. Do you think he'd talk to Nancy and me?"

"Maybe. I'll ask him."

"Not unless I go with you. If we bring him back, he'll be shot, so he's on his own for a couple of days. Got it?"

"Got it."

Chapter 20

I had to find Betsy. She was a sitting duck or maybe a cooked goose, a dying quail, a squatting swan, or something equally as fowl. If The Minimalist got to Betsy before I did, he'd squeeze her like a custard frog on St. Beadle's Day. I took the stairs two at a time, carefully wiping my mouth as I got to the bottom. Right then and there, I made a solemn vow. Fishy Jim had been a good bass, and his skeleton would get the burial it deserved.

Marilyn was waiting for me with the car running.

I hopped into the jump seat. "What are you doing here?" I asked, curious as an altar boy at a "True Love Waits" convention.

"I thought you could use a little help. You wanna get some dinner?"

"No thanks. I just ate."

"Okay. Where to?"

"Let's get over to Moby Mel's. I need to find Betsy."

"Harumph. I don't know what you see in her."

"Other than a drop-dead gorgeous face, a body that Aphrodite would envy, a personality that makes Katie Couric seem like Leona Helmsley, a double-doctorate in Anthropology and Medieval English, and seventeen million dollars?"

"Yeah. What's she got that I haven't got?"

"Other than a drop-dead geor..."

"Shut up," said Marilyn.

"When do they announce the Bulwer-Lytton contest winners?" asked Meg.

"Next week. It could be as early as Monday."

"So I'll have to take you all out sometime next week."

"Yes, I suppose you might if you happen to win. However, I had an e-mail from Scott Rice, the head of the contest. He's very impressed with *my* submissions."

"Is that the one that says 'Your submissions have arrived and will receive the treatment that they deserve?'"

"Umm...yes, that's the one. But then he sent another e-mail as well."

"Did it say 'You latest inflictions have arrived?'"

"Yes," I sighed.

"So," said Meg. "You received two *form* e-mails."

"Well...okay, but it's the *way* he said it. Your latest *inflictions* have arrived."

"Ah yes. Now I see. I shall start quaking in my Reeboks any moment."

I was at the Police Department at 7:30 in the morning with Moosey in tow. I knew that the Slab wouldn't be open, so we stopped by a fast-food place at the edge of town and loaded up on our minimum-daily-requirements of sugar, carbohydrates and grease. Moosey was still finishing one of his cinnamon rolls as we got out of the truck and walked into the station. Dave, usually here every morning at seven sharp, was nowhere to be seen. Nancy, however, usually in her chair no earlier than nine o'clock on a normal morning, was front and center, her uniform starched and as crisp as a new dollar bill.

"Good morning," I said, ushering Moosey into one of the visitor chairs.

"Morning," said Nancy. "I need to ask you something."

"Okay, shoot."

"Can we...uh...talk alone?"

"I'd like to, but I have to keep an eye on this one." I gestured toward Moosey. "There's a gorilla loose, and there'll be hunters galore in a couple of hours."

"Soon as people read the paper," said Nancy, handing me a copy of the *Watauga Democrat*. "Page four."

I flipped the paper open and saw a full-page ad. It looked like a "Wanted" poster from the Old West. There was a gorilla's picture in the middle of the page. Across the top was emblazoned "Wanted—Dead." Underneath the picture were the details. I read them quickly, but carefully.

"$5000 reward to whoever kills this wild gorilla. 5' 8" tall—480 lbs. Extremely dangerous. Last seen at the animal shelter in St. Germaine, NC. A warrant has been issued to destroy this animal and a hunting license is needed. A Gorilla License is available at the Courthouse in St. Germaine for $80. Dogs okay."

At the bottom was added, "Bounty paid for by Bennett Shipley, St. Germaine, NC. Collect from Mayor Peter Moss, St. Germaine Courthouse."

"Holy cow," I said.

"Can I see?" asked Moosey. I walked over and handed him the paper.

"I called the courthouse," said Nancy. "There's already a line outside the door waiting to buy a Gorilla License. They won't open up until eight, though. Pete said that Bennett Shipley came by his house last night and gave him a certified check for five thousand dollars."

"Well, if they don't get Kokomo today, we may want to talk with him tomorrow."

"Shipley?" asked Nancy.

"No. The gorilla."

"You know where he is?"

I gave a nod in Moosey's direction. Moosey smiled as innocent a smile as I've ever witnessed.

"Ahh," said Nancy. "Can't we just go bring Kokomo in?"

"I don't think so. If we did, he'd have to be destroyed. I think he's better off taking his chances."

"Okay, let's hope he's as smart as everyone thinks he is." Nancy thought for a moment. "You know," she said, "I really, *really* like Dave. I always have."

"Yeah," I grinned. "I know."

"But I didn't know he was going to call the wedding off. That's a lot of pressure. What if this thing between us doesn't work out?"

"That's life," I said. "Sometimes it doesn't, but you have to give it a chance."

"Hey," called Moosey, still sitting in his chair, and holding up a section of the newspaper. "Look here at this picture. What's this called?"

I walked over to where he was sitting and looked down at the paper. He was pointing to a photo of a couple of American soldiers on a dusty Iraqi street.

"What? The soldiers? They're the ones stationed in Iraq."

"No, this here." He pointed to the woman behind them, clad head to toe in black.

"That's called a burka. It's what some of the women wear in the Middle East."

"Ain't it hot?" asked Moosey.

"I suppose it is."

"Sheesh. I wouldn't wear it if it was as hot as it looks," said Moosey, flipping the paper open to the comic page. "Lookie here at Snoopy. He's up on the doghouse again!" He giggled. "Hey, when are we going to go fishing?"

"You think Moosey has ADD?" asked Nancy, softly, when I returned to the other side of the room.

"Maybe a little," I replied.

There were two workmen outside the Slab Café, replacing the plate glass window, when I wandered down the sidewalk to see how Pete was faring. I looked in the door. The glass had been cleaned up, and the food was off the floor and into the garbage. Noylene was leaning on a mop, a strand of red hair hanging down into one eye.

"Hey there, Chief," she said, with a smile. "We've almost got it cleaned up. Took about five hours last night, though."

Pete came out of the kitchen, wiping his hands on a towel. "I need to get back in business. Those gorilla hunters are going to come back hungry."

"How about the dishes?" I asked.

"Already on the way. Darla's Restaurant Supply in Asheville. They should be here in an hour."

"Toasters?"

"Toasters, cups, mugs, sugar shakers...the whole enchilada," said Pete. "My insurance guy was here this morning at six. He said they wouldn't pay for the damage unless I brought charges against Collette. I told him to forget it."

"How much is it going to be?" I asked.

"Probably two or three grand," said Pete. "I've got it covered. I needed new plates anyway."

"I'm in for half," I said. "I'd hate to have to arrest Collette. By the way, did you see that line outside the courthouse?"

"Yep. I called over to see how we were doing. We'd sold two hundred fifty or so as of nine o'clock."

"I'm hoping they don't find him for a while," I said.

"That might be a vain hope," said Pete. "A bunch of those guys had their dogs with them."

"Ah. But dogs don't know what a gorilla smells like," I said, with a smile.

"Can't they just go over to the animal shelter and sniff around the cage?"

"Well, I suppose they could," I said. "And they'll get a scent, sure enough. It might even have been a gorilla's scent if someone hadn't cleaned out that cage last night, hosed it down and replaced all that straw with used hay from Seymour Krebbs' camel stall."

"Heh heh," chuckled Pete. "As I recall, that camel doesn't care for dogs."

"Hey!" called Billy Hixon. "Hayden! C'mere a second."

Billy was in the parish hall, pouring a cup of coffee when he spotted me walking by the outside back doors. I joined him at the coffee pot.

"We've got some real coffee," he said. "*Finally!* That other stuff was just...bleah."

"I agree." I poured myself a cup, and we walked over to one of the tables. "'Because thou art lukewarm, I will spew thee out of my mouth.'"

"What?"

"Nothing. A verse from Revelations."

"I didn't know John the Revelator had anything to say about coffee. Huh," he grunted. "You learn something new every day."

"Absolutely," I agreed.

"I've been helping Kimmy Jo Jameson with the funeral arrangements," said Billy, sipping his Apocalyptical brew. "It's going to be quite a service."

"Is Gaylen presiding?"

"Yeah, she is. Junior's being buried in his car, you know."

"I heard that," I said.

"Elaine's going to be one of the scripture readers," said Billy proudly. "Wormy's going to wire the car radio up with *Eternizak*, we've got a forty-foot crane rigged to lower the racecar into the ground, and guess what?"

"What?"

"The American Academy of Piping and Drumming started last weekend in Valle Crucis. We're going to have a whole bagpipe band. Kimmy Jo asked that the St. Barnabas choir be there, and we're renting the electronic organ from the Cliff Hill Music Company. You remember—the one Cliff sent over for that tent revival. We're hooking it up to an old Marshall amp and set of speakers that Bob Solomon had in his storage building."

"That's the organ I'm playing?"

"Yeah! Kimmy Jo is faxing music to the church. She wrote a song, then paid some guy in Virginia to arrange it for choir and organ."

"Oh, Lord. I don't suppose I can get out of this?" I sighed.

"Nope," said Billy. "We want to stay on their good side. I don't want any problems getting our money back. By the way, it's all going to be televised."

I sighed again. "Of course it is."

I walked into Bootsie Watkins' office, wearing my sternest look and my new badge hanging visibly on my belt.

"Can I help you?" she said smartly, in her best secretarial tone.

I stood in front of her desk and stared at her for a full thirty seconds without saying anything. She started to squirm.

"Can I help you, Chief Konig?" she asked again, this time a little less sure of herself.

"I think that maybe you can," I said, after a long moment. "Why don't you come with me into the pastor's office? Bring the key with you. And Brother Kilroy's appointment calendar."

"Okay," she said, in a very small voice.

I walked quickly down the hall, Bootsie dogging my steps, trying to keep pace with me. We came to the door of Brother Kilroy's office. The stained-glass window in the door was still broken. I tried the door. It was locked. I gestured to the handle. Bootsie put the key into the lock and clicked it open. I pushed down on the handle and the door swung open.

"Let me get you a chair," I said, as I picked up one of the upholstered armchairs in the alcove. I carried it into Kilroy's empty office and set it in the middle of the room. Then I came out of his office and brought in a matching chair, leaving the alcove empty except for a small table on which rested a hymnal. I set the chair opposite the first, close enough that when we were both sitting, our knees would almost touch. It was an awkward and uncomfortable situation—which is what I wanted.

"Let's take a seat," I said. "I have some questions."

Bootsie sat, knees tightly together, her arms crossed in the classic defensive position. I sat across from her and leaned in.

"I'm curious, Bootsie. How many keys are there to this office?"

She chewed on her lip. "Just one."

"Just the one that you used to open the door?"

"Yes."

"How do you know?"

"I got it out of the door the morning after the...umm...accident. I put it in my desk until you asked for it when you came back. Mona asked Brother Kilroy for a copy at least twice that I remember. He always told her that she didn't need it. I *never* had a copy. He always kept that one on a separate key-fob—not on his regular key ring."

I held out my hand, and Bootsie dropped the key into my outstretched palm. I held it up and looked at it.

"Where's the key-fob?" I asked.

"It wasn't with the key. The key was stuck in the lock, but the fob was missing."

"What did it look like? The key-fob, I mean?"

Bootsie raised her eyebrows. "It was a Bible. Not a full sized one. One of those miniatures, but it had both the Old and New Testaments. And the Psalms. It had a little silver clasp—maybe two inches wide and a little longer than that." She held up her fingers, showing me the dimensions that she remembered. "It was black with a little silver chain and a silver clasp." She was chewing on her lip again.

"Have you seen it since Brother Kilroy was killed?"

"No. No, I really haven't. Can I go to the bathroom?"

"In a minute," I said. "What about Brother Kilroy? I want to know what kind of a man he was. What kind of husband?"

"He was a good preacher."

"That's not what I'm asking."

Bootsie nodded. I waited without saying anything. Finally she spoke.

"He was a good man and a good husband, and he doted on Mona. He could be a little self-righteous, but he was a Man of God. It was Mona..."

I waited again. Bootsie sighed heavily.

"Mona wasn't ever satisfied. She wanted him to make more money, drive a fancier car, take expensive vacations—stuff like that." Bootsie lowered her voice. "She wasn't well-liked."

"Was she having an affair?"

"Good heavens!" Bootsie exclaimed. "I can't imagine it. She worshipped Brother Kilroy. Not literally, of course."

"How about that Bennett Shipley fellow? He follows her around like a puppy."

Bootsie squirmed. "No. Mr. Shipley is the head deacon. He was required to go into confession with Brother Kilroy every week. I've never seen him and Mona together. To tell you the truth, I'm not sure that Mona had much use for any man other than Brother Kilroy. She told me once that she could never marry again because Jimmy was so good that he'd ruined all other men for her." Bootsie blushed.

"Is Shipley married?"

"Oh, yes. He's married with five children."

"So, to your knowledge, neither Brother Kilroy nor Mona was involved with anyone else." Bootsie shook her head. "Neither one of them was having an affair?" I continued. "There wasn't any hanky-panky going on in the hot-tub in that palatial bathroom of his? Brother Kilroy wasn't engaging in any late-afternoon private counseling sessions with female church members?"

"No, he was not." Bootsie lowered her arms, pushed up her beehive, and straightened her blouse. "I'll tell you this much. Whenever Brother Kilroy had a female member in for counseling, Mona always sat in. It was something he insisted on."

"Can you tell me who had appointments with Kilroy before he was killed?"

Bootsie opened the appointment book. "How far before?"

"A week."

"Well...let's see here. He was killed on a Sunday. On the Monday before, Dave Vance and Collette came in for their weekly marriage counseling session. Brother Kilroy went to the hospital in Asheville in the afternoon—Gina Catlenburg was having some surgery. On Tuesday morning he was at a prayer breakfast at seven, then into the office for a staff meeting, lunch, a meeting with Bennett Shipley, the head deacon, at two, Men's Bible study at four. That's all that was on the calendar. I usually leave at four."

"How about Wednesday?"

"On Wednesday, Brother Kilroy never came in before noon since he has Wednesday Night Prayer Meeting. At three o'clock, he had a meeting with the praise-team leader. At four, our Wonderful Wednesday programming starts. He's here, but he wanders all over the church checking on things."

I nodded. Nothing interesting, as far as I could tell.

"On Thursday morning, he plays golf with a foursome from the Ministerial Association in Boone. At 1:30, he went over to Watauga Medical Center to check on our hospitalized members. We have three. Then he came back here to work on his message for Sunday. He usually worked on it—undisturbed—on Thursday afternoon and Friday morning. Then he took Friday afternoon off."

"So he didn't have any appointments on Friday morning?" I asked.

"Well, yes, actually, he did have one," said Bootsie, looking down at the book. "At eleven o'clock. A young man named Burt Coley. He's not a member of this church."

"Was he wearing a police uniform?"

"Why, no. But, come to think of it, I think I've seen him before."

"He was one of the policemen that came from Boone on Monday when you called 911," I said.

"Yes! That's why he seemed familiar. I was so upset, though."

"I understand. Does it say why he wanted to see Brother Kilroy?" I asked.

"It doesn't say, but I remember exactly. We had a very pleasant conversation before he went in. He was going to enter the ministry, and Brother Kilroy was on his discernment committee. He was such a nice young man."

184

"I shall have to talk to Officer Coley," I said. You've been very helpful. I'm going to borrow this key for a little while."

"We have a couple of puzzles," I said, "that need un-puzzling." Nancy, Dave and I were sitting at a table in the Bear and Brew. "The first one is the locked door."

I laid the key on the table, and we all looked closely at it. It was three inches long, black with age and substantial.

"The door was locked from the inside. Apparently, this is the only key. Bootsie told me that Mona had asked for a copy numerous times, but that Brother Kilroy always refused."

"Could she have made a copy on the sly?" asked Dave.

"Nope," said Nancy, picking up the key and looking at it closely. "Look here. This is a double-bitted key. A normal key from this time period would have the head dropping from one side of the shaft. This has two heads—one going up and one going down. Not only that, but do you see the cutting on both sides?"

We looked and nodded.

"Look how the metal returns back on itself, making a small 'L.' A regular tumbler lock uses a set of levers to prevent the bolt from moving in the lock. Usually, the key lifts the tumbler above a certain height and allows the bolt to slide past. But this key opens a double acting lever lock. *This* key would require two turns to lock or unlock the door. The first turn allows the first bit to unlock one lever; the second turn does the same with the bit on the opposite side. A double lock, really."

"Huh," I said. "Two turns, eh? I never tried it."

"How do you know this stuff?" asked Dave.

"I pick locks for a hobby," said Nancy. "It's one of the many things you don't know about me. This lock would be very difficult to pick."

"Could you do it?" I asked.

"Sure. It'd take me probably fifteen minutes. But that's just unlocking. I'm not sure you could lock it back without a key."

"Why couldn't Mona have made a copy?" I asked.

"I guess she could have. People can do anything in this day and age. But this is a forged key, not a cut one. She'd have to make a careful impression and send it off to a forge somewhere to have another copy made. Very expensive—I'd say eleven or twelve hundred dollars for the mold, the pouring, all the extras."

"Twelve hundred bucks?" said Dave. "Sheesh."

Of course, if she had twenty keys made, the price-per-key would go down considerably," said Nancy.

"I doubt she'd need twenty keys," said Dave, "but it's not impossible."

"It *is* improbable," I said. "She might have done it, but it implies a level of premeditation that I don't think exists."

"What if she did it a year ago, just to have a copy?" Nancy offered. "In case she needed it."

"I guess it's possible," I admitted. "But expensive. Here's a thought. What if we took the lock apart? If a new key was used, would there be evidence of it in the lock?"

"Absolutely," said Nancy. "Any new key would probably have been made of brass, and new brass always leaves a trace."

"You two go and check it," I said. "We'll meet back here this afternoon. And stay out of the dumpster."

Chapter 21

The line over at the courthouse had dissipated and all the heroes were merrily about the task of big game hunting. I could hear the baying of beagles up in the hills to the north of town. Gathered in the park were a couple of small groups of orange-clad men going over topographical maps of the area, planning out their strategy. Most had their deer-rifles slung over their shoulders, but I saw one with a .50 caliber muzzle-loader and several packing large pistols. I recognized Sergeant Todd McCay and Burt Coley from the Boone P.D. walking across the park toward their pick-up.

"Hey there, fellow peace officers," I called. "Doing a little gorilla hunting?"

Burt shrugged sheepishly, and Todd gave me a big smile as I walked over.

"Hey, it's five grand, we're both hunters and it's our day off," said Todd. "We might as well give it a try."

I nodded, said goodbye and walked over to the Slab. I had left Moosey with Pete with instructions to put him to work around the restaurant until I returned. He was busy sweeping the floor when I walked in. The Slab was back open and ready for business.

"Hayden," Moosey called out. "Pete let me pick out anything on the menu for lunch!"

"Wow! What did you have?"

"A piece of coconut cake, and a donut I found in the fridge, and some blackberry cobbler, pumpkin pie, and pancakes with chocolate ice cream on top for dessert! It was great!"

"Sounds very healthy." I shot Pete a nasty look, but he ignored me.

"The donut had green sprinkles on it," said Pete. "That counts as a salad."

"Miss Farthing came by," said Moosey, "and she said that I could go over to her house this afternoon and help Miss Ruby with a jigsaw puzzle."

"That sounds like fun." I was relieved that I didn't have to keep an eye on the boy. Two gunshots echoed through the stillness of the afternoon, and Moosey suddenly became less animated and very quiet.

"Don't worry," I whispered. "Those were close to town. Not more than a half-mile away."

Moosey nodded and continued to sweep, but I could tell he was anxious.

I left the Slab and walked down to the Police Department where I dropped into my chair and picked up the phone. Seven digits later, Kent Murphee picked up the line.

"Afternoon, Kent. This is Hayden."

"I saw the ad in the paper. You have many hunters out your way?"

"Yeah. Pete sold a bunch of licenses. Maybe four hundred or so."

"Wow!"

"Wow is right. How's Penelope holding up?"

"Not well. She doesn't want to drive back to St. Germaine. Just in case...you know."

"Yeah. I understand."

"Did you find out who took Kokomo?"

"Umm," I said. "It's an ongoing investigation. Tell Penelope to try not to worry."

My next call was over to the new forensic lab at Appalachian State. It was a good lab and part of their criminal justice program. A voice I recognized as Jillian Crocker answered the phone on the third ring.

"Hi, Jillian," I said. "This is Hayden. Do you have anything for me on that pipe that Nancy brought over?"

"I do," said Jillian. "I hear that you have quite a safari going on in your neck of the woods. Is this information going to clear Kokomo?"

"Depends on what you tell me."

"Well, then. There's a smudged partial print. Not enough to make an identification. But, where there's a print, there's DNA. I got two good samples. One was from the victim—I matched it to a sample sent over by Kent—and the other is from an unknown donor."

"You ran it through the system?"

"CODIS. Yeah. The FBI's Combined DNA Index System. No

match. So, we have the DNA but until we can match it to someone, it doesn't do us any good."

"So what can you tell me?"

"The DNA is from a male human—not a male gorilla. That's about it until you have something I can match it to. Then it's a slam-dunk. I can't believe the perp left the pipe sitting there."

"It was wedged between the sound-board and the cast-iron plate of the grand piano. We never would have found it if Kokomo hadn't broken the piano in half."

"Wow," said Jillian.

"Wait a minute," I said. "Did you just say *perp*?"

"Uh...no."

"You did! You said *perp*!"

"I didn't! And don't you ever tell anyone, either! Hey! Hang on a second. Nancy's here."

"Oh, yeah. She has something else for you to look at. Can you do it right away?"

"Absolutely. I like that gorilla."

Nancy plopped down at our table at the Bear and Brew. "We took the lock off the door, carried it over to Jillian, took it apart and looked at it under the microscope. There is absolutely no trace of any key other than this one."

She dropped the key onto the table.

"And this one," she continued, "is made of nickel."

"Nickel?"

"Yep. And there isn't one chance in a million that any duplicate would be made of nickel as well. First of all, no one would know the original was made of nickel unless they tested it. Secondly, no one would cast nickel unless they had to. Jillian checked the inside of the lock looking for scratches that left a trace of any other metal other than nickel. Nothing. This was absolutely the only key that opened this lock."

"Hmm. Where's Dave?"

"On his way. He had to pick up his dry cleaning."

I spread the blueprint of the church across the table. "Okay. First question. The door was locked. How did the murderer get out?"

Dave walked up and sat down beside Nancy. "What did I miss?"

"Not a thing, Snookie-Pie," I said. "Now pay attention. The door was locked, and the key was in the lock *inside* the office. How did the murderer get out?"

"Air vent?" Nancy said, looking at the blueprint.

"Nope. They're all too small. The duct work is flexible pipe about a foot in diameter."

"Maybe the killer was really, really thin," offered Dave. He was answered by an elbow and a snort from Nancy.

"How about a drop ceiling?" said Nancy. "Maybe he pushed a panel up and got out that way."

"It's a drywall ceiling," I said. "I checked when I was there this morning."

"Secret tunnel?" asked Dave. "Maybe he was hiding under the piano?"

"He would have been seen if he was still in there when Nancy and I arrived. It was a mess, but I doubt that we could have missed him. And there's no secret tunnel in the blueprints. We went around that office and the outside of the church pretty thoroughly. Frankly, I don't think that New Fellowship Baptist would have spent the money to put a secret tunnel in for Brother Kilroy's use."

"Good point," said Nancy.

"How about this?" said Dave. "The key is magnetic, right? What if the killer used some sort of magnet from the outside to turn the key?"

"Can't be done," said Nancy. "Yes, nickel is magnetic, but the door's too thick, the lock's too tight and anyway, it's a double bit key."

"How about the gorilla?" Dave said. "Could Kokomo have locked the door behind the killer?"

"I don't know," I said. "Let's find out."

I pulled out my cell phone, dialed Kent Murphee and posed the question.

"Let me call Penelope. She drove back to Maryland this morning, but she'll be back tomorrow. I'll call you right back."

We were on our second beer when my phone rang.

"Monkeys," explained Kent, "have a wrist joint that restricts the

190

movement plane of their wrist in the same way that we restrict the movement of our foot. Now that's great if you're in the trees. But if you come down to the ground and think about running around with a foot that has this kind of floppy motion, you won't last very long. What apes did, when they came down from the trees, is develop an odd form of locomotion called knuckle-walking. It's the way that they can deal with this wrist problem."

"But they still have the wrist problem?" I asked.

"Absolutely."

"So, could Kokomo work a key in a double lock?"

"Not a chance. It'd be like you trying to lock it with your toes, even if you *could* hold the key steady. Your foot just doesn't turn all the way around."

"So, we're back where we started," I said, after I thanked Kent and flipped my phone closed. "So the first question is 'How did the killer get out of the locked room?' Second question—Brother Kilroy always kept his key on a ring with a miniature Bible key-fob attached. What happened to the Bible?"

"Maybe it got pulled off in the fracas," said Nancy.

"If that had happened, part of the key ring would have still been attached. Nope. The key was in the lock, but there was no key ring. I find that very odd."

"A clue perhaps?" said Dave.

"Perhaps," I said. "One of you guys is going to need to go through the dumpster again. See if you can find that miniature Bible and the key chain."

"Aw, man " said Nancy.

"Just Dave this time," I said. "It shouldn't take more than a couple of hours. Okay, that's the first part of the puzzle. The *How*. We also need the *Why*. We need a motive."

"It might be easier to discover how and then we'll know why," said Nancy.

"Jillian gave me a DNA report on the pipe," I said. "Kilroy's DNA is at one end and our killer's at the other. No match in the system, though."

"Fingerprints?" asked Nancy.

"Nothing we can use," I said. "One thing we do know. Our killer is male."

"Nuts," said Nancy. "I had a feeling it was Mona."

"Well, she may be involved, but she wasn't the one that hit him with the pipe. But here's another person-of-interest. It seems that Officer Burt Coley had an appointment with Brother Kilroy on the Friday before he was killed. Burt is going into the ministry, and Kilroy was on his discernment committee."

"Really? You think Burt might be involved?" said Nancy. "I've known him since he was eighteen."

"Yeah, me, too," I said. "Anyway, I'll talk to him tomorrow. Don't forget, Dave—dumpster duty, first thing in the morning."

"I hate to go into a dumpster by myself. I have dumpster-phobia. Nancy should really come with me."

"In a pig's eye," I said. "You know, Bootsie Watkins sure was jumpy at the beginning of that interview. Then she relaxed. Maybe I just didn't ask the right questions."

"Let's go interview her again," said Nancy.

"We will. Tomorrow morning, while Dave's in the dumpster. Right after we interview Kokomo."

I barged into Moby Mel's Fish Emporium like a smelt on National Smelt Day at the Fish Emporium. I looked into the display case and there they were—basses from every choir in the city, stretched out on the ice like Nancy Kerrigan after her attempted Triple-Mooseflip during the long program at the '94 Olympics. They'd been cleaned and cleaned good.

"Oh, those poor things!" said Marilyn, coming in behind me.

"Don't look, Babe. It's not a pretty sight."

"Why'd they do it?"

"Two reasons. First, they don't want any four-part singing. That's obvious. Just praise choruses. And with the basses gone, the tenors don't stand much of a chance. Sure, they'll wander around for a while, trying to find tonic, but eventually they'll just give up and go home."

"How about the altos?"

"They might hang on a little longer. Try to harmonize. But they won't last."

"What's the second reason?" Marilyn asked.

"They needed those scales. Look there," I said pointing to the naked corpses. "There's Larry Lydian. That one's Phreddy Phrygian." I sighed. "Mick Solydian, A.O. Leon, Linc Locrian. What a waste."

"Who did it?"

"The Minimalist," I said.

"You're referring to me?" came a voice from behind us. It was him—and I was caught with my waders around my ankles.

Choir practice began promptly at 6:45 during the summer months. That being the case, everyone was in his or her seats and ready to sing at 7:18.

"Everyone sit down and let's get started," I called out. "We have a lot to do. I have an announcement to make. Also, there's some music on the organ we need to look at."

"Pete sent this," said Rebecca, holding out a brown paper grocery bag. "I stopped by the Slab for supper before choir, and Pete said to bring this bag on up."

"What is it?" asked Bev.

"His new Communion Fish," said Rebecca. "They're really tasty! Try one!" She passed the bag down the row of altos. "This flavor is *Tongues of Flame—Cajun Spicy*. I'm going to need something to drink, though. These are hot!"

The bag made its way across the section, each alto reaching into the bag of Communion Fish and coming up with a handful.

"Isn't this sort of sacrilegious," mumbled Tiff, her mouth full of crumbs. "I mean, isn't this the body of the Lord?"

"Not until it's blessed," I said. "Till then, it's just crackers. Cajun-spicy fish crackers. Let me try one of those."

"Hey, these are great," exclaimed Marjorie when the bag had made its way to the tenor section. "I vote we use these all the time."

"I agree," said Mark Wells. "Delicious!"

"Is there a rule that communion bread has to taste bad?" asked Fred. "And be stale to boot?"

"I don't think so," I said. "There's no rule."

"I think the vestry should vote on these," said Elaine. "They're very tasty, and look—they have a little cross on the side. How cute!"

"Do they come in other flavors?" asked Georgia.

"I'm afraid so," I said. "I'm afraid so."

"What's this thing?" asked Meg, looking askance at the Xeroxed music she'd picked up off the organ.

"It's the anthem for tomorrow afternoon," I said. "That's the announcement I have to make. As you know, Junior Jameson died on Sunday in a car accident. He won the race, but then crashed into the wall. Anyway, we've been asked to sing at the funeral. It's going to be televised."

"That's *great!*" said Mark. "We'll be on national television. The St. Barnabas choir will be famous!"

"What are we going to sing?" asked Georgia. "How about something from the Brahm's Requiem? *How Lovely Is Thy Dwelling Place?*"

"Nope."

"How about that thing they sang at Princess Di's funeral?" said Rebecca. "The 'flights of angels sing thee to thy rest' song. It's really pretty."

"*Song for Athene,*" I said. "No, not that one."

"What about *Never Weather-Beaten Sail,*" said Phil. "That's the one I'd want at *my* funeral."

"I'll make a note. But alas, Kimmy Jo Jameson has sent over the piece we'll be singing. She wrote it *specially.*"

"Not this?" said Meg in horror, her eyes scanning the page.

"Oh, yes," I said. "And if I have to do it, you all have to do it with me. Would you pass them out, please?"

Meg took the stack of music off the organ and passed it down the rows of choir chairs. There were a few snickers as people started reading through, but the snickers broke into full-fledged guffaws even before everyone had their hands on the anthem.

"She can't do this," said Meg. "Isn't it under copyright?"

"I was hoping so. That would have certainly been an easy way out for us. But, no. The song was written in 1922, so it's in the public domain. She can do whatever she wants with it."

"Do we have to sing it with a straight face?" asked Phil Camp.

"Yes, we do. That's why we're practicing it tonight," I said. "Now, we need a soloist. Who wants to be on national TV singing a solo?"

There were no hands.

"C'mon," I said. "This could be someone's big break. How about you, Tiff?"

Tiff shook her head in terror.

"Okay. We all know the chorus. We can do the verse in unison. How many of you know how it goes?"

No hands.

"You're lying," I snarled.

"Why don't you sing it, Hayden," said Bev. "From the console. We'll get you a mic."

"Yes, yes!" came the enthusiastic cheers from the choir. "Exactly! Perfect! That'll be great!"

I slumped forward, my head hitting the keys of the top manual with a thump. My goose was cooked, and I knew it.

"Fine," I said. "I'll do it."

I turned on the organ, punched a couple pistons and started crooning in my best Frank Sinatra imitation.

Praying is never wasted,
It's a fine habit they say;
All the glory I've tasted,
Just seems to fade away.
I believe that God answers our prayers,
So standing with Jesus, I'll say:

The choir was howling with laughter. I ended on the dominant chord, growled at the choir and they took off singing. The tune, familiar to everyone in North Carolina, had been arranged in four parts with an oom-pah accompaniment. It wasn't difficult and wouldn't take much rehearsal—maybe just enough to work the giggles out.

Nothing could be finer, laid to rest in Carolina
in the morning,
It'll be like Eden, with my Jesus, when I meet him
in the morning.
Where the morning glories,
Wrap around my grave,
Whispering the story,
I know I've done been saved!

Strolling with my Savior, where there is no bad behavior
in the morning,
Angels all will kiss me and my loved ones ne'er will miss me
at the dawning,
If I knew my life was done, and had time to pray,
I'd close my eyes and here's what I'd say:
Nothing could be finer, laid to rest in Carolina
in the morning.

"Hahahahahahaha!" screamed the choir.
"We've got to sing this?"
"On national television?"
"Oh...my...GOD!"
"I can't do it!"

"Oh, you'll *do* it, all right" I said. "You'll do it with a straight face and a tear in your eye! The funeral's at two o'clock. We have to be there by 1:30. Wear your robes and don't be late!"

Chapter 22

Nancy met me at the McCollough trailer at 7:30 in the morning. Her Harley growled to a stop on the dirt driveway just as I was knocking on the door for Moosey. The door opened, and Ardine greeted me.

"I'm just on my way to work," she said. "Moosey's coming. He wouldn't tell me what this is all about. You sure he's okay?"

"He's fine," I said. "Don't worry."

Ardine smiled a tight smile and went down the steps to her old car. I waved as she drove off, heard the slam of a screen door, and looked down to see Moosey right beside me, happily munching on a Milky Way bar. He had a brown paper grocery bag in his other hand. The top was rolled shut.

"Y'all ready?" he asked. "I've got some food for Kokomo."

Nancy pulled her bike up on the stand, took off her helmet and put it on the seat.

"I guess we're walking," she said.

"Yep," I answered. "Moosey says it's about a mile."

"Let's get going then. Before the hunters are up and about."

"They're already out," I said. "I saw three or four pick-ups beside the road on the way into town. They're looking up closer to Gwen's clinic, though."

"C'mon," said Moosey impatiently. "Let's go. I hope Kokomo's all right. I haven't seen him for a couple days."

We walked into the woods behind Moosey's home, following a path cut years ago by a logging truck. The summer morning sun shone through the overhanging branches, dappling the forest floor with splashes of light that danced as the light breeze played in the trees. The path turned up the mountain, climbing at a steep angle, and Nancy and I were breathing hard in a few moments despite our high level of donut conditioning.

"How far did you say?" huffed Nancy.

"Almost...there," I puffed back.

"You're lying."

I *was* lying, but after about twenty minutes, we came to a sharp bend in the path, and Moosey announced that we had arrived.

"We're here!"

"We're where?" asked Nancy. "Where's here?"

"The bus is back over there," said Moosey, with a grin. He pointed into a huge thicket of mountain laurel. "Nobody knows it's in these woods anymore."

"How'd they get it up here?" asked Nancy.

"They probably drove it up, back in 1952," I said. "Way back when this was a road. I would have never found it."

"C'mon," said Moosey. "I wanna see if Kokomo is okay."

We picked our way through a hundred feet of thick laurel and finally saw the outline of a pale green school-bus. The tires had rotted to shreds, the hood was up and most of the windows were broken. Some of the panes had been replaced by pieces of old plywood. On the side of the bus was painted "Homewood Four-Square Church" in faded white letters. The door was standing open. Moosey ran up the steps in a flash.

"Kokomo!" we head him call from inside the bus. "Kokomo!" He stuck his head back out of the door. "The food's almost gone, but Kokomo's not here." He sounded very worried.

"Come out here and call him," I said. "Maybe he just went out for a stroll."

"Humph," said Nancy. "Yeah, that's it. A stroll."

"Kokomo!" Moosey called from the steps of the bus. "Kokomo! Come here! I've got some food for you!"

Without warning, there was a tremendous crash right behind us, as the gorilla burst through the thicket. Nancy and I both jumped, adrenaline sending our hearts into overdrive. This time, however, our pants remained dry. At least, mine did. I couldn't speak for Nancy.

"Jiminy Christmas!" I said through clenched teeth, hoping I hadn't screamed it. "I wish he wouldn't do that!"

"There he is!" Moosey sang out. "Kokomo! Come over here."

The gorilla grunted and lumbered toward Moosey on all fours. He sat down in front of the boy and began to run his fingers through Moosey's hair.

"I think he's looking for bugs," said Moosey. "But Mama says I don't have 'em anymore. Not since the school nurse sent home that shampoo." He reached into his pocket and pulled out a Milky Way candy bar. Kokomo snatched it out of his hand, delicately peeled away the paper, and nibbled on it like an old lady eating a watercress sandwich at a tea party.

"Moosey," I said. "See if he'll answer some questions for us."

"He says 'yes,'" said Moosey, intently watching Kokomo's gestures.

"I forget he understands what we're saying," whispered Nancy. "Man, I just can't get used to this."

"Kokomo," I said. "Do you know who hurt Brother Kilroy?"

"That's it," said Nancy, under her breath. "Get right to the point. No use beating around the bush."

"That red," signed Kokomo, brushing Moosey's shirt with his free hand."

"Yes," said Moosey. "That's red. Did you see who hurt Brother Kilroy?"

"Friend," signed Kokomo.

"Yes, he was your friend," said Moosey. "Who hurt him?"

"Tiger bad," signed Kokomo.

"He says 'Tiger bad,'" said Moosey. "Just like I told you."

"You mean Tiger, your cat?" I asked.

"Tiger man," signed Kokomo.

"Tiger man," translated Moosey.

"Tiger man friend hit," signed Kokomo. Moosey translated again. "No like tiger man. Kokomo dream tiger man devil scared. Red."

"Red again?" I asked. "Blood? The water was red?"

"Water red," came the answer. "Friend red. Devil Tiger."

Suddenly Kokomo stood up to his full height, pounded on his chest and, with a roar, disappeared back into the thicket with a crash and the sound of breaking limbs.

"That went well," said Nancy. "At least *my* pants are still dry."

"Ditto," I said. "Does he have enough food?" I asked Moosey. "I don't want you coming back up here alone until we have this sorted out."

"Oh, I almost forgot. I brought this." Moosey held out his brown paper bag. I opened it up and looked inside. It was full of Communion Fish.

"They're *Barabba-que,"* said Moosey, pronouncing the name carefully. "Pete thought that Kokomo would like 'em."

"I'll bet he will," I said.

Dave came into the office about mid-morning, dropped into a chair, pulled a handkerchief out of his back pocket and wiped it across his brow.

"It's hot."

"Yes, it is."

"Did you and Nancy interview Kokomo?"

"Yep. All we got was 'tiger man, devil tiger, water red'—that sort of stuff. Nancy has it all written down."

"How about Bootsie Watkins?"

"Bootsie Watkins," I replied, "is conveniently out of town until Monday."

"Huh," grunted Dave.

I looked out the front window, past the reverse, dark-blue lettering on the glass spelling out 'St. Germaine Police Department,' and into the park. I quickly counted thirty-four hunters—some going over maps, a few talking in groups of two and three, some walking toward their four-wheelers. Pete's office was still selling gorilla licenses at the rate of about ten an hour. After the first rush, the hunters came in slowly but steadily. Even some of the residents of St. Germaine, who didn't hunt on a regular basis, had bought a license, just in case—as L.L. Sutherlin put it—"I happen to see that gorilla walking by my bedroom window."

"What a mess," I said. "They're going to find Kokomo eventually. We can't stop them."

"What if we can find the real killer?" asked Dave, mopping his brow again.

"That would help. Then we could get a judge to rescind the warrant. But the problem is that everyone won't *know* it's rescinded. Our best bet is to find the killer, arrange to have the warrant lifted, and then get that gorilla out of the state. Hey! Did you find that miniature Bible?"

"Nope. It wasn't there. I went through the whole mess. I threw every piece of trash from the new dumpster back into the first one.

I was careful. As far as books were concerned, there were a couple full sized Bibles, some hymnals, some kind of Bible dictionary, a complete set of New Testament commentaries—all twenty-six volumes, and a bunch of other stuff. But no miniature Bible."

"All right, then. I'm on my way over to talk to Burt Coley."

"Hey, Burt. It's good to see you again." I said, shaking his hand. "I didn't get much of a chance to speak with you when we were busy with that gorilla. How have you been?" Burt had sung for me in the St. Barnabas choir about ten years ago. He'd been a good tenor enrolled in the music department at Appalachian State. He was one of my scholarship singers.

"Pretty good," said Burt. "I got out of music and into law enforcement. Following your lead, I guess."

"Ah, but I never got out of music," I said, with a smile. "Just changed it to an avocation. Listen Burt, I've got to ask you some questions about Brother Jimmy Kilroy."

"Yeah," said Burt. "I know."

"You want to just tell me what your relationship was and why you were there on the Friday before he was killed?"

Burt took a deep breath. "Okay. I've been called to the ministry. I guess you know that."

I nodded.

"There's a discernment process that I have to go through to get into the school that I want."

"What school is that?" I asked.

"Tabernacle Bible Institute. It's a conservative Bible college in Kingsport. Anyway," Burt continued, "there are three pastors on my committee. The college contacts three ordained men of God from your area, and they interview you and listen to your testimony. Then they decide if the Lord has actually called you to the ministry." He shrugged.

"So, what did your committee say?"

"Two of the pastors said I was fine. Brother Kilroy wasn't so sure. He wanted me to come in every Friday for three months to talk."

"So did you?"

"I tried to. I did it for a couple of weeks, but then we got busy. I can't just take every Friday morning off for three months."

"And so you told him you were going to stop coming?"

"I told him that I couldn't come in every Friday. He said that if I wanted to be a pastor, there was nowhere I needed to be that was more important than in his office every Friday."

"What did you say?"

Burt shrugged again. "I didn't say anything. I just left. I called the Institute. They said I could reapply in the fall."

"I'll bet that made you mad."

"It made Todd madder than it made me. He's my uncle, you know. Mom's brother. Dad died when I was eleven."

"Sergeant Todd McKay? Your partner?"

"Yeah. Todd's not a religious man, but he's been really good to me and Mom."

"No, I didn't know. I'll bet he's proud of you," I said.

I was driving back to town when I passed the Piggly Wiggly and saw the commotion. There were half a dozen people in the parking lot, including Roger the manager, the three checkout girls, Hannah, Grace and Amelia, and a guy dressed in a stocker's uniform whom I didn't recognize. As I pulled up, I saw Hannah, a sixty-two-year-old grandmother, hold up her pistol, drop the magazine out of it into her free hand, check it, and snap it home. I turned off the truck and got out.

"Hannah, put that thing away! What's going on?"

"That gorilla just came into the Pig!" said Roger. "He was huge!"

"Yeah, he's a big one," I agreed. "What happened?"

"We didn't see him come in. We've got these automatic doors, you know. Then Hannah spotted him down by the pickles on aisle three."

"I knew it was the gorilla," said Hannah. "Although he looked a little like Beaver Jergenson, but with more hair. Luckily, us girls got these pistols from Ken's Gun Emporium a couple of months ago. We keep 'em under our registers."

"Can I see it?" I asked, holding out my hand. Hannah handed

me the gun. It was a Beretta .38 caliber automatic—a lightweight pistol with quite a punch.

"You all have one of these?" I asked. The three checkout girls nodded.

"I don't," said the stocker, "but I wouldn't mind having me one. Look at my arm! That gorilla hit me with a pipe!"

"You're not getting a gun," said Roger. "Only the cashiers. That's store policy."

"He hit you with a *pipe*?" I asked.

"Yeah. He ran by the feminine hygiene products, turned the corner and hit me. I just saw him out of the corner of my eye. It was a gorilla though. He was aiming for my head, but I threw up my arm like this." The stock boy demonstrated. "It may be broken," he said. "I'm going to have to get about six weeks off. With pay, of course."

"Shut up, Wally," said Roger. "You're not hurt."

"Did you see him?" I asked Roger. He shook his head.

"Where are *your* guns?" I asked Grace and Amelia. They both sheepishly produced pistols of their own from behind their backs. I shook my head, cleared Hannah's pistol, clicked the safety on and handed it back to her.

"Did you shoot him?" I asked her. "Did you shoot the gorilla?"

"Well, I tried to," said Hannah. "Once I started firing, though, he took off through the store. I think that I hit a bunch of pickle jars."

"You sure did," giggled Amelia. "I shot all my bullets at him, too. How about you, Grace?"

"I'm pretty sure I missed him. I saw him over there on the cookie aisle. I fired a couple of times, but I was just too nervous."

"It sounded like a war!" exclaimed one of the customers. "I heard gunshots and breaking glass. I hit the floor."

"Me, too," said a lady wearing a flowered scarf over hair rollers. "I saw that gorilla run right past me with a package of Oreos."

"I saw him run out the door," said a male customer. "I was at the back of the store. He didn't even wait for it to open. He just hit it with his shoulder."

"Anyone hurt inside?" I asked. "Y'all didn't shoot anyone in the store by accident did you?"

"Oh," said Hannah, in surprise. "I don't think so. I hope not."

I looked over at Roger, and he'd gone white at the suggestion.

"Let's go and check," I said. "The rest of you wait here, please."

"Can we leave?" said the lady in the scarf. "I'm in kind of a hurry."

"Not yet," I said. "It'll be just a few more minutes."

Roger and I went through the Piggly Wiggly, looking for any accidental victims of the checkout girls' shoot-fest. The only victims seemed to be jars of pickles, relish, and some dairy products. I expected that they'd be finding products containing bullet holes for several more days, but at least no one was hurt. We went back outside, and I let the customers go after I got their names and phone numbers, just in case. Then I called Roger and the checkout girls over to the side.

"It's not against the law to shoot a gorilla inside the Piggly Wiggly, is it?" asked Amelia, defensively.

"Depends," I said. "Do you have a gorilla license?"

"Yep," said Amelia. "We all do. We bought them yesterday."

"Then, according to the law, you can shoot him wherever you want."

"Great!" said Grace. "Just let him come back here again! We'll be ready for him next time!"

"But," I continued, "I suspect that the P. Wiggly Corporation has certain rules about employees hunting inside their stores." I looked over at Roger.

"Well, if we don't, we damn sure will this afternoon!" he said, glaring at the three women.

"And I imagine that if this happens again, you'll all be fired," I said. Roger took the hint.

"Absolutely! Terminated immediately!"

"I also might suggest that, although it's certainly not against the law for the checkout girls at the Piggly Wiggly to be packing heat, you might want to rethink your policy on arming the staff."

"Hmm," said Roger. "We sent them to a firearms responsibility class. But I'll think about it."

"And ladies," I said, addressing them. "You realize that if you'd shot a customer, or one another, even by accident, you'd be in jail right now, and you wouldn't be coming out for a long, long time."

"Huh?" said Grace. "Oh. I never even thought about that."

"We won't shoot at gorillas in the store anymore," promised Amelia.

"Nope," said Hannah, shaking her head. "Just robbers. The gorilla's not coming back anyway. Do you think any of us hit him?"

"I don't think so. There isn't any blood. Just a lot of pickle juice."

"I think he's around here, though," said Amelia. "Those hunters are looking on the wrong side of town. They're all up by Seymour Krebbs' place, but I'm going to look around here. You girls want to come?"

"Sure," agreed Grace and Hannah.

"Wait a minute!" said Roger. "Who's going to ring up the customers?"

"You do it, Roger," Grace called back over her shoulder. "We'll be back in a little while."

Chapter 23

It was one o'clock when Meg and I drove up to Kenny Frazier's old farm. I'd been back to the office, after my stop at the Piggly Wiggly, and in the last two hours, St. Germaine had come alive with people. They were going in and out of shops, arms full of packages. There was a queue at the Beautifery, and there wasn't a table to be had at any of the eateries. The Altar Guild had even arranged a tour of St. Barnabas and there was a waiting line out the front door.

"Are all the people in town here for the funeral?" asked Meg, as my truck made its way up the drive.

"Except for all the hunters. They're here to shoot a gorilla."

"Why'd we come over so early?" asked Meg.

"I have to check the set-up, the organ, make sure my microphone works—stuff like that. Anyway, the choir will be here in half an hour.

"I understand. I'm so proud of you, honey. Singing on national TV. What an honor."

"One more word, and I'll be singing at *your* funeral."

"Okay," said Meg. "But I'll want the same song."

Meg and I passed a large hand-painted sign announcing that we had arrived at Woodrow DuPont's Bellefontaine Cemetery— otherwise known as Wormy Acres. We parked the truck in the field designated for mourners (by another hand-painted marker), gathered up our vestments, and walked up the path leading, we presumed, to the burial plot. From where we had parked, it was a lovely gravel path, winding through the trees, and finally opening upon one of Wormy's fields. He'd torn down the old house and barn and mowed the grass. The landscape looked beautiful. The gravesite, however, did not. Not because it wasn't a pretty place. It was. But it seemed to be set up for something other than a funeral. A circus, for instance. Billy came up to us as soon as he saw us.

"I was hoping you'd be here a little early. Let me show you the set-up."

"Please," I replied.

He led us toward the gravesite. There was a huge pile of dirt at one end. We stood at the edge and looked down into a hole that was ten feet deep, ten feet wide and about sixteen feet long. Hanging eight feet above the hole was Junior Jameson's purple racecar—Number 17. The crew hadn't fixed the damage, so the front of the car was crushed. We couldn't see the St. Barnabas crest on the hood or the huge gold cross painted on the roof—the car was up too high—but we could still read Junior's words of wisdom to his fellow drivers. The two signs were lit up in electric lights. It was hard to miss the twin messages—"The wages of sin is death," and "Do you know where you'll spend eternity?" I looked up at the car and saw Junior's face looking out the front windshield and out into the sky. He had his helmet and his racing glasses on. His two hands were gripping the steering wheel.

"That's creepy," said Meg, with a shudder. "Look at him sitting there, just waiting to go into the ground."

"Once they lower the racecar," said Billy, "everyone will be allowed to throw a shovelful of dirt on top of the car."

"How do those signs light up?" I asked. "The ones on the back bumper."

"Wormy wired the car up to a new battery. Everything else has been stripped. They sold it off, I guess. The engine's gone. Transmission, brakes...everything but the body and the wheels. The battery will run the lights for a couple of hours. The radio, too. Wormy doesn't have the *Eternizak* wired up yet, but he hooked the car radio to work with a CD player. The car will be playing *The Show Must Go On* by Queen as they lower him down and cover him up."

I watched Meg shudder again. "How does that song go?" she asked. "I've never even heard it."

"You know," said Billy, clearing his throat and crooning a tune that had no discernible pitch whatsoever.

Show must go on! Yeah! Show must go on!
I'll face it with a grin! I'm never giving in!
On with the show!

"I can't remember how it starts, but it goes something like that."

"How awful," said Meg.

"It's on the *Best of Queen* CD. I love it!" said Billy, then switched to his singing voice. *"On with the show!"*

"Stop it this instant," said Meg.

"Okay, okay. Follow me over here."

We walked around the grave. On one side was a grandstand that looked as though it would seat about three hundred folks. Directly across the pit, a stage had been erected with black bunting around the edge. The electronic organ was placed in the middle. It was caddy-cornered to the choir chairs—about twenty in all—that were set in a semicircular pattern. There were at least ten microphones set up to amplify the choir, including one right in front of the organ that I was supposed to use for my big solo. On the back of the instrument was a sign proclaiming "This Organ Courtesy of the Cliff Hill Music Company." Behind the choir, and off to the sides, were four giant Marshall speakers—dinosaurs left over from the 70's. They were stacked two on a side, and two high, putting the tops of the speakers about eight feet off the stage. I also noticed two deer stands, one beside the crane, and one beside the choir stage, each holding a tripod and a large video camera, but I didn't see any videographers yet. At the far end of the grave, the end opposite the huge pile of dirt, was another, smaller dais. A lectern and microphone were set up for Gaylen and another two mics off to the side.

"Who are those for?" I asked, pointing to the mics.

"The banjo players," said Billy. "I thought you knew."

"Knew what?"

"They're here playing the *Banjo Kyrie*. It's in the program."

Meg giggled.

"Maybe you should show me a program," I said.

"Okay. Sure," said Billy. "I've got one right here." He reached into his back pocket, pulled out a folded piece of paper and, grinning, handed it over.

I looked down at the program and saw where the choir was singing—right after the reading of the 23rd Psalm. I also had to play *Amazing Grace* with the bagpipes for the congregation to sing during the *Tossing of the Lug Nuts*. I did a double-take to make sure I read it correctly.

"*The Tossing of the Lug Nuts*? What the heck is that?"

"Everyone is getting a lug nut when they walk in," explained

Billy. "The car gets lowered down while we play *The Show Must Go On* through the car speakers. Then, when the hymn starts, everyone sings and throws their lug nut into the grave."

"On top of the car?"

Billy nodded. I looked at Meg. She was biting her lip to keep from laughing. I looked back at the program, saw the *Banjo Kyrie* and realized, to my relief, that the service didn't include communion. At least I didn't have to worry about the service music.

"Give me that back," said Billy, taking the program out of my hand. "It's my last copy. Anyway, I put enough for the whole choir on top of the organ. Go get your duds on and try out that bad boy."

I did as Billy suggested—got into my robe and surplice, turned on the organ and tried a few chords. I didn't bring the music to *Amazing Grace*, but that was no problem. That was a hymn that I, and every other organist, knew from memory. I did have Kimmy Jo's composition, though, and I spread it on the music rack. I didn't have a whole lot to do during the funeral, so I thought, all in all, it'd be a relaxing afternoon. That was the thought going through my head when Billy walked up.

"By the way, Hayden. Kimmy Jo was wondering if you'd be so kind as to start playing at 1:30. Just some background music while the people are gathering."

"*What?* That's in ten minutes! Why didn't you tell me? "

"Sorry. I must have forgot. Gotta go."

"You have some music in the truck, don't you?" asked Meg.

"Behind the seat," I growled. "There's a volume of Bach. That should go over *really* well."

"I'll go get it," said Meg. "You take a few deep breaths."

"Hey," I said. "Wait a minute. I think there's an old *Cokesbury Hymnal* under the seat that I was using to keep the springs from falling through. On the driver's side."

"I'll get it."

The choir started arriving at 1:30 along with the rest of the congregation. "Congregation" was a loose description of the crowd gathering for the funeral service. There were some members of St. Barnabas, to be sure, but most of the four hundred or so mourners were NASCAR fans, drivers, or friends of the Jameson family. "Junior's fans will come," said Pete, when he declined to attend. "They'll come like lambs to the mint sauce."

It was my lucky day. The 1938 *Cokesbury Worship Hymnal* had a wealth of old, familiar hymns, and I flipped my way through the book, improvising on one tune right after another. I looked over at Kimmy Jo and the family, all who were ushered in at about a quarter till two, and she nodded, smiled at me, and gave me a little wave of acknowledgement. At two o'clock, I wrapped up my extended prelude with *His Eye Is On The Sparrow*, closed the hymnal, and settled back for a few minutes.

Gaylen, clad in her best white vestment and chasuble, stood up at the lectern, raised both hands and proclaimed, "I am the Resurrection and the Life, says the Lord. Whoever has faith in me shall have life, even though he die. And everyone who has life, and has committed himself to me in faith, shall not die for ever."

"Wow!" whispered Bev. "Look at the way the sun is hitting her white hair. She looks like the angel of the Lord."

Gaylen continued. "Happy from now on are those who die in the Lord! So it is, says the Spirit, for they rest from their labors." She paused for a moment, then said, "The Lord be with you."

"And also with you," answered the Episcopalians in the stands.

"Let us pray," said Gaylen. "O God, whose mercies cannot be numbered, accept our prayers on behalf of your servant Junior Jameson, and grant him an entrance into the land of light and joy..." She finished the collect and added the traditional 'Amen.'

"Amen," echoed the crowd.

That was the cue for the *Kyrie*, and the banjo players were ready. They were already standing at the microphones, and the unseen sound-man cranked them up. When they started playing, the banjos could have been heard in three counties, and with two banjos on the program, it didn't take much imagination to know what was coming next.

"Plink-a-plink plink plink plink plink plink plink," went the first banjo, playing the opening of the well-known tune from the movie *Deliverance. Dueling Banjos.*

"Ky-ri-e e-le-i-son," sang the banjo player, in imitation of his instrument.

"Plink-a-plink plink plink plink plink plink plink," went the second banjo followed by a second "Ky-ri-e e-le-i-son." The two banjo players traded licks a few more times, and then they were at it, hammer and tongs, playing more notes than seemed to be possible. "Lord, have mercy!" they interjected at appropriate moments. "Christ have mercy! Lord have mercy!"

The people in the stands were on their feet, clapping along and stamping to the beat. I looked over at the choir. They were trying to remain reverent and serious, but there were more than a few toes tapping. I looked again into the bleachers, and suddenly froze. I caught Meg's eye and pointed across the pit to the top row. There was Moosey. And sitting next to him was a five hundred pound Muslim woman in a black burka.

Elaine Hixon stood up at the lectern, adjusted the microphone and began reading the 23rd Psalm. I tried to watch her, but I couldn't take my eyes off of Moosey and his date.

"Hayden," hissed Meg. "Pay attention. Elaine's almost finished. We're next!"

I snapped my attention back to the job at hand, opened my music, adjusted my microphone, and pulled a couple of pistons just as Elaine said, "And I will dwell in the house of the Lord forever." The choir stood up, I poised my fingers on the keys and then began.

Praying is never wasted,
It's a fine habit they say;

I was amazed at how loud my voice was, coming through those Marshall speakers. Luckily, it was a short solo, and I managed it without too much embarrassment. Then the choir came in.

Nothing could be finer, laid to rest in Carolina
in the morning,
It'll be like Eden, with my Jesus, when I meet him
in the morning.

We sang the chorus through twice. The words had been printed in the program, and the second time through, the choir was joined by the entire congregation.

*Strolling with my Savior, where there is no bad behavior
in the morning,
Angels all will kiss me and my loved ones ne'er will miss me
at the dawning.*

The congregation was swaying back and forth, and singing at the top of their lungs. We finished, and the crowd burst into applause. I glanced back into the stands, looking for Moosey, and spotted him right away. He was standing with the others, and his burka-clad companion was sitting next to him, stuffing handfuls of Communion Fish under his veil and into his mouth.

I was expecting a short sermon from Gaylen Weatherall, but she remained in her seat. Instead, rising from a chair beside the stage and making his way up the steps toward the lectern, was a short, round man with one of the finest comb-overs ever seen in North America. His one sprig of hair was probably two feet long, although we couldn't tell for sure. It began just behind his left ear, swooped forward toward his brow, turned right, and circled his head once—then twice—before being sprayed tight to the top of his pate. As a professional statement of faith, it was breathtaking. The crowd hushed in awe of this magnificent comb-over, but this was just one of his many gifts. This was Dr. McTavish—Brother Hog, to those who knew him—and he was the featured evangelist of *Brother Hogmanay McTavish's Gospel Tent Revival.* He'd been to St. Germaine before.

"Brothers and Sisters," he started. "When Kimmy Jo asked me to preach at Junior's funeral, I was at first reticent."

"Hallelujah!" came a voice from the stands. "He was *reticent!*"

"I asked Kimmy Jo how long I'd have to preach to y'all," said Brother Hog. "She told me, 'Take as much time as you need. It's more important for these folks to come to Jesus than for us to get over to Boone for fried chicken!'"

"Fried chicken!" yelled a voice. "Hallelujah!"

"But I'm going to keep it short. Whenever I'm asked how long I'm going to preach, I say that my sermon's going to be like a woman's skirt—long enough to cover the essentials, but short enough to keep you interested."

This brought a huge laugh from the crowd. I looked over at Moosey. He and his companion seemed to be doing fine.

"My text today is from the Second Book of Kings. Listen here to God's Word." He opened his well-worn Bible.

"As they were walking along and talking together, suddenly a chariot of fire and horses of fire appeared and separated the two of them, and Elijah went up to heaven in a whirlwind. Elisha saw this and cried out, 'My father! My father! The chariots and horsemen of Israel!' And Elisha saw him no more. Then he took hold of his own clothes and tore them apart."

Meg glanced at me with a questioning look. I shrugged. It wasn't one of the traditional funeral scriptures.

"Now, ya'll see that Junior is like Elijah. He was taken to heaven in a fiery chariot."

"Amen," said several voices from the stands.

"And Kimmy Jo is like Elisha, even though she's not a man, and women shouldn't be prophesyin' no how. But when she heard that Junior was taken up in a fiery chariot, she took hold of her dress and tore it right down the middle." Brother Hog grabbed hold of his lapels and mimicked the terrible scene. "Like this!" The crowd gasped.

"Tore it!" called a voice. "Tore it down the middle!"

"Luckily," said Brother Hog, "Sheila DeMoss was right there to offer her a cover-up or Kimmy Jo would have been standing there in her all-togethers—an *abomination* to the Lord!"

"An abomination!" came several shouts. "Amen!"

"Now, it is appropriate that Junior Jameson is the first person buried in the No-Smoking section of this fine cemetery. We all know that Junior is up there today..." Brother Hog held his Bible skyward. "...Driving his racecar past the Pearly Gates and zooming up and down those streets of gold—praising Jesus and laughing at Satan as he drives by—even though his earthly body is sitting behind the wheel of that racecar right there." Brother Hog pointed to Junior.

"Hey," whispered Meg. "Wormy has a No-Smoking section."

"I heard. I'm signing up."

"We know," continued the preacher, "that Kimmy Jo will, one day, go to join Junior in the eternal Winner's Circle." His voice got soft, and he moved in close to the microphone. "But what about you, *friend*?" Brother Hog snaked a finger out over the pulpit, pointing accusingly at every unsaved soul in the congregation.

"Will you join Junior and Kimmy Jo, or will you be cast into the fiery pit-stop where there shall be weeping and gnashing of teeth?"

"Amen!" came the cries from the crowd. "Not there! Not the fiery pit-stop!"

Brother Hog continued. "Let us close our eyes for a moment and think on this. And while every eye is closed and every head bowed, if you haven't given your heart to Jesus, now is the time. While the organ plays two verses of *Softly and Tenderly, Jesus Is Calling,* y'all raise your hand if you've made a decision for the Lord. And if you raise your hand, you'll have to seek me out after the burial and I'll pray with you. We're not having any of y'all coming down and falling into this grave and meeting Jesus before you need to. Let us pray."

My mouth had dropped open at the words "while the organ plays" and I grabbed for the hymnal, hoping that *Softly and Tenderly* was in there somewhere. I needn't have worried. As Brother Hog prayed, I turned on the organ, threw the tremolo stop, and two verses later, let out a sigh of relief.

"That was a close one," said Meg. "Any more surprises?"

"I don't think so," I said, but I was wrong.

The pipes and drums had been standing behind the bleachers, and now they marched out to the strict click of a drumstick on the edge of one of the drums. "Twelve pipers piping" and "eight drummers drumming" might not have followed the numeric directive set down in the Christmas carol, but they were a fine sight, standing at attention in full Scottish regalia, kilts rustling in the breeze. They lined up at the head of the grave in three neat rows. One of the pipers gave a nod, and with a *whoosh*, the bags filled with air, and an amazing sound uttered forth—the sound of a dozen geese with their necks caught in a washing machine.

"They're from the Academy," I said, gritting my teeth. "They're still learning."

"What are they playing?" shouted Meg. "I can't tell. Is it *Amazing Grace?*"

"No," I said, shaking my head. "*Rocky Top.*"

There's an old joke—why do bagpipers usually walk while they play? Why, to get away from the noise. The racket was such, that I didn't hear the dogs at first. Hannah had gone into town and told everyone she saw about her confrontation with the gorilla inside the Piggly Wiggly, and it didn't take long for the hunters with dogs to bring their scent-hounds over to this side of the mountain.

When the pipes and drums had finished their tune and the last bagpipe had wheezed uncomfortably to a stop, the dogs, that were a good half-mile away when I had first spotted them, were now closing rapidly on the gathering, and, having caught the scent, baying at the top of their lungs. I pulled my surplice and cassock off over my head and reached under the organ bench for my 9mm pistol. It wasn't there, of course. It was under the bench back at St. Barnabas.

"Rats!" I said to Meg. "All these organs should come with a pistol under the bench."

Everyone turned to watch the dogs. I estimated the pack at thirty. There were beagles, coon hounds, some indistinguishable mutts, and several Carolina dogs. The pack ran around the perimeter of the gathering, then turned toward the bleachers and, barking as though their canine lives depended on it, sent the mourners scattering as they clambered over bodies in their fever to reach Kokomo, still sitting with Moosey on the top tier of the grandstand. Moosey screamed in terror.

Kokomo had no such reaction. He stood up, still wearing his black burka—only his eyes visible through the draped fabric—let out a roar and jumped, aiming for the spot that had just been vacated by the people fleeing the hounds. He landed on the second tier of the bleachers and discovered, in his own gorilla way, that the aluminum construction of the bench was no match for his five hundred pounds. The bench crumpled under his weight like a piece of tin foil and the dogs, heading for Moosey, did an about-face as the gorilla soared over their heads, and came racing back down the steps. Kokomo grabbed the nearest dog, a good-sized coon hound that was close enough to snap at him, and flipped it over his shoulder like a rag doll. The unfortunate dog flew half-way up the stands, yelping all the way, and landed on a large man wearing a purple baseball cap with the number 17 embroidered on the front—a NASCAR haberdasher's tribute to Junior Jameson. The coon hound untangled itself from the startled fan, resumed its barking and headed back down the steps. Now there were shouts coming from the stands, as the shock of seeing a pack of barking hounds racing up the bleachers wore off, and people realized what was happening.

Kokomo took a step, crouched and leapt from the stands across the twelve-foot gap, the makeshift burka not hindering him in the least. He caught hold of the back bumper of Junior's car that was hanging eight feet above the grave and supported by a single cable. The boom of the crane swung ominously, compensating for the sudden added load of a full-grown gorilla. Jimbo, the operator, had locked the boom, so it didn't move much, but Kokomo's jump had added a significant "pendulum" effect. The suspended car swung crazily toward the choir, then back toward the congregation, and I heard gasps and screams coming from both sides.

"My God!" exclaimed Rebecca, watching Kokomo pull himself up onto the top of the car. "I didn't know a Muslim woman could jump that high!"

"I think that, legally, she's a Baptist," said Meg. "She's been dunked, you know."

"Oh," said Rebecca. "That explains it."

The dogs had run back down the bleachers and were now circling the grave, looking up at Kokomo, and doing a fine job keeping any stray cats away with incessant barking.

Jimbo, meanwhile, not wanting to take a chance on a catastrophic accident, had begun lowering the car toward the hole. It was still swinging side to side and people were scattering well out of its way as it descended. Kokomo was standing on top of the car, one hand grasping the cable, the other hand beating his chest. Just as he gave another roar, the cable gave way and the car dropped the last ten feet and landed with a crash in the bottom of the hole.

Later, Jimbo explained that the cable didn't break, but rather, the winch on the crane couldn't handle the added stress produced by the swinging racecar and a five hundred pound gorilla. In such cases, the winch will allow the cable to drop ten feet or so before the automatic brake engages. Since the car was only ten feet above the bottom of the grave, the brake never engaged and the racecar hit the bottom with a tremendous crash.

From our vantage point on the stage, the entire choir leaned forward and tried to look down into the hole, but all we could see was the top of Kokomo's head. The crash caught the dogs by surprise, and when it happened, they backed a few paces, startled and seemingly confused—unsure of how to proceed. Then they returned in full force, buoyed by a pack mentality, and deciding, as a group, to attack en masse. The first dog to jump was an extra large Carolina dog, an aggressive breed that reminded me of an Australian dingo. He leapt at Kokomo with a growl that we could hear from the stage. Kokomo slapped him aside with a roar, and the dog skidded, yelping, off the roof. The rest of the pack hesitated for a spilt second and then followed the Carolina dog into the pit. Most of them didn't make it to the roof of the car, landing instead in the fresh dirt. The ones that did land on the roof were quickly batted away. A couple of the beagles landed on the hood and tried to scramble up to where Kokomo was waiting, but fared no better than their brothers. In a few seconds, the whole pack was at the bottom of the grave, baying like mad, with just enough room to make their way noisily around the car.

When the racecar landed at the bottom of Junior's final resting place, it was the sound-man's cue to push the "play" button on the CD player hooked up to Junior's car radio. Music blasted from the amp, sub-woofer and four extra speakers that Wormy had placed in Junior's car. The *Eternizak* song listed in the program was *The Show Must Go On* by Queen, but the soundman must have pushed the wrong button. The song was still by Queen, but this track was a different song. Blasting out of the stereo with enough sound to make the remaining windows rattle, came the unmistakable words:

Another one bites the dust,
Another one bites the dust,
And another one gone and another one gone,
Another one bites the dust.

"That's an unfortunate choice of songs," Georgia said. "I thought Billy said they were playing that other one."

"Hey!" said Meg, pointing up toward the sky. "What's that?" I hadn't heard anything because of all the racket, but now, looking skyward, I saw a bright yellow biplane coming in about a hundred feet above the ground.

"It's Five-Dollar Frank," I said.

"What's he doing?"

"I have no idea."

Five-Dollar Frank dropped down another fifty feet, skimmed the crowd, waggled his wings and dumped a box of paper out of his plane. Several thousand leaflets came floating down on the congregation and most people, including the choir, reached up and grabbed one.

"It's an ad!" exclaimed Fred. "For Woodrow DuPont's Bellefontaine Cemetery. Look here! We can get a plot for twenty percent off!"

Five-Dollar Frank swung around again and circled the crowd one more time, dropping another box of leaflets.

"You know," I said. "If I had hired Frank to drop leaflets advertising my cemetery, I would have had him take that banner off the back of his plane." Sure enough, as soon as Frank made his last turn, the banner that had been secured at the beginning of his flight, came loose and opened behind the yellow plane, proclaiming in large white letters, "WE GOT WORMS!"

Kokomo ripped off his burka—in reality, a black blanket with a hole cut in the middle—dropped it on the top of the car and then, with a mighty leap, cleared the edge of the pit and landed beside one of the bagpipers, who promptly fainted.

"He's out!" cried Bev. "And look. The dogs are trapped."

Another one bites the dust, another one bites the dust, sang Queen.

The roar of the plane was suddenly joined by the sound of the hunters' ATVs. They'd been following the pack of dogs, but had been a couple of miles behind them, tracking them with radio collars. Now they roared up to the edge of the funeral and turned off their engines, not sure how to proceed. Right behind the leader, driving a Kawasaki Mule—a four-seater—were Hannah, Amelia, and Grace.

"There he goes!" hollered Hannah, pointing in Kokomo's direction, but Kokomo had already made it to the near woods and had disappeared into the trees. All three ladies jumped out of the ATV, pulled out their pistols and emptied their guns into the forest on the off chance that one of their shots might hit the gorilla. The other hunters looked startled at this breach of hunting etiquette and, when the guns clicked on empty chambers, jumped on the three grandmothers, wrestled them to the ground, and disarmed them.

"You know," said Meg. "As funerals go, this one's a doozy!"

It took a good half hour before the tumult subsided and one of the hunters could get a ladder down into the pit to rescue the dogs. They had to be carried out, one at a time, and were put on leashes, much to their dismay. The crowd hadn't left. The family and friends were still on the dais, and Brother Hog was now fanning Kimmy Jo with his program. I looked up to where Moosey had been sitting, but he was nowhere to be seen.

Finally Gaylen got up and walked over to the microphone. "Let us pray," she said.

"O God, whose blessed Son was laid in a sepulcher in the garden: Bless, we pray, this grave, and grant that Junior Jameson, whose body is to be buried here may dwell with Christ in paradise, and may come to your heavenly kingdom; through your Son Jesus Christ our Lord. Amen."

"Amen," echoed the crowd.

I took my cue and played the introduction to *Amazing Grace*, then heard the bagpipes squawk into action as everyone began singing.

Amazing grace! How sweet the sound
That saved a wretch like me!
I once was lost, but now am found;
Was blind, but now I see.

When we've been there ten thousand years,
Bright shining as the sun,
We've no less days to sing God's praise
Than when we'd first begun.

We finished, and a sudden silence fell over the field. Five-Dollar Frank had flown off, the dogs had calmed down, and the hunters were politely waiting for the service to end before resuming the chase. It seemed that even the birds had decided to take the rest of the afternoon off. Or, and this was more likely, they had flown off terrified. Then, in the stillness of the moment, I saw something fly through the air and catch a glint in the afternoon sun. With a startling clank, it landed in the grave and banged off the hood of the car. The clanking sound was followed by another. And another. In three seconds, the air was full of lug nuts, each of them tossed by a mourner into the grave of their fallen hero.

"My work is done here," I said to Meg. "I've got to get back."

"I'll come with you," said Meg. "Can we get out without being seen?"

"Yeah. Everyone will be consoling Kimmy Jo. We'll be fine. Let's go."

We made our way back down the path, got into my truck, started it up and pulled out of Wormy Acres and onto the highway.

"Hey," said Meg. "What do you have in the back?"

"Nothing. Why?"

"I saw a tarp in the back of the truck when I got in."

"I didn't notice," I said, looking in the rear view mirror. Meg was right. There was a dark green Army tarp in the back of the truck and as my eyes darted back and forth between the rear-view mirror and the road in front of me, I saw it move. Then I saw a face—Moosey's face. When I looked again, there were two faces, and they were both laughing.

Chapter 24

I turned around slowly and saw The Minimalist standing in the door. I'd seen him before and I racked my brain like a set of elliptical billiard balls trying to figure out where. He had a Tommy gun trained right on my boutonniere and suddenly I felt as dumb as a box of rocks with all the good ones taken out. Behind him was Moby Mel, smiling a fishy smile and smelling like last week's relatives.

"Where's Betsy?" I asked.

"Don't you worry about Betsy," smirked the Minimalist. "She's about to sleep with Davy Jones. We got her some cement Manolo Blahniks. She always did like to be stylish."

"I wouldn't mind a pair of those myself," said Marilyn. "Not cement, though. I wouldn't have anything to wear with them. And really," she added, "it's nobody's business who Betsy sleeps with."

The Minimalist's mouth dropped open in surprise, revealing an underslung jaw, and two outer mandibular barbels--"whiskers" in laymen's terms. I knew I'd seen him before. It was Carpy. Carpy Deeum. The Minimalist was a bottom-feeder.

I dove behind Moby Mel's aquarium, just as Carpy cut loose with the Tommy gun. I grabbed Marilyn and pulled her down beside me. The gun clattered like a bunch of lug nuts being thrown into an open grave.

"Whadda we do now?" she squealed, as the aquarium burst into a thousand pieces and covered us with water, angelfish and extra-fancy guppies.

"Something will come up," I said, lighting a stogy and brushing a Delta Red out of my hair. "It always does."

"Brilliant work, detective," Meg said, leaning over my shoulder as I sat at my typewriter and giving me a smooch on the cheek. "I especially like the thing about the lug nuts. Any word from the Bulwer-Lytton competition?"

"I checked on-line this morning," I said. "Nothing yet."

"You should have seen it, Pete," I said. "It was spectacular!"

"Well, I haven't watched it yet," said Pete, "but I taped it. The whole thing was on ESPN2, and the gorilla swinging on the car made it to the top ten sports highlights."

Dave and Nancy came into the Slab, saw Pete and me, and joined us at our table.

"Hi there, Casanova," said Pete, when Dave sat down. "Have you heard from Collette? I need her to get back to work.'

"I called her mother, and she said that Collette had gone to Spartanburg to stay with her cousin for a while," said Dave. "Then she cussed me out."

"Oh, that's just *great*," said Pete. "I *need* Collette!"

"Speaking of girlfriends," Nancy said. "How're you and Molly doing? I haven't seen her around for a week or two."

"We broke up," said Pete. "She didn't appreciate my manly lifestyle."

"You showed her your bathroom, didn't you?" I asked.

"Not on purpose. She walked in without permission." Pete shrugged, then changed the subject. "Well, since I'm the only one here, what'll you have for breakfast?"

"Surprise us," I said. "Make it easy on yourself."

"No problem there. You're all getting oatmeal. It's already made."

"I love oatmeal!" said Dave.

"Okay," I said. "Let's figure this thing out. What do we know?"

"Brother Jimmy Kilroy was killed when he was hit on the head, fell into the water and drowned," said Nancy.

"The killer was a man," added Dave.

It was Nancy's turn, and she had her pad out. She flipped a couple pages and skimmed them quickly. "The door was locked from the inside with a key. The key was in the lock, and there wasn't another one. Kokomo was the only other person...er...animal in the office. He was being baptized by Brother Kilroy, and he was freaked out when we got there," added Nancy. "No tunnels, no air vents big enough to crawl through, no false ceiling. The room was sealed."

"And Kokomo couldn't have locked the door from the inside," said Dave. "Because he's a gorilla, and gorilla's wrists don't work that way."

"So, we only have one witness," I said. "Kokomo."

Nancy consulted her notes. "Kokomo says, and I quote, 'Tiger man friend hit. No like tiger man. Kokomo dream tiger man devil scared. Water red. Friend red. Devil tiger,'" she concluded. "We just need to find the Tiger Man."

"Will Kokomo's testimony hold up in court?" asked Pete, who walked up to the table carrying a tray with three bowls of oatmeal. "Here's your oatmeal, but you can get up and get your own coffee."

"Snookie-Pie, would you get the coffee?" asked Nancy sweetly. Dave grunted and got to his feet.

"Kokomo's testimony wouldn't be allowed in any court that *I* know of," I said. "But we have a definite DNA sample from the pipe. We just don't have one to match it to. If we knew where to look, we could find the killer without any problem."

"The killer doesn't know we found the pipe," said Nancy. "That's a point in our favor."

"Then he doesn't know about the DNA either," I said. "As far as he's concerned, the police suspect that something is not kosher, but we don't have any evidence. He also doesn't know that we talked to Kokomo, so he probably still wants to shut that gorilla up."

"Suspects?" asked Pete.

"Hard to say," I said. "There's Mona. She is singularly unlikable, but she's not the killer. The DNA on the murder weapon—an iron pipe—is from a male. There's Burt Coley, the second officer at the scene. He was trying to get into a Bible College and Brother Kilroy was keeping him out."

"Burt didn't do it," said Nancy. "I know Burt. I've known him for years."

"I tend to agree, but we can't rule him out," I said. "Then there's Sergeant Todd McKay, Burt's uncle and partner. He's been looking out for Burt since his father died, and I heard that he was a whole lot madder at Brother Kilroy for blackballing Burt than Burt was himself."

"Mad enough to kill him?" asked Pete.

"Maybe. I haven't questioned him yet."

"How about Bootsie Watkins?" asked Dave. "The church secretary?"

"She's out of town until Monday. She knows something that she's not telling, that's for sure," I said. "And don't forget Bennett Shipley, the head deacon."

"How about Dr. P.A. Pelicane?" offered Dave. "Let's say she found out that Brother Kilroy had stolen Kokomo. She'd try to go over there and get him back. She might have been so mad that she hit Kilroy in the head with the pipe."

"She's a woman," said Nancy. "The killer is a man."

"We *think* she's a woman," said Dave.

"Oh, she's a woman all right," Pete said. "I can vouch for it."

"And then there's Tiger Man," said Nancy. "It may be someone we know, but it may be somebody else entirely."

We sat in silence for a long moment, looking down at our breakfast. Then we all picked up our spoons.

"We've forgotten something," I said, tasting my oatmeal. "Hmm. Needs a little salt. Oh yeah—the miniature Bible key fob. We never found it."

"So?" said Pete.

"It's relevant," I said. "It couldn't have just fallen off. It was attached with a short chain and a key ring. The chain might have broken, but the ring would have stayed with the key. Now, why would it have been removed? The Bible wasn't in the dumpster, so someone took it out of the office. I'll bet that person is the killer."

"Makes sense," said Nancy, with a nod. "But why?"

"Why, indeed?" I said.

"Do you know where Kokomo is?" asked Pete. "Billy told me he ran into the woods."

"I think he's safe enough for now," I said. Pete looked at me and I gave him "the eyebrow." It was enough.

"I hope so. I'd hate to see him stuffed and holding umbrellas in someone's entrance hall."

"What about 'tiger,'" I asked. "Could Tiger Man be someone that reminds Kokomo of his cat?"

"I thought of that," said Nancy. "I was trying to come up with descriptive words for the cat that maybe we could apply to the suspects. Look." She pulled a piece of paper out of her notebook, unfolded it, and handed it across the table. It was a printout of one of Kokomo's website pages. He was sitting in his cage, holding a gray cat. "How would you describe that cat?"

"Furry," I said. "Gray, Green eyes."

"Short hair," contributed Pete. "He's got claws...he's cute."

"Hey," said Nancy. "*Burt's* cute."

"That's not funny," said Dave. "*I'm* cute."

"No help there," I said. "If only I could figure out why that miniature hymnal was taken off the key."

"You mean 'Bible,'" said Pete.

"Yeah. Bible. What did I say?"

"You said 'hymnal.'"

"Hymnal..." I was quiet for a moment. "The question is, how did the killer get out of the office and relock the door from the inside...?"

"What's he doing?" whispered Dave.

"Shhh," said Nancy. "He's thinking."

"Son of a..." I said suddenly, slapping my hand down on the table and making the silverware jump. "Of course! Dave, call Judge Adams. We need to get a warrant and go make an arrest."

"Do we have probable cause? 'Cause we can't get one on Kokomo's say-so," said Nancy. "You know that, right?"

"We don't need it! The answer was right in front of us!" Then I poured myself another cup of coffee and spilled the beans.

Chapter 25

Nancy and Dave met me an hour later with the warrant in their hands.

"Judge Adams is on vacation. We got this from Judge Minton, but he wasn't happy about it," Nancy said.

"It couldn't be helped," I said. "Even if it is a Saturday afternoon, we want this all legal."

"Oh, that's not the reason he wasn't happy," said Dave. "He's a member of New Fellowship Baptist Church. Judge Minton said that he was going to call this guy and give him a chance to turn himself in."

"What?"

"We asked him not to," said Nancy, "in no uncertain terms. But he is a judge. We couldn't ask him too hard. Luckily, in the end, he agreed not to."

"We'd better get going then. I've got Meg's car. Nancy, you come with me. Dave, you wait here. We'll call you if we need anything."

We were on the way out to the house when Nancy got a call from Dave on her cell phone.

"We've gotta go back to town," said Nancy, as soon as she hung up the phone. "Kokomo was seen outside of Noylene's Beautifery. Wormy was outside on the sidewalk, putting away his table, when Kokomo came up behind him and hit him in the head with a pipe."

I was stunned. "That's not possible."

"Well, we didn't think it was, but Wormy saw him right before he got hit. Noylene saw the gorilla, too. Through the window."

"Anyone else see him?"

"Not that I know of. Dave's over at Noylene's now. Wormy's there too. He says he isn't going to the hospital."

"It wasn't Kokomo," I said.

"How do you know?" Nancy asked. "He ran into the woods at the funeral."

"Because Kokomo's at *my* house."

The town square in St. Germaine was empty—typical for a late afternoon on a summer Saturday. The shops were closed and the few cars that dotted the parking places were probably there for the evening. Dave was waiting for us inside Noylene's Beautifery when we pulled up. Nancy and I walked in and saw Wormy stretched out in Noylene's beauty chair. He was still dressed in his best black funeral attire, although his tie had been loosened. Noylene was holding a Ziplock bag of ice held to his head.

"Hi, Wormy," I said. "Are you okay?"

"I guess," grumbled Wormy. "I wish someone would go ahead and shoot that gorilla."

"Did you see him?"

"Yeah. I turned just as I saw him. You know—out of the corner of my eye. I sort of ducked, but he hit me. Hit me with a pipe. It happened real fast."

"I saw him, too," said Noylene. "I saw him right through the window. He hit Wormy and then run off. I ran outside, but he was gone."

"Listen, Wormy," I said. "You've got to go to the hospital to get checked. You might have a concussion. Noylene, can you take him over to the emergency room?"

"Sure."

"C'mon then. We'll help you get him into the car. Then Nancy and I have to run."

We helped Wormy stand up and walked him outside to Noylene's car. Nancy opened the passenger door, and Dave and I sat Wormy on the cracked vinyl seat and fastened his seatbelt. Then we heard a shot, and all our heads swung around and our eyes focused in the same direction. The courthouse.

Dave, Nancy and I left Wormy with Noylene, ran across the park and up the courthouse steps. The front doors were open, but they generally stayed open until dark during the summer, even though the offices were closed. Coming down the steps to meet us was Hannah, the pistol-packing grandma.

"I got him! I got him!" she cheered.

"Got who?" I asked, knowing the answer, even before I posed the question.

"I got that dang gorilla, that's who! I'm gonna be rich!"

"Where is he?" I said.

"Inside. I was dropping off my check to the gas company, and there he was. I pulled out my roscoe and let him have it."

"Your roscoe?" said Nancy.

"You know," said Hannah. "My heater. My rod."

"Yeah," I said. "I know. Now where's the gorilla?"

"Inside. He went in the door to the clock tower, but I peeked in and there he was. So I shot him."

"What was he doing?"

"Well," said Hannah. "He was holding up a pair of pants." She suddenly looked puzzled. "That's seems strange, doesn't it?"

"C'mon," I said. "Let's go see."

We followed Hannah as she led us inside and showed us the door to the bell tower.

"I've been up there before," she said. "A couple of times. Our senior group took a tour of the courthouse a few years ago. Usually it's locked, but I saw the gorilla go in. So I tried the door and there he was."

I slowly opened the door and saw him lying on the floor by the narrow steps leading up to the clock, a moaning sound coming from his mouth. Nancy and I were bending over him in a second. I bent down, and lifted his head off the floor. Then Nancy grabbed the hair on the top of his head and pulled. The mask came off.

"Where are you hit?" I asked.

"My head."

"Well, you were lucky," I said, looking at his wound. The bullet just grazed your scalp. You'll need some stitches, but you'll be fine.

"I didn't think anyone was around. The square was empty."

Dave and Hannah joined us in the small alcove.

"You mean I shot *you*?" said Hannah. "Oh dear. Oh dear me. I was aiming for the gorilla. I'm so sorry!"

"That's okay," Nancy said. "No harm done."

"What do you mean, no harm done," spat the man. "She shot me in the head!"

"You shouldn't have been running around in a gorilla suit," I said. "We were just on our way over to your house to arrest you anyway."

Chapter 26

I pulled out my heater and waited for Carpy's Tommy gun to run out of slugs. I didn't have to wait long. I heard the tell-tale "click" of the hammer on an empty chamber and jumped up like a Lutheran at a snake revival.

"Freeze," I said, pointing my .38 at Carpy. Then Moby Mel got my attention. Moby Mel was a whale of a man and the bazooka looked small in his flippers--small like a toy bazooka, or maybe a miniature bazooka developed by elves so that the Keebler Republic could defend itself. I grabbed Marilyn, slung her across my back and dove behind the fish-freezer like Ben and Jerry on prom night at Harvey Milk High School.

"Come out, come out wherever you are," sang Moby, his voice, the beautiful and timeless song of the Humpback.

"Blow it out your blowhole!" I called back.

"Say goodbye, Flatfoot," sang Moby.

We closed our eyes and waited for the explosion. It never happened. Instead, we heard a grunt, then another grunt; the same, yet different, the first grunt being whale-like and the second grunt being more of a carpish grunt--followed by the Zen-like sound of one fin flopping. Marilyn and I peeked over the top of the freezer.

There they were--Carpy Deeum and Moby Mel, laid out like a couple of Episcopal handbell players at a Christmas party with an open bar. They both had harpoons sticking out of them and standing in the doorway was Cleamon "Codfish" Downs.

"Hey there, Codfish," I said. "We're glad to see you. But I thought that Toby Taps dropped a piano on your head."

"Nah," said Codfish. "He missed me by two octaves."

"You didn't wreck my car did you?" asked Meg, when she answered the phone at my cabin.

"Nope. Listen, can you put Moosey and Kokomo in the back of the truck, throw the tarp over them, and drive them down to the Slab?"

"Sure," said Meg. "They're in the den, but, quite frankly, that ape scares the daylights out of me. One night's stay in the Hayden Konig Monkey House is enough."

"How's Baxter doing?"

"He hasn't barked at all since last night. He and Kokomo are getting along just fine."

"It's been a busy morning," I said. "We got the arrest warrant, Nancy and Dave went over and served it, and the judge rescinded the warrant on Kokomo. I don't want to take any chances, though. Those hunters don't have any way of knowing that his death sentence has been lifted."

"Why are we bringing him to the Slab?"

"Penny Pelicane and Kent are on their way over from Boone. She'll take him back to the biology department, put him in the motor home, and take him on back to Maryland."

"Can Mom come over and meet Kokomo before he goes back?"

"Absolutely. Tell her to meet us."

"So," asked Meg, "whom did you arrest?"

"I'll explain it all when you get here," I said.

"Don't you dare hold out on me! Who did it?"

"Oh no," I said. "It's a surprise. In fact, I have two surprises for you."

The Slab Café was full. It was noon on Friday, and there was the walk-in crowd, several hunters taking a break for lunch and the usual customers. Pete had reserved us the big table in the back. Noylene had been commandeered to help with the waitressing chores, and Pauli Girl McCollough, who had taken Collette's place, was serving coffee.

Nancy and Dave were waiting outside for Meg to arrive. I sat at the table with Billy and Elaine Hixon and Pete. Ruby and Gaylen

Weatherall walked in at the same time, and I waved them both over to our table.

"Have a seat," I said. "It's a beautiful day, isn't it?"

The two women smiled and sat down.

"It certainly is," said Ruby.

"Absolutely," agreed Gaylen. "I must say, by the way, that y'all certainly know how to put on a funeral in St. Germaine."

"We do, don't we?" said Billy. "By the way, Wormy was so pleased with the entire thing, he gave me four free plots. Me and Elaine are now looking forward to our interment. You and Meg want the other two? We'd be neighbors. We got into the No-Smoking Section."

"You bet!" I said. "Wormy Acres, here we come!"

"Wormy was *pleased*?" asked Gaylen, incredulously.

"Why, hell yes! He's gotten over seven hundred phone calls just since yesterday. And ESPN is going to air the service again tomorrow night. He was released from the hospital, by the way."

"The hospital?" said Gaylen. "Why was he in the hospital?"

"Well, he was beaten in the head by a gorilla," said Noylene. "But the doctor says he's fine. No concussion."

The bell on the front door jangled, and we looked over to see Dr. Pelicane and Kent Murphee come in. They spotted us right away and came over to the table.

"Is Kokomo all right?" asked Dr. Pelicane.

"Kokomo's fine," I said. "And you have Moosey to thank for it. He's the one who snuck into the animal shelter and let him go. Then he kept Kokomo up in the mountains until we could clear him."

"Moosey should have brought Kokomo to me," said Dr. Pelicane angrily. "I could have taken him back to Maryland."

"No," said Kent, gently taking her hand. "The university would have had to destroy him."

Dr. Pelicane bit her lip. "I guess. One thing's for sure. We're not coming back *here* again!"

We heard the bell jangle again, and this time, gasps erupted from all the tables. Dave and Nancy came in first. Behind them was Moosey, holding one of Kokomo's hands. Bringing up the rear and holding the gorilla's other hand, was a very nervous Meg.

I saw the four hunters that had stopped for lunch jump to their feet. They didn't have their rifles with them, and they couldn't get to the door with the gorilla blocking the path.

231

"Take it easy boys," I said, showing them my badge. "The hunt is over. There's no reward, and anyone who shoots this gorilla is going to jail for a long time."

"Who says?" challenged the largest man, a big guy with a four-day beard wearing an orange hunting vest.

"This document right here," I said. I held up Judge Minton's order rescinding the warrant on Kokomo. The large man took it from me, read it over and handed it back.

"That's it then boys," he said to his companions. "We're done here. Let's finish up our lunch and head on back to Virginia." He looked Kokomo up and down. "I guess it would have been a shame to shoot that animal anyway."

Dr. Pelicane had been waiting nervously at the table, waiting to see what the hunters would do. Now, she leapt to her feet and ran over to Kokomo. Kokomo saw her coming, vocalized a greeting, and wrapped her in his arms like any long-lost son greeting his mother.

"You've had quite an adventure," said Dr. Pelicane. Kokomo just grunted. Then she turned to Moosey. "Young man, I want to thank you. You saved Kokomo's life."

Moosey looked down at his ratty tennis shoes and blushed. "Twarn't nothin'," he said softly.

"Three cheers for Moosey," called Pete from the table. "Hip Hip..."

"Hooray!" yelled the crowd at the Slab. "Hip Hip Hooray! Hip Hip Hooray!"

Moosey didn't say anything—just grabbed Kokomo with outstretched arms and hid his face in the gorilla's hairy chest.

"Come over and sit down," I said to the group. "And we'll tell you what happened."

"It was a slam-dunk," said Nancy. "Just like Jillian said. When we arrested him and showed him the DNA evidence, he confessed to the whole thing."

"Who?" asked Meg. "Who did you arrest?"

"I believe you mean *whom*," I said. "*Whom* did you arrest? You forget that I am a writer and a grammararian."

"Grrrr," growled Meg.

"We arrested Bennett Shipley, the head deacon at New Fellowship Baptist Church," said Nancy. "He got shot in the head, but the bullet just grazed him. We took him down to the Watauga Medical Center. He just needed a couple of stitches and a bandage."

"You shot him?" asked Meg.

"No," I said. "If Nancy shot him, he'd be dead. Hannah shot him. He dressed up like a gorilla and hit Wormy with a pipe, but Hannah saw him go into the courthouse. She followed him and shot him."

"Why'd he do that?" asked Pete.

"He was getting desperate. He thought that if a few people saw the gorilla hitting people with a pipe, they'd never believe, no matter what Kokomo said, that he didn't kill Brother Kilroy."

"So, it was Bennett Shipley in the Piggly Wiggly? Not Kokomo?"

"Right," I said. "No one got a real good look at him. The gorilla suit wasn't perfect, but if you only caught a glimpse of it, it'd fool you—especially if you knew a gorillas was running around loose. He also didn't expect the checkout girls to be armed to the teeth."

"He's now in the county jail," said Dave. "Once we presented him with the evidence, he confessed."

"He was having an affair with the church secretary," said Nancy. "Bootsie Watkins. But he says it was over and done with."

"So?" said Pete.

"So," continued Nancy, "as head deacon, Shipley had to go to confession every week. He finally confessed the affair to Brother Kilroy, told him it was over, and that he wanted to be forgiven. Brother Kilroy said 'fine,' but that he'd have to confess to the congregation as well, and he'd be removed as head deacon."

"And then his wife would know," said Pete. "Now I see."

Nancy nodded. "But Shipley pretended to go along."

I took up the narrative. "He knew that Brother Kilroy was going to bring Kokomo over to get baptized. He even arranged to help him when he got to the church. He went into the bathroom with Kilroy and Kokomo, but when they were in the water, Shipley hit Kilroy in the head with the pipe. Then he broke his neck and hid the pipe in the piano. He had no idea that Kokomo would trash the office and break the piano in half."

"We're with you so far," said Elaine. "But how did Bennett Shipley lock the office from the inside and then get out?"

"Easy," I said. "He didn't."

"Huh?" said Pete.

"When Nancy and Bootsie and I got to Kilroy's office that morning, Bennett Shipley was already there, pounding on the door. The door was locked. I told Nancy to shoot the lock off, but before she could do it, Shipley smashed the window of the door with a hymnal. A *carefully placed* hymnal."

"I don't get it," said Gaylen. "Why was the hymnal carefully placed?"

"He needed something handy to smash the window with. Something that was common enough that it wouldn't draw any attention," I said. "He broke the window with the hymnal, reached inside, told us that the key was still in the lock, unlocked the door, and we went in."

"I *get* it!" exclaimed Meg. "The key was never in the lock!"

"Exactly. The key was always in Bennett Shipley's hand. And the reason the miniature Bible key fob had been removed, was that it made the key too difficult to hide."

"So Shipley was just waiting for witnesses to arrive before he 'broke in' to the office," said Pete.

"Not only witnesses," I said. "*Police* witnesses."

"What about Kokomo?" asked Meg. "He kept saying the Tiger Man did it."

"His hair," Nancy said. "Shipley has dark brown hair with a white stripe running through it. Kokomo was telling us about the stripe." She shrugged. "At least we think he was."

"Shipley's also the one who put the bounty on Kokomo's head," added Billy. "I guess that when he found out Kokomo could talk, he didn't want to take any chances."

"Yep," I said.

"That's quite a story," said Dr. Pelicane. "I never should have let Kokomo out of my sight. I won't do it again."

"Well," said Noylene, who had been standing against the back wall listening to the tale. "It's a shame that things went so wrong. The good thing is that Brother Kilroy is with Jesus and that Mr. Shipley's sins, no matter how grievous, can be forgiven. All he's got to do is ask."

"I'm sure that if they meet in heaven, they'll have a lot to talk about," said Ruby.

"Yeah," said Noylene. "And maybe they'll walk on over and say 'hello' to Kokomo. He'll be there, too. Y'all don't forget. He's done been saved."

Dr. P.A. Pelicane and Kent Murphee took Kokomo out to Kent's SUV, and after a goodbye hug to Moosey, Kokomo climbed into the back and they drove off. We all stood outside the Slab and waved goodbye until the truck was out of sight. Then we walked back into the restaurant.

"How's your Communion Fish venture going?" I asked Pete, as we made our way back to our table.

"We already have orders from eight hundred churches. They're small orders," Pete acknowledged, "but once they taste them, we're going to be home free."

"I actually like the Communion Fish," said Gaylen. "I don't know why we can't use them."

"Hurrah!" said Pete. "My fortune is made! We've been endorsed by the priest who officiated at Junior Jameson's funeral!"

"I have another surprise," I said. "I was on the Bulwer-Lytton website this morning."

"The results are posted?" said Ruby.

"Yes. Yes they are."

"Did one of us win?" asked Elaine.

"Yes. Yes, one of us did."

"It wasn't you, was it?" asked Meg, disgust clouding her voice.

"Yes. Yes it was."

Chapter 27

It was Saturday morning and I picked Moosey up at five a.m. Five a.m. comes early, but we were determined that Old Spiney would be seeing his last sunrise, and we'd be there to share it with him. It was dark as we parked the pick-up and walked down the path toward the dock.

"I've got a surprise," I whispered, lighting up a cigar, and puffing away in the early morning. "There's no way he's getting loose this time."

"What is it?" asked Moosey.

"You'll have to wait and see," I said.

We trudged down to the water, carrying our tackle and life jackets, and saw Pete's rowboat bobbing on the lake. The sun was just beginning to send some light flickering across the water, but it wouldn't make its appearance above the trees surrounding the peaceful scene for another half-hour or so. It was a cool morning, or would be until the sun was up, and both of us were wearing sweatshirts.

We climbed into the red boat and got settled. I dropped the oars into the oarlocks and waited while Moosey untied the boat and pushed us away from the dock. The birds were just starting to make some sounds, and we could hear squirrels beginning their morning chatter as well. I gave a pull on the oars and sent us gliding across the glassy surface toward the deepest end of the lake.

"Okay, what's the surprise?" asked Moosey.

"I got some worms," I said.

"I've got some too," said Moosey. He held up his coffee can. "A whole bunch of 'em."

I lowered my voice to a whisper. "I've got *professional* worms. I got them down at Uncle Jerry's Bait Shop."

"*Wow!*" said Moosey. "Can I see one?"

"Just as soon as we get over there," I said, pointing to an old oak tree that had fallen half into the water. "Old Spiney doesn't stand a chance."

"We're gonna get him this time for sure!" said Moosey.

An hour later, we'd caught two small bass and a small striped turtle that had a taste for professional worms. The sun was above the trees, and Moosey and I had stripped off our sweatshirts. We kept the bass, vowing to eat them for breakfast and were about to throw the turtle back when Moosey thought of a better idea.

"I can keep him for a pet!"

"It's a water turtle, Moosey," I told him. "It'll die if it's not in the water."

"I can keep him in the bathtub," said Moosey. "then I'll take him out on Saturdays if anybody wants to take a bath."

"Well, at least the morning's not a total loss," I said.

"Yeah," Moosey added cheerfully. "I got me a pet turtle!"

"Your mother will be thrilled."

We reeled in our lines, put my professional worms in the coffee can with Moosey's amateurs, stored the poles under the seats and decided to call it a day. Our two breakfast bass were in a twenty-five gallon ice chest I'd brought to carry home Old Spiney. They looked pretty small, but, I thought, maybe we'd have some pancakes as well. I'd started to row for the dock when there was a tremendous splash on Moosey's right. He was so startled that he dropped his turtle into the bottom of the boat. The splash was immediately followed by the sight of a giant fish leaping out of the water, his skyward path taking him directly toward Moosey. So great was the fish's leap that had Moosey not been sitting where he was, the fish might have sailed over the boat and landed in the water on the other side leaving us with nothing but a good fish story. But Moosey let out a yelp and threw up his hands, hitting the fish on the nose with a loud smack and causing him to end up flopping in the bottom of the boat.

"WE GOT HIM! WE GOT HIM!" shrieked Moosey at the top of his lungs. "WE GOT OL' SPLINKEY!"

"Spiney," I said. "Old Spiney. You sure got him!"

"Wow! Look how big he is," Moosey said. "He's HUGE!"

"I brought the scale," I said. "Let's weigh him."

I reached into my tackle box and pulled out a digital fish scale. Then I made my way down the boat to where Moosey was sitting and looking at Old Spiney.

"Look at all those hooks," Moosey said. "They must hurt him."

I lifted the fish's head and looked into his gaping mouth. "I count four," I said. "No five. One is mine. See, here's my lure."

"Can we take them out?"

"Yeah. I think we can."

I went back up to my tackle box and got a pair of pliers and some snips. When I got back, Old Spiney was lying still.

"Is he dead?" asked Moosey.

"No. Look here. See. His gills are still moving. He'll be okay."

Very carefully I removed three of the hooks with the pliers. The last two, I pushed through Old Spiney's lip, snipped the barbs and backed them out.

"There we go," I said. "Good as new."

"We're going to let him go, aren't we?" asked Moosey.

"It's up to you," I said. "You caught him."

"Let's let him go."

"Okay, but we're going to weigh him first."

I lifted the great bass up by one of his gills, and slid the hook of the scale under my finger and let him dangle. The scale read twenty-one pounds, ten ounces.

"Wow," I said.

"Is that a world record?" asked Moosey.

"I don't think so. It may be a state record. But in order for it to count as a record, you have to catch him on a line. You caught him out of the air."

"It's good we're going to throw him back then."

"Yeah," I said. "He'll be here next year. And he'll even be bigger."

"And we'll get some more professional worms. Those work great!"

"That's a plan."

I lifted Old Spiney off the scale and lowered him into the water, holding him dorsal-up while the water passed over his gills. He was still for a moment, then gave a shudder and with a snap of his tail, he was gone.

Postlude

"Have you seen Betsy?" I asked Codfish as the three of us walked down the street toward my office.

"Yeah," said Codfish. "She's at your place. I stashed her there. She said she was gonna cook you supper. Something about roasted woodchuck and chicken skins."

"How about you, big boy?" cooed Marilyn, looking down at Codfish from her five-foot-three-inch stature. "You having dinner with anyone?"

"I've got some minnows in the fridge," said Codfish.

"Looks like we're all going to be singing two-part music for a while," I said, lighting a stogy.

"Heinrich Schütz never had any basses either," piped up Marilyn. "They were all out fighting the Hundred Years War."

"How do you know?" I said. "You're a secretary."

"Oh, I know stuff. Lots of stuff."

"I'll bet you do," said Codfish. "C'mon Doll-Face. I'll show you why we always swim upstream."

"I see that you didn't win the Grand Prize," said Meg.

"No, I didn't. But I did place in my category, and my winning entry is on the internet until next year. There it is, in black and white."

On the computer screen in front of us was my brilliantly composed ode to the Valedictorian Brandi and her unfortunate t-shirt.

"I concede," said Meg. "You're a worse writer than I am, and I will graciously consent to you taking all of us out to the Hunter's Club for dinner."

"Hmm," I said. "But I didn't win the two-hundred dollars."

"No, Sweetie, you didn't."

"It's lucky I'm rich then."

"Yes," said Meg, giving me a kiss. "You're a lucky man."

About the Author

Mark Schweizer lives and works in Hopkinsville, Kentucky, where he composes music, writes books and directs a church choir. He has the distinction of receiving a Dishonorable Mention in the 2006 Bulwer-Lytton Fiction Contest (www.bulwer-lytton.com).

The Liturgical Mysteries

The Alto Wore Tweed
Independent Mystery Booksellers Association
"Killer Books" selection, 2004

The Baritone Wore Chiffon

The Tenor Wore Tapshoes
IMBA 2006 Dilys Award nominee

The Soprano Wore Falsettos

The Bass Wore Scales

A note from the author

In the fall of 2001, I began what I hoped would be a funny little book about an Episcopal choir director/detective that had a flair for bad writing. Now, five years later, that book, *The Alto Wore Tweed,* is going into its sixth printing and the rest of the quintet (bad writing aside) are working hard to catch up. Thanks to all of you, Hayden Konig mysteries continue to make their way into the hands of mystery lovers and across church choirs, one reader and singer at a time.

If you've enjoyed this book—or any of the other mysteries in this series—please drop me a line. My e-mail address is mark@sjmp.com.

Also, if your book club is reading one of these mysteries, I'd love to hear from you. If you'd like to arrange a time to for your club to call (via speakerphone), it would be my pleasure to open a *Schwabbling's*, light up a stogy and chat with your group. Invite me! I'll come!

Cheers,
Mark